INSTANT FAMILY

INSTANT FAMILY

ELISABETH ROSE

THORNDIKE PRESS
A part of Gale, Cengage Learning

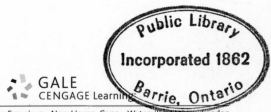
GALE
CENGAGE Learning

Detroit • New York • San Francisco • New Haven, Conn • Waterville, Maine • London

GALE
CENGAGE Learning™

Copyright © 2010 by Elisabeth Hoorweg.
Thorndike Press, a part of Gale, Cengage Learning.

LIBRARY OF CONGRESS CATALOGING-IN-PUBLICATION DATA

Rose, Elisabeth, 1951–
   Instant family / by Elisabeth Rose.
      p. cm. – (Thorndike Press large print gentle romance)
   ISBN-13: 978-1-4104-3678-8 (hardcover)
   ISBN-10: 1-4104-3678-0 (hardcover)
   1. Brothers and sisters—Fiction. 2. Architects—Fiction.
3. Large type books. I. Title.
PR9619.4.R64I57 2011
823'.92—dc22
                                                 2011007488

Published in 2011 by arrangement with Thomas Bouregy & Co., Inc.

To Colin, Carla, and Nick

CHAPTER ONE

Alex sat up abruptly in bed, wide-eyed in the darkness. A noise. Outside. A siren wailed in the distance. Not that, something else. Closer. Loud enough to wake him.

Silence.

A thud, scuffling feet, a scraping sound.

Ears straining, he tossed back the sheet. Two strides and he was at the window, peering carefully through the slats of the vertical blind at the narrow view of the front garden. Nothing.

Hot. Dark. Still. Deep shadows from the liquidambar tree created black holes in the night.

Frowning, he let the blind fall into place and groped for the bedside light switch. Better check on Steffie while he was awake. No real need, just the freely admitted pleasure of having her under his roof on their fortnightly weekend together. Short snatches of time to delight in his daughter.

Alex padded across the passageway to the spare room, where the elephant-shaped night-light cast a soft yellow glow. One of Steffie's softly rounded hands rested on the pillow. A tumble of dark, silky hair obscured her face. A smile stretched his lips as he touched fingers to his mouth and blew her a kiss from the doorway.

Crash!

What the — ? At the side. Glass breaking. Steffie stirred, rolled over, settled back into sleep.

Alex darted for the family room and the sliding door. The outside sensor light hadn't come on, but the quarter-moon cast enough of a silvery glow to show dark, fleeing figures, maybe three.

Precious moments lost fumbling with the lock, a muttered curse, the door finally dragged open. Alex sprinted across the tiled terrace, leaped the low hedge of ornamental lavender and thyme, landed on grass, prickly and dry underfoot. Ran.

The catch on the side gate slowed the intruders and gave him time for a desperate lunge amid swearing and panicked cries of, "I can't open the gate!" "Hurry! He'll get us!" *Kids.*

The gate swung wide, and the dark mass of bodies moved. Alex's fingers clutched cloth and hung on.

Briing-briing. Briing-briing. Briing-briing.

Chloe stretched out a leaden arm, flopped it about in search of the phone, made contact, somehow managed to find the button, and silenced the unbearable shrieking.

"Hello," she croaked, eyes closed.

"Constable Brent Burrows from the City Watch House. Sorry to disturb you. Is this Chloe Gardiner?"

"Yes." Chloe's brain and body sprang to alert. Her pulse rate trebled in an instant, and the hand holding the phone began to tremble. Cold sweat beaded her face and body. A suddenly closed throat choked her words. "Has something happened? An accident?"

Unbearable, unthinkable, that such crushing disaster could happen again.

Her mind ran frantically through the possibilities in the second it took the officer to respond. Katy. Asleep. Julian and Seb. Asleep. Grandmother Simone. Definitely at home at . . . Chloe's fearful gaze shot to the red numbers on the bedside clock: 3:15. She switched the reading light on, blinking painfully at the sudden onslaught of vision.

"Not an accident, Miss Gardiner. We have your brother Sebastian here. He was caught trespassing, and there's been some vandalism. We'd like you to come to the station, please."

Chloe sprang out of bed, her body stiff with indignation. "That's impossible. He's at home, asleep."

"Would you check, please, miss?" Patient almost to the point of boredom.

But Chloe was already charging along the corridor to Seb's room. The hall light came on, and Julian stood there yawning and rubbing his eyes, straw-colored hair amok.

"What's up? Who's on the phone?"

"The police think Seb's a vandal." Chloe pushed the bedroom door open. "I told them he's asleep."

But her voice faded on the last word, because Seb wasn't asleep. He wasn't in bed at all. He wasn't in the room. She raised the phone slowly to her ear, hand trembling. "He's not here."

"I know," replied Constable Burrows. "He's here."

"I can't come," she said, floundering in the waves of disbelief. "I have children — eleven and fourteen — in the house." She stared at Julian. What did he know about this?

"We'll be all right. Go, please, Chloe." Julian's eyes brimmed with tears. He jammed

10

his fists into his eyes, blinked, sniffed.

"I'll be there as soon as I can." She disconnected. "Did you know, Julian?" A surge of rage overtook the fear. "Did Seb tell you he was sneaking out? How often does he do that? What did he say to you?"

He shook his head. Too quickly. Her eyes narrowed. Julian didn't tell lies. Neither did Seb. . . .

"Anything?"

"No."

"Don't cover for him." Her voice rose on a crest of anger. "It won't do him any good. Who was he with?"

"I don't know." Almost a wail.

Chloe didn't know either. The boys had lives she knew nothing about, and the realization came with the shock of a sandbag to the chest. They weren't frightened nine-year-olds any more, clinging to her, trusting her as their lifeline for survival in a world turned completely and cataclysmically upside down.

"But you can guess, can't you?"

His clear blue eyes skated away from hers, and his mouth took on a very familiar, stubborn line. He scratched his elbow absent-mindedly, a nervous reaction. The stalling tactic fueled her rage.

"Come on, Julian. You're twins. You share

11

everything — you always have."

"I don't know," he insisted with a rare flash of anger.

"Think about it while I get dressed." She turned away with a pounding heart stealing her breath and a deep sense of dread sitting malevolently in her belly.

Chloe entered the neon brightness of the police station foyer on legs trembling with delayed shock. A square-jawed constable listened to her query through a narrow space in the security-glass panels that separated them. "Take a seat." He'd already returned his attention to papers on the desk.

The straight-backed chairs had hard, uncomfortable seats, even more noticeable because she had been dragged from the comfort and oblivion of sleep in her own bed. Chloe sat clutching her black and red Chinese bag on her denim-clad lap, her clammy right hand running constantly over the smooth, shiny surface.

Her wandering gaze landed on her T-shirt front — rumpled. A red tomato stain glared at her from the mint green fabric — the same shirt she'd worn yesterday, the first garment at hand. Should have had a shower, grabbed clean clothes, pulled her hair back into a pony tail, and brushed her teeth, but at three-thirty in the morning she wasn't thinking much beyond Seb and what he might have done. And that he needed her. And that she was, in some way she couldn't fathom, responsible.

A tall, gangly, dark-haired man in uniform appeared through one of the doors leading from the reception area. He glanced about with weary eyes in a pale, angular face and walked straight to Chloe.

"Miss Gardiner? Brent Burrows."

Chloe jumped to her feet and shook the proffered hand, warm and dry in her unpleasantly damp palm. The Chinese bag slipped to the floor, spilling her keys with a clatter onto the gray tiles. She scooped them up hastily while he waited with an expressionless face. He ushered her through a door, up some stairs, and along a pastel gray corridor to a small interview room, where he indicated she should sit on a chair only marginally more comfortable than the ones downstairs. Then he perched himself casually on the edge of the desk.

"Is Seb all right?" She tried to swallow, but her mouth was so dry, her voice rasped. Surely this constable could hear the thumping of her heart. She wanted to scream at him to get on with it and tell her, don't spare her feelings, don't be tactful.

"He's scared stiff." A tiny, swift smile darted across his mouth and lightened his tired face. His front teeth overlapped, and the slight imperfection made him seem friendly, approachable. "Has he been in trouble before?"

Chloe shook her head vehemently. "Never."

"That's what we thought." He paused and licked his lips thoughtfully. "He said you're his guardian — he's your half brother. That your parents —"

"Yes," interrupted Chloe. She glared at him, daring him to suggest that this escapade was her fault. Due to her negligence or lack of care. "What exactly did he do? Is he being charged with something? Was he alone?"

The idea that Seb would creep out at night by himself and vandalize someone's property was incredible. Why would he do such a thing? And without Julian. They were inseparable. Weren't they?

"He was caught running from a backyard."

"Where?"

"Aranda. Nungara Street." Their own suburb but the far side. "The householder thinks there were three, but he only managed to catch Sebastian. Your brother won't

14

give us names. There's been vandalism in the area, but we're not sure if they're responsible for all of it. Letter boxes smashed, cars scratched, graffiti, stuff like that. Common in summer. Hot nights, bored kids. Broke the sensor lights in the front and back garden. That's what woke the householder."

"But nothing was stolen?"

"No. Not from that house."

Hot blood scorched through her veins. *This was all wrong. Not Seb. It couldn't be.* She sprang to her feet. Sitting down, she was dwarfed. He had her at a disadvantage, staring down at her like that. "What do you mean? They'd been on a crime spree? Did he have anything on him? Any evidence?"

"No."

"Are you positive it's my brother?" she cried in a last vain attempt to return some sense to the situation. But Constable Burrows remained unmoved, sitting casually with arms folded. He nodded with determined firmness.

Chloe subsided onto the chair under the inescapable truth. "Does he need a lawyer?"

"We'd prefer a family conference, but the victim may press charges against your brother. The damage was considerable — broken letter box and sensor lights, spray-painting on the driveway. They seem to have gone along the street doing the same thing at random."

"I'm positive Seb has never done any of that before. Positive."

"That's what most parents say." Burrows tilted his head with a skeptical little close-mouthed smile.

"Will the man press charges or go for the conference?" Family conferencing must mean talking, coming to a mutually agreeable conclusion. No court appearance.

"He's very angry at the moment. His six-year-old daughter was asleep in the house at the time. Can't blame him. The whole area's been suffering from the problem. They've had enough. So have we."

Chloe's face crumpled. Her eyes filled with tears. "I'm sorry." She groped in her jeans pocket for a tissue. A sweet-faced six-year-old asleep in her bed. "Seb's a good boy at heart. I know he is. He wouldn't hurt anyone and never a little girl. He loves his little sister. Katy's eleven." She blew her nose and sniffed while Constable Burrows watched calmly. "Can I talk to him?"

"Sure." He stood up. "We think your brother was led into something that got out of his control. In this case you're probably right that he'd never done it before. He's very scared, and we'd like to keep him that way for a while." The tired smile appeared again at Chloe's outraged gasp. "So he learns a lesson he won't forget. We'd like to know who the others were, if you can help us find out. He won't tell us."

Chloe followed him out the door. A female officer accompanied by a stern-faced man with dark-stubbled chin and cheeks appeared from a room farther along the short corridor, headed for the stairs. An incredibly good-looking man. The physical reaction came from nowhere, sudden as a body blow, a cricket bat to the knees. Chloe's step faltered as her brain scrambled under the overload of buzzing hormones and thudding heart. But Burrows was surging on ahead. She forced her legs to move, knowing she'd been staring, knowing the most attractive man she'd ever seen would pass her by, barely registering her presence.

But piercing blue eyes raked her uncomfortably from head to toe as she neared the pair. He had a natural air of authority, radiated an instinctive assumption that his way was right. The best. The only way.

Some sort of high-ranking officer? A detective? He'd think she was scum, a criminal, brought in off the streets for interrogation. Her rumpled jeans and T-shirt virtually developed rips, and the tomato stain grew larger and more grotesque as he stared.

By stark contrast his khaki slacks and white open-necked shirt hung crisply and neatly from broad shoulders and narrow hips. Close-clipped hair didn't dare stray out of line. The unshaven chin gave the only indication of the bizarre time of night.

The female officer and Burrows exchanged a meaningful glance, but they didn't speak. Chloe stood aside as the constable passed, but the man stopped, his face and body rigid with anger, she realized with an astonishment that drew her out of the whirlwind of her thoughts.

"You're here for that young hooligan, aren't you?" The eyes bored into her like lasers. Chloe recoiled from the venom, shrinking against the wall. "The Gardiner boy."

He almost spat the name into her face.

Chloe nodded while Burrows placed a placating hand on the man's arm, restraining gently. "Now then, sir."

"I'm sorry," Chloe managed to say. "I had no idea."

"People like you never do, do they? You have no idea what your kids get up to. Running around the streets in the middle of the night, terrorizing the neighborhood. People like you should be banned from having children."

"That's enough." Burrows rapped out the words. He took Chloe's arm and propelled her down the corridor while the other officer said, "Insulting Ms. Gardiner won't serve any useful purpose, sir."

His voice followed her down the corridor like a cloud of toxic gas. "Completely irresponsible. She must've been a teenager herself when she gave birth."

Chloe wrenched her arm from Constable Burrow's grasp. Spinning around, she yelled, "He's not my son. He's my brother, and he's a good boy. I'm sorry for what he did, and I'm positive he's sorry too. Haven't you ever made a mistake or done something stupid? Are you so perfect?"

"Come on, Chloe." Constable Burrows placed a firm arm around her shaking shoulders and marched her around the corner.

Alex stared after the pair, his anger fizzling and dying under the weight of the girl's extreme and all too real anguish. *"Haven't you ever done something stupid?"* The scalding memory of an incident he'd thought long forgotten. How old? Twelve or thirteen. His father's uncomprehending

19

rage, his own humiliation. Then the more recent idiocy. Marriage.

"Is that true?" He turned to Constable Wright, whose expression clearly told him she agreed with the girl's summation of his character. "He's the brother? Where are the parents?"

"Bevan and Rose Gardiner were killed in a terrorist bombing in Indonesia, along with Ms. Gardiner's older sister, Terry, five years ago. Chloe Gardiner took on the care of the three younger children — half siblings. It was in the papers at the time. The community raised a lot of money to help them." She spun on her solid black leather heel and marched toward the stairs, her back stiff with disapproval.

Five years ago he'd been dealing with a failing marriage and struggling to establish himself as an architect with his own company. He remembered the bombings, of course. Every Australian did. But names, individual cases? It hadn't touched him personally. Now, somehow, this stern-faced policewoman made him feel guilty for not losing a loved one. "I didn't realize. No other relatives?"

"I'm not sure."

Alex followed her downstairs and through to the reception foyer, deep in thought.

"Thank you for coming in, Mr. Bergman."
He recognized the officially polite tone as
one he used himself — with clients he
particularly didn't like.

"I'm sorry." It seemed inadequate. Perhaps it was. She waited, her face a blank
mask. "Sorry I reacted that way."

"You were naturally upset, sir." She extended her hand. "We'll be in touch."

"Look — you mentioned a conference."

"Yes?" She wasn't going to make it easy
for him. Especially considering his earlier
reaction to the suggestion, which on her
part had been more of a strong recom-
mendation, he realized now. *"Lock the young
thug up, and throw the key away, for all I care,"*
sounded harsh and uncompromising in the
extreme as the words resounded in his head.

"Do you think it might work for this kid?"

Constable Wright nodded with a marginal
increase of warmth in her manner. "We see
boys like Sebastian Gardiner all the time,
especially in the summer holidays. They're
basically good kids. They go out with their
mates or fall in with a rotten crowd, and
before they know it, someone's suggested
something they'd never do on their own.
The ringleaders aren't the ones who get
caught most often."

"I suppose we should give it a try." The

sister's face flashed through his mind. Very pretty. Young and vulnerable with soft, pink cheeks under a mess of gold blond hair falling in disarray to her shoulders. Obviously straight out of bed, bewildered, uncomprehending. The shock, the responsibility shadowed eyes that had already seen too much sorrow. Then his cruel and vicious words hurled at her. "I should apologize."

"Yes."

"Could I wait?"

"It's up to you, but to tell you the truth . . ." She paused as if deciding whether to say what she'd intended. Decided. "She could be here for some time, and if I were Ms. Gardiner, I wouldn't want to speak to you right now."

Alex stared, and his skin prickled uncomfortably as her meaning sank in. "I suppose not. I should go home. Thank you," he said abruptly. Jeannie from next door was babysitting, but she was due at work in the morning and wouldn't be sleeping too well on his couch.

Chloe, still shaking with indignant fury at the monstrous suddenness of the attack and the complete demolition of her gross and irrational attraction to such a cruel individual, allowed Constable Burrows to propel her around the corner.

"I'm sorry about that, Chloe."

"Horrible . . . horrible man." After the torrent of angry words, she could barely speak now. The blue-clad arm still lay comfortingly around her shoulders.

"He was upset, but he had no call to say what he did."

"He'll never agree to a conference, will he?" Chloe stopped and gazed up into the gray eyes of her protector. He stepped back quickly as if realizing how intimate his consoling gesture had been.

"He may when he calms down." Constable Burrows paused with his fingers on the handle of the door they stood next to. "Ready?"

Seb sat slumped on a chair in the small interview room with his head cradled in his hands. His expression changed from alarm to delight when he saw Chloe appear from behind Constable Burrows, then almost immediately collapsed into apprehension. Red-rimmed eyes, a deep pink staining the cheeks contrasting starkly with alabaster skin, rumpled T-shirt, shaking fingers now clutching and plucking at the fabric. So young, so helpless and scared. Chloe spontaneously held out her arms, and he launched himself clumsily into her embrace.

"I'm sorry, Chloe, I'm sorry." Between sniffles. He was as tall as she and bony under her fingers. How long since she'd held him, hugged him? Or Julian.

"What on earth were you doing?" She released her hold and stepped back. "Who were you with? Julian said he had no idea. Does he? Or has he been lying for you?"

Seb stared at her, his mouth moving wordlessly. His cheeks had deepened from pink to a dull red.

"Tell me, Seb! You're the only one they've caught, and you're the one who's going to be in court over this."

"Court?" Seb's eyes flashed to Constable Burrows, who stood watching with his back against the door.

"What did you expect? That the people you robbed and whose property you wrecked wouldn't mind?" Chloe glared at him as the complete stupidity and insanity of the whole affair reignited the rage.

"I didn't rob anyone."

"You tried," put in Constable Burrows. "One of you dropped a chisel."

"Not me. I didn't want to break in, but they —" He stopped, glanced at Burrows, then back to Chloe. Couldn't hold her gaze.

"Who?" she asked.

Seb sat down. He folded his arms across

24

his chest in a feeble act of defiance. His baggy jeans had dirty marks on the knees. The T-shirt with his favorite band logo had been a birthday present from his grandmother, Simone. What would *she* say? Whatever it was, it would be endless. Chloe stood over him. "Tell me, Seb."

"I'm not ratting on them." His voice shook despite his determination to maintain the tough act.

Idiot! Chloe exhaled noisily.

"So you think it's all right for those others to get away while you take the blame for something you didn't even want to do in the first place?"

"And you're the one we'll charge, seeing as you're the only one we've got," put in Burrows.

"How did you get there?" Chloe demanded. "How long have you been sneaking out?"

Seb stared at his feet. His arms hung by his sides.

"We found a white Commodore abandoned behind the shops. We'll be fingerprinting it."

"Stealing cars as well? Seb!" Tears sprang to her eyes. She blinked rapidly.

"I didn't steal any cars." But his face had turned almost green with fear, his hands

25

shaking uncontrollably.

"Were you *in* the car? For heaven's sake, Seb, don't take all the blame for this if you didn't do it. You owe those kids nothing!"

"Will you protect me if I tell?"

Seb looked up at Constable Burrows, and a flash of something almost like amusement crossed the policeman's face before he said sternly, "Tell us what we want to know, and you'll be better off — trust me."

Straight from a TV show — Mafia versus the good guys. Did Seb think they'd put out a contract on him? What sort of kids were they? What were their parents thinking? Where were *they?*

The furious face of the home owner flashed through her mind. She was one of those irresponsible guardians.

Seb blurted, "Zak Simic got the car. He and his brother, Alan, do it all the time."

"I've never heard of them," said Chloe. "How do you know them?"

Constable Burrows shushed her with a subtle hand gesture as he stepped forward. "Were they both with you tonight?"

Seb shook his head. "Only Zak. He wanted to prove to Alan and his mates that he's as tough as they are."

"As stupid, more like," muttered Chloe.

Seb's eyes were fixed on Constable Burrows, tall and imposing as he towered over him in the chair. His face showed an anxiety now, to cooperate. He must remember how good the police had been to the distraught children on that horrendous day.

"Who was the third boy?"

"Cameron Jarvis."

"Give me names and addresses." Burrows sat down at the desk and fired up the computer.

"You did the right thing. Eventually," said Chloe as she drove a completely exhausted Seb home at seven that morning. He said nothing, sagging in the seat beside her with eyes closed, head resting against the door. The burst of cooperation had subsided into sullen silence after they'd left the police station, Seb released on Chloe's cognizance — not to leave the house alone, to have no contact with anyone connected with the gang, to report in tomorrow.

She glanced at him. His cheek and jaw retained the softness of childhood, but he wasn't a child any longer. His voice had deepened in the last year, and both he and Julian gained several centimeters each time she turned her back. The previously smooth skin sported the occasional teenage spot. The boys were growing away from her, and she didn't know how to deal with them anymore.

"I'm sorry, Seb." Blinking tears, she turned her attention to the road again.

He didn't reply. Breathing heavily. Asleep.

Julian flung the front door open as soon as Chloe turned into the driveway. He jumped the couple of steps from the front terrace and ran to the car, hovering anxiously as she turned off the engine. Seb stirred, and Julian wrenched the door open, nearly spilling his brother onto the ground.

"Hey!" He saved himself by grabbing the seat belt.

"Sorry. What happened? Where were you?"

Chloe slammed her own door. "We've been at the police station doing a deal so Seb doesn't go to jail," she said harshly. A wave of tiredness hit her. "Any coffee going, Julian?"

"I'll make it."

Chloe stalked to the house with Julian and Seb following her in a huddle, whispering together as they'd done all their lives. It had never bothered her before, but now she spun around and in a burst of fury yelled, "What are you two whispering about? You'd better not be telling Julian stuff you didn't tell the police, Seb, or so help me I —" She clamped her trembling lips into a tight line as her voice shook uncontrollably.

"Chloe," ventured Julian tentatively. "He's —"

"Don't." She chopped her hand down. "Don't say anything. I've had enough. I should let the police lock you up, Seb, the way that man wants. You might learn something about being responsible."

She registered Seb's pale, exhausted face and Julian's identical, pale, shocked one in the brief moment before she turned on her heel and charged up the steps and in through the open front door.

Chloe slammed into her bedroom and flung herself onto the bed, fighting the overwhelming rush of tears. Why did she have to deal with this stuff? She couldn't cope with teenage boys. How could Seb do this to her? Why? She jammed clenched fists into her eyes. A couple of salty tears found their way down her cheeks and into her mouth.

She'd failed. Failed to bring up the boys properly. All those people who'd said she couldn't do it, she was too young, were right. Simone would have another weapon in her armory. Chloe could hear her now. *"Katy should live with me. You can't cope with three."* Or, *"The boys need a man in their lives. You should get married, Chloe."*

As if that would be her sole reason for marrying. A father for the boys. She'd given up everything for the kids. Dropped out of Uni, dropped out of her old carefree life to be a single parent. Sure, she'd like a boyfriend, but how could she meet someone, and who would want her, knowing he was to be surrogate father to a ready-made teenage family? Including, as of today, a would-be criminal. Look at the reaction of that staggeringly attractive man. He despised her.

Chloe drew a deep, shuddering breath. The Simone issue wasn't black-and-white. Nothing was. What Simone said, she said out of love and a genuine desire to help, however impractical and ineffective. She'd been grieving too. She'd lost her only son.

The bedroom door cracked open an inch.

"Chloe?" Two blue eyes wide with alarm peeped timidly around the door from under a fringe of flyaway brown hair. "What's happening?"

Chloe patted the bed beside her. Katy darted across the room, a slim, bony little figure in pink shorty pajamas, and snuggled next to her.

"Seb snuck out last night and went in a stolen car with some boys. They were vandalizing people's property, and Seb got

30

caught. The police called me."

Katy's eyes grew even wider. "Is he in jail?"

"He's home. But he's in big trouble."

"What will happen to him?"

"I'm not sure. The man who caught him is very angry. I think Seb . . ." Chloe bit her lip as tears threatened again. "I don't know, Katy. We have to wait and see."

Julian appeared in the doorway holding a mug. "I made coffee for you, Chloe."

"Thanks." She sat up. Julian placed the mug carefully on the bedside table, then sat on the end of the bed. Chloe took a long slurp. The hot, sweet liquid hit her system with a revitalizing jolt.

"Seb's in big trouble," announced Katy. "He might go to jail."

"I know," said Julian. "But he won't go to jail."

"He might."

"You don't know anything." Julian's lip curled in disdain.

"I know you shouldn't vandalize people's things and steal cars."

"Shut up, Katy!" Julian cried.

"Where's Seb?" asked Chloe.

"Asleep."

"I need a shower." Chloe slid off the bed.

"I have to go to work. I'll ring Gran to come over."

"Why?" Katy asked.

"Because Seb is only home on the proviso there's an adult here." Chloe's stomach churned, a feeling that had become uneasily familiar in the last few hours. There was no easy way to break the news to Simone. Cold turkey was best. Straight out, no frills. The reaction would be much the same whichever way the shock was delivered.

But Simone amazed her. "I'll be over straightaway, lovey. Don't you worry."

Perhaps it was another of her acts. This time she was being the competent older woman calmly stepping into the breach and holding things together, ever reliable, as the crisis crashed around her family. If only that were true for more than five minutes.

CHAPTER TWO

Chloe stood behind the counter at The Music Room serving the trickle of customers on automatic pilot. Twice before lunchtime she phoned Simone to make sure Seb was actually in his bed.

"Go and check," she insisted when Simone protested he was fast asleep.

"He's not leaving this house, Chloe, and when he wakes up, he'll have to explain himself to me. We've never had a thief in the Gardiner family, and we're not starting now." Simone's voice had resumed its normal volume, so she must have left the bedroom and the sleeping sinner. "I've cleaned the bathroom properly for you, and Katy and I are making muffins when she gets home from tennis."

"Thanks, she'll love that." Julian had cleaned the bathroom yesterday with his usual meticulous care, leaving taps and tiles gleaming, towels hung neatly and new soap

33

in the holder.

Tiredness slammed into her, mid-afternoon. Luckily the hot weather discouraged shoppers, and The Music Room was virtually empty. She sat on the one stool trying to keep her eyes open while her colleague, Tran, scoured the online catalogues for a customer inquiry. With her mind in its current overwrought state she'd chosen a soothing New Age CD to play through the sound system. Maybe she should have gone with Tran's preference for jazz instead. Wind chimes, rain, and gently lilting flutes were soporific in the extreme.

What would happen to Seb? Would that man insist on a trial? How could she cope with work and monitoring Seb with two weeks of school holidays left? She'd have to tell the boss she couldn't work as much. Or Simone would move in. *Horrors.*

A customer asked for a recording of Carmina Burana. Chloe roused herself, slid off the stool, and led her to the correct section.

A man entered accompanied by a little dark-haired girl. Chloe glanced at the pair, then looked again. The same surge of attraction swamped her in the instant before she could clamp down on it. It was him. Seb's victim, the very angry man, wearing the same shirt and slacks, clean-shaven now, gazing about the shop, those penetrating blue eyes searching for something. *Her? Impossible.* It was a nasty coincidence.

He didn't look angry now, but he might when he saw who worked here. Chloe hurried around the end of the row so an Andre Rieu promotional display obscured her hot-cheeked, shaking self from sight. She couldn't face another scene here in public. Or anywhere, for that matter. In a couple of minutes they'd be gone. He was talking to Tran at the counter. The New Age tinkling drowned out their words.

"Chloe." Tran's voice pulled her reluctantly from her hiding place. "Someone to see you." He went back to the computer.

They were walking past the COMPLETE OPERA section. Her eyes flitted to the door. Could she make a run for it? Ridiculous. She forced herself to stand her ground. He didn't look nearly as intimidating now, especially holding a small child's hand. The daughter?

"Hello, Chloe." His voice was surprisingly gentle, deep, and smooth. But she knew he had another voice, one that cut with sarcasm and bit with anger, went for the throat and the heart. Ruthless.

"May I help you?" Her smile wouldn't work when faced with the memory of his venom. Her mouth dried in an instant. He was too handsome; he attracted her too much. She couldn't stand it, knowing what viciousness he was capable of. She looked away from the unbearably false intimacy of his gaze, to the child.

The little girl stared up at her through gray eyes in a disgruntled, round face topped by straight brown hair cut in a bob. Definitely not pleased to be dragged into this boring shop. The white T-shirt strained over the stomach, and the yellow shorts revealed solid brown thighs and knees. He must spoil her rotten. She was probably as used to getting her own way as he was.

Chloe gave her a brief smile, then shifted her attention to the father. This man who seemingly had sought her out, here at work. Was he allowed to do that? His blue eyes were assessing her again, still piercing, still disconcerting. But she'd regrouped in those few moments, donned some fragile armor against his charm, against her own weakness.

"I wanted to talk to you," he said.

"How did you know where I work? Surely the police didn't tell you."

The words tumbled out, made her sound young and foolish and incompetent, certainly incapable of raising a teenage boy

36

adequately. Chloe bit her lip. She'd backed up against PIANO CONCERTOS and eased herself away from the support. She wouldn't appear weak in front of this man and his grumpy child, but she glanced to where Tran was still engrossed in the computer screen. All she need do was call out for him to ring the police.

"I found you in the phone book. The lady I spoke to directed me here." No doubt Simone thought it was a boyfriend at long last. She'd have been extremely helpful. Probably told him all about Chloe's non-existent love life.

"Did you tell her who you were?"

His name would mean nothing to Simone. Or to herself. Who was he? The police didn't say; she hadn't asked. After that exchange she didn't want to know. And why had he come searching for her if not to continue his attack?

"No. I asked for you." The child pulled at his fingers. He ignored her.

"Why?"

He licked his lips but met her gaze directly. "To apologize."

Chloe stared at him. *Apologize? Completely out of left field. Completely out of character?*

"For the way I spoke to you this morning.

37

I'm sorry." He had her impaled. The eyes, the expression, the broad chest, the sheer presence of the man. Overwhelming. Unrelenting. That gaze too intimate for this place, with his daughter as unwilling observer.

"Who are you?" Chloe asked abruptly. "What's your name?"

"I'm sorry," he said again but in a different, almost disconcerted tone. "I didn't realize. Alex Bergman. This is Stephanie." He extended his hand, and Chloe was forced to grip it briefly or seem churlish and rude. His fingers held hers for a split second. Large, warm, masculine fingers — strong, used to work, but not rough-skinned with ingrained grime or damaged nails.

"Hello, Stephanie." Why had he dragged a six-year-old along while he made his apology? Was this just a quick stop before grocery shopping or the movies? A quick appeasement of the conscience before getting on with more interesting things, family things? Was the wife waiting impatiently somewhere, tapping her foot and looking at her watch while he did what he saw as this duty?

"Hello," Stephanie murmured grudgingly. She tugged at his hand. "Daddy, I want to go now. Come o-o-o-n-n-n." The last word

38

dragged out in a singsong whine.

"In a minute, hon." He smiled down at her, then looked at Chloe again. "It's not the proper time or place, I know, but I needed to tell you how sorry I am. I didn't know your situation, and I'm mortified. Will you forgive me?"

The lips creased in an appealing smile, which faded when she didn't immediately respond by capitulating. But she was over the first shock of attraction now, had her emotions under control. Pity about the manner. He anticipated her acceptance as automatic, a given. And why did her "situation," whatever that meant, matter? Very tempting to tell him to get lost.

"Thanks," she said. "But I don't see what my 'situation' has to do with your rudeness."

What else could she say? Forgive him? Salve his conscience for him when really she should be apologizing to him for the behavior of her brother? But she'd done nothing wrong. Seb had, and he was taking responsibility for his actions.

The blue eyes seemed to peer right into her soul. He didn't say anything, didn't react. Just frowned slightly.

"Daddeeee." Stephanie yanked at his hand. Her face wore a sulky pout, and she glared at Chloe as if it was her fault their outing had been interrupted.

"I'd better go." A smile flicked on and off. The eyes softened. His expression sought understanding. One parent to another. Except she wasn't a parent, technically.

"Yes. Good-bye, Stephanie."

But Stephanie was already dragging her father toward the door. Chloe returned to the counter.

Tran said, "Can't stand whining little kids."

She stared across to the door. The pair had left the shop. Disappeared. "Me neither."

But that brief flicker of a smile lingered in her mind long after it should have. In that instant she'd caught a glimpse of a completely different man. In that breathtakingly attractive physical package. And he needn't have sought her out to make an apology. Maybe he wouldn't be as inflexible in his attitude toward Seb as she'd thought.

Making the apology to Chloe Gardiner didn't make Alex feel any better. It was patently obvious that he terrified her. From the moment she'd glanced up and recognized him, he saw fear. Fear and dislike. Her whole body was poised for flight. The anxious gaze flew from the door to her colleague. He had her cornered, he knew, but he could only go ahead with the words he'd practiced silently on the way to the city center in the car.

Apologies weren't really his thing. He didn't make them often. Not to adults, anyway, as Lucy was fond of pointing out to him when they were married. But with this young woman, Chloe, he hadn't hesitated. He'd maligned her in a most insulting and vicious way. Quite uncalled for and inexcusable. The memory of his words and her face as he shouted at her replayed constantly in his head, twisting his brain and his stomach into knots until they both ached. Seeing her face-to-face and speaking his contrition would, he'd thought, be the only cure. Except it hadn't worked. His stomach still harbored the dull pain of nervous tension.

"Daddy, I want popcorn."

Alex looked down. Steffie was becoming very plump. Lucy had told him last year that she was teased at after-school care but hadn't done anything about it diet-wise.

"You can have a popsicle and juice or water, hon. We've only just had lunch, so you can't be hungry."

"But I always have popcorn at the movies."

The queue shuffled forward three steps. "Not today."

"Daddeee." She stamped her foot.

Alex squatted down to her level, conscious of the critical glance from the mother in front of them. "Stephanie, I said no. Please don't whine, or we'll go home."

Her bottom lip protruded in a fierce pout, and tears started in her eyes. "I don't like you, Daddy," she said loudly.

Alex straightened. Sometimes these weekends seemed endless. He tried to take her out, keep her amused, because if they stayed at home, he had to think of ways to entertain her. She became bored very easily.

Five minutes later with Steffie firmly in tow, he headed for the Theatre 3 entrance clutching two popsicles, two chilled bottles of fruit-flavored sparkling water, and straws, prepared for a couple of hours of torture.

A matinee session of an animated hit movie on a hot afternoon was his idea of hell, or close to it. How anyone could follow the story or hear the dialogue over the chatter of young voices, numerous toddlers who began running up and down the aisles, and the crying of babies was beyond him.

After about fifteen minutes his attention wandered from the screen. Chloe Gardiner. How old was she? At least twenty-three, because to take charge of the younger children five years ago she'd have been eighteen, minimum. How on earth would a girl that age cope with three children? Plus deal with the trauma and grief of losing her parents and sister in that one, shocking, mindless act.

Alex closed his eyes and groaned. How could he have said what he did to her? And she was right when she'd asked what her situation had to do with his rudeness. An insult was an insult however you dressed it and whomever you addressed it to.

What a headache.

Plus the town house project was running behind schedule. He should be out there now checking what was going on. Maybe they could go after the movie. He yawned. His eyes drifted shut and flicked open as a roar of childish laughter jerked him awake.

Chloe must be exhausted, working all day from presumably nine this morning and having spent most of the night at the police station. Her face had showed the signs of strain — pale cheeks with dark smudges under her eyes, accentuated because she'd pulled her hair back, held somehow with a tortoiseshell clasp. Pretty eyes. Deep green with brown flecks. Emphasized by the hairstyle and the white blouse. The fine bone structure made her appear waiflike. An orphan. He hadn't noticed that last night. Too busy being an angry and abusive victim.

That boy Sebastian had better get his act together. He should be helping his sister, not causing trouble. Perhaps he should press the charges of trespassing and give him a taste of court. But that was excessive. The kid needed a chance to straighten himself out.

"Who was he?" demanded Simone as soon as Chloe set foot inside the house after work that evening. "Did he call you at the shop?"

"Is Seb at home?" countered Chloe as she dumped her handbag on the hall table and headed for the kitchen with her green bag of groceries.

"Of course. They're all in the pool, plus a few extras."

"Which extras?" Seb wasn't to have his mates around for about fifty years, and he knew it.

"Matty and Andrew." Julian's friends.

Simone peered into the shopping bag. "You shouldn't buy butter, Chloe. You'll clog their arteries."

Chloe took the offending article and opened the fridge. Mum had been brought up on a dairy farm and couldn't abide the taste of margarine. Buying butter was one small, private gesture in her memory. Simone handed her the groceries. Chloe stacked without comment. There was no point.

"Who was he? Did you meet him at work? No, you couldn't have, because he didn't know where you worked. Grab the lemon squash while you're in there, lovey. And some ice."

"Didn't give him the third degree?" Chloe removed the lemon squash bottle, which Simone must have brought with her, knowing Chloe didn't buy soft drinks, took the ice tray from the freezer and shut the fridge.

Simone unscrewed the cap. Her nails were purple today. Chunky slip-on sandals revealed matching purple toenails.

"What do you take me for?" she retorted. "You look exhausted. Sit down, and I'll fix this."

Chloe peered through the kitchen window and counted heads bobbing in the blue water. Four, plus she could just see Katy's feet as she lay on the recliner in the shade. The water beckoned. Might wake her up and give her the energy to cook dinner.

"Thanks." She took the tall glass from

45

Simone and drained half in one long swallow.

"Lovey, don't blame yourself for what young Seb got up to. Boys will be boys. I gave him a good talking to when he woke up." Simone nodded firmly with fuchsia lips pursed. "He's very sorry about the whole thing. I made sure of that!"

"Constable Burrows told me that the police wanted to give him a fright. They didn't think he was a bad kid. I hope —" Chloe swallowed. An image of Alex Bergman's furious face flashed through her mind.

"What?"

"That man who rang. He was the one who caught Seb. The man whose place they were caught trashing."

Purple-tipped fingers flew to Simone's mouth in horror. "Did he cause trouble? Why didn't you tell me?"

"Tell you what? I didn't know his name." Chloe finished her drink. "It was odd. He came into the shop with his daughter. I thought he was going to be angry again, and I was ready to call the police, but he came to apologize for what he said this morning."

"And so he should!" Five feet four of outraged grandma had bristled with righteous, protective indignation when Chloe

46

recounted the incident before she left for work.

Chloe smiled and stepped forward to hug her tightly. "Thank you, Simone. Thanks for coming over and . . . everything."

"And what else would you expect?" The fingers stopped patting her back and gave her a little shake.

Chloe said nothing. What she had expected was a round of "I told you so's," but she'd been wrong. Maybe she was too inflexible, had assessed Simone years ago and never bothered to form a second opinion. Maybe the strain of bringing up the kids had made her difficult, narrow-minded, and too quick to make assumptions. Like that man, Alex Bergman. She'd done it with him too.

He'd done it with her, and it had been extremely unpleasant.

Chloe took Sebastian to the police station on Sunday to check in as ordered. The officer on duty said, "Constable Fields will be down shortly."

Nice Constable Burrows would be the night shift.

Constable Fields, when she appeared, towered over both Chloe and Seb, and she was almost wider than both of them put together. Dark hair so short it must have had a shave recently added to the imposing presence.

She sat them opposite her in one of the interrogation rooms. "I've good news and bad news." Chloe caught Seb's fearful eye. "Good news is Mr. Bergman has accepted that Sebastian undergo an official Police Caution. Be here at ten tomorrow."

She glared at Seb, who quailed under the flinty stare.

"Is that family conferencing?" asked Chloe. "Constable Burrows mentioned it could be an option."

"No, a Caution is our first step with cases such as this. We prefer the deterrent effect to locking young people away." Again the chilly gaze lighted on Seb, who shrank farther into his chair. "Bad news is the owner of the car you stole isn't so accommodating."

"But I didn't steal it," cried Seb.

"The judge will decide that, but given your cooperation and the fact that the others have been in trouble with us before, you'll probably get off with a suspended sentence and good behavior."

"When will he go to court?" asked Chloe. "Do we need a lawyer? I can't afford . . ." She stopped, biting her lower lip. She

48

couldn't afford anything much at all.

"Here's the Legal Aid number. He'll have to appear in court tomorrow for a trial date to be set."

She handed Chloe a card and stood up. The steely-dagger gaze pinioned Seb once more. "I hope I don't see you in here again, young man."

He sprang to his feet, shaking his head.

"I'd suggest you get hold of a lawyer quickly and ask for Sebastian to be tried separately from those others. They're a bad bunch."

"Thank you," said Chloe, gratified and surprised to see a glimmer of sympathetic warmth in the private look Constable Fields gave her as she opened the door.

"Thanks," muttered Seb as he scuttled out ahead of them.

Alex picked up the phone on Monday afternoon, the third interruption since he'd sat down to work. If it was another telemarketer, the phone at the other end would melt when his language hit the wires.

"Bergman Design," he barked.

"Hello, may I speak to Alex Bergman, please?"

He recognized the voice. A slight hesitancy in the tone betrayed nervousness, as if she'd screwed up all her courage to make the call but now found that resolve failing her. He swiftly moderated his tone.

"Alex speaking." Chloe Gardiner deserved gentle treatment. Especially from him.

"Oh, hello," she said again. "I'm sorry to bother you at work. I'll call later if you'd rather."

"No, it's fine. I work from home, so I'm my own boss." He added a chuckle to show he truly wasn't annoyed.

"I'm Chloe Gardiner."

"I know." Alex waited.

"How are . . ." he began as she said, "I wanted to . . ."

Silence again.

"Sorry," she said.

More silence.

"Thank you." The words erupted into his ear. "For not pressing charges against Seb."

"I thought he needed a chance."

"He does. I just hope the judge sees it that way."

"Judge?" Surely he'd prevented that, hadn't he?

"The owner of the stolen car is taking them to court. The trial date was set this afternoon. It's in March." Her voice trailed away, and he heard the anxiety, but she added briskly, "But that's not your problem.

I was wondering — his grandmother suggested — insisted, actually — she's very persuasive and very angry with Sebastian . . . Anyway, Simone wants him to apologize to you in person, and she thinks he should repair the damage. Maybe work off the cost of the lights and whatever else needs replacing."

Giving the boy a chance was one thing, but did he want him hanging around? How did he know he wouldn't case the place for another nocturnal visit? And he'd have to come into the house to use the bathroom. Not a desirable state of affairs.

"I'm not too sure."

"Seb won't cause any more trouble. He's not allowed to see those boys again. He's grounded for the rest of the holidays, and he doesn't go to the same school as they do." The words tumbled into his ear, a little breathless, very worried, anxious to convince.

"I'd need to give it some thought." Alex pulled a face as he considered how to extricate himself from this very awkward situation.

"I understand." Chloe's voice was formal now, formal and reserved. "I'd like to bring him over to apologize, though."

"Of course. When?" He heard himself

almost gushing in the effort to appear reasonable in making this small concession.

No trace of nervousness now when she said, "Whenever suits you. I'd like to do it as soon as possible. We won't bother you again."

"This evening?" How did she manage to make him feel guilty?

"Is six-thirty all right?"

"That's fine. Do you have the address?"

"Seb knows where you live," she said dryly. "Thank you. Good-bye." The line clicked.

Alex replaced the phone with precise care. He sucked in air between pursed lips. An apology. He could accept that. Shake hands with the kid.

He stood up and immediately sat down again. He had to finish the kitchen plan. Almost done. He picked up his pencil, twiddling it between thumb and forefinger. Chloe's voice was sweet. Very unexpected in his ear. He frightened her. He must try hard not to when she brought her brother over this evening.

Alex glanced at his watch. He dropped the pencil and stood up. He went to the small kitchen area he'd installed in his office and filled the electric kettle. Six-thirty, she'd said. About two and a half hours. He leaned against the counter, waiting for the kettle to boil. It must have taken a lot of courage for Chloe to call. He could hear it in her voice. She was a very courageous girl — had to be to take on what she had. All by herself. Except for the grandmother.

He dumped a green-tea teabag into a mug. She'd have a boyfriend for sure, Chloe. A girl as pretty as she was. An image of her face floated into his mind. Beautiful eyes with delicately arched brows framing them. A mouth with soft, full lips. Hardly any makeup. Didn't need it. Her skin was perfect.

She gave the impression of extreme fragility, but he suspected that was quite wrong. Interesting to discover whether he was right. A thrill of anticipation rippled through him. She'd be here in a few hours.

The steaming kettle clicked itself off. Alex poured water into his mug and wandered back to his desk in a pleasant state of daydream. Then he remembered why Chloe was coming. And he had yet to decide what to say to her about Sebastian.

CHAPTER THREE

"It's best if just Seb and I go," Chloe said for the third time.

"But he won't be able to get violent if I'm there." Simone took a bite from one of the few remaining chocolate chip muffins she and Katy had made.

"A grandma bodyguard, you mean?" Chloe brushed crumbs from Simone's blouse. "He won't be violent. Seb's apologizing to him, remember? Anyway, he has a wife and child."

"He might be a wife beater." Simone pressed a fingertip onto a crumb and transported it to her mouth.

"Doubt it. He sounded quite —"

"What?" The gray eyes flashed to Chloe's face.

"Subdued." Chloe thought for a moment. "Normal." He probably *was* a normal man. People under extremes of emotional stress reacted in all sorts of unpredictable ways.

Simone popped the last of the muffin into her mouth, chewed, and swallowed. "He had a lovely voice on the phone. Very sexy." She smiled, but her expression suddenly became serious, and she took Chloe's hand in hers. "I worry about you, lovey. You're too serious, and your pretty face is always worried. You've missed your youth, my pet. Old before your time."

"I didn't have any choice," Chloe managed to say through the choking in her throat. Simone was right. Too serious, too stressed, her life and her focus too narrow. But she had responsibilities, and they weren't going away anytime soon. Katy was only eleven. Anyway, Chloe loved her half siblings dearly — they were all she had.

Simone sighed. "All I mean is, you don't give yourself much of a chance to fall in love. Katy told me you haven't been out on a date in years. Not since that Lachlan —"

"I'm only twenty-six," interrupted Chloe before Simone could get started on Lachlan's failings. Lachlan, who'd found dealing with a grief-stricken girlfriend completely beyond his capabilities or his love. But her protest was a weak effort, and they both knew it.

"I'm not desperate to find a man," she said firmly. "And Katy's as bad as you are.

She raved about the really cool teacher at school until he got married and she had to rethink her plans." Chloe laughed wryly.

"You should finish your degree," said Simone with an abrupt switch of attack. This conversation had been had before, many times. The answer was always the same.

Chloe shook her head. "I can't, not yet. When Katy's in high school, I'll think about it."

"That's two years away."

"I can't afford not to work. It was tough enough when I was a student and there was just me to think about. It'd be impossible now." She'd love to go back to full-time study, finish her performing-arts degree, immerse herself in that musical world again. At the moment it was a dream shoved to the furthest reaches of her mind.

"You could use some of the inheritance money," suggested Simone.

Chloe firmed her mouth into a straight line and folded her arms. "No. You know I won't dip into that if I can help it. They'll all need it when they grow up. We have the house unencumbered, and, thanks to that amazing public donation, we can scrape by on my earnings." She would *not* fritter away the children's inheritance on daily living.

Not when the money would set them up for good educations and a nest egg when they reached twenty-one. Bevan and Mum would have wanted that.

"I wish you'd let me help," grumbled Simone. "Bevan wanted you to have everything he could provide for you. He loved you and Terry as his own."

"I know, and we loved him. He was our father, far more so than the real one."

"Bevan told me you were Honors material. You play so beautifully. He was extremely proud of you. He'd be very disappointed that you let it slide this way."

Chloe bit her lip. That remark had so much wrong with it, was so unfair and thoughtless, she couldn't begin to correct Simone. Best ignore it. She wouldn't have knowingly disappointed Bevan in a million years. She wouldn't have dropped out of university in an ideal world, but life wasn't ideal, as they'd learned so painfully.

Bevan had died. Mum and Terry had died. Simone was an emotional mess for the first two years after the bombing, hardly any help at all. Three young children were left with only their big half sister to care for them. They needed full-time love and a full-time, stay-at-home replacement mother. A stable routine. Chloe had done her best to provide it. And Simone had rallied eventually.

"You do help," Chloe said. "We couldn't manage without you."

Seb fidgeted constantly in the passenger seat beside Chloe. As soon as she started the engine, he tuned in music full blast, nearly blowing the windows out with a thudding bass beat and screaming lead vocalist.

"Turn it down!" she yelled.

He twisted the dial a fraction. Now just her body vibrated rather than the whole car. "Seb!" Another twist. Silence, and she could think.

"You didn't need to switch it off." She braked at the stop sign at the end of their cul de sac, peering both ways before easing out into the road.

"Not much point having it on if you can't hear it." He stared out the window with his arms folded hard across his chest. Chloe gritted her teeth. Why did teenagers always overreact to every little thing? And where did he get off doing this sullen, defiant routine? This whole situation was his doing.

Owning up to bad behavior took courage, no two ways about it. Alex Bergman had had the courage and the moral integrity to make an apology to her. Maybe she owed him an apology too. Chloe smiled to herself.

Everyone could apologize to everyone. They'd all be falling over themselves to be polite.

Alex's street was close to the major arterial route from the city center, screened by towering gum trees and raised above the traffic by the natural rise of the land. The whole suburb spilled down the gentle slopes of Black Mountain, the houses nestled in dense, original bushland thick with gums, wattles, and native vegetation.

Bevan had bought their own house when he'd married her mother sixteen years ago. He'd wanted to live in Aranda because it was close to the university where he lectured in Asian Studies — said they'd need a big place because they planned to have more children so Terry and Chloe would have siblings. And ultimately they'd been a big happy family in that sprawling house, all seven of them, until the older girls had moved out to share a house with fellow students.

"Stop." Seb sat upright to twist in his seat, jolting her into sudden awareness. "You've gone past."

She slowed and hauled the big sedan through a turn in a neighbor's driveway. Alex's house was set back with a long, sloping lawn, dry and turning brown in the summer heat, as were most people's at this time of year. Drought conditions and water restrictions made their dusty mark on Australia's bush capital. She parked in the shade, and they both got out and stared at the low white house for a moment. It sat sheltered from the weather in a cool nest of trees and shrubbery with a large liquidambar dominating the front garden. That tree would be glorious in its autumn colors.

Chloe walked up the driveway. The accumulated heat of the day radiated through the soles of her sandals. Seb shuffled behind her. Someone had spray-painted a hot pink obscenity on the blanched white concrete.

"It wasn't me," said Seb as she paused, staring at the word beneath her feet. "It was Cameron."

Chloe exhaled in disgust, shook her head, and moved on.

The liquidambar stood in the middle of a loop at the top of the drive. An arched gateway led to the rear between the double garage and the house. A small sign said OFFICE with an arrow pointing through the gate. Stone pavers shunted the social visitor between low shrubs to the front door. Small black solar sensor lights were set along the path. All broken.

A pair of birches shaded the front of the

house; their leaves, cool and green, rustled gently in the slight breeze. Two steps up onto the wide front porch, the gray slate surface cooler underfoot. The front door stood open, but the security screen door was closed. A polished wood floor lead into the dim recesses of the house.

"Ready?" Chloe paused with finger poised on the bell.

"Yeah." His upper lip wore a sheen of perspiration. Probably not from the heat of the afternoon. *Good. He darn well should be nervous.* She was.

Alex was in the kitchen preparing salad for dinner when the bell rang. He wiped his hands, took a deep breath, and went to open the door. They stood side by side on the porch, their outlines blurred by the screen. Chloe wore a pale pink sundress that revealed lightly tanned, bare shoulders and slender legs. She'd pulled her hair back again, but wisps drifted across her brow and cheeks. She stood stiffly straight, clutching her car keys and a small black purse before her with both hands. Looked as though she were awaiting execution.

He wanted to set her at her ease, invite her in for a drink, make her smile and see he wasn't the ogre she thought he was, but the boy was there, slouching, trying to look

61

cool. Failing dismally.

The kid had thrust his hands into the pockets of baggy black shorts, but he fidgeted from one thong-clad foot to the other and licked his lips nervously when he spied Alex approaching. He immediately stared at his feet.

Alex unlatched the screen and pushed it open toward them. "Hello. Come in."

"Thank you." Chloe ducked her head in a kind of greeting and stepped awkwardly past him. The boy followed with a brave attempt at a swagger.

They stood crowded together in the entry foyer while Alex closed the screen door. A light fragrance hung in the air. Her perfume. Tantalizing with a hint of warm female skin. His eyes strayed to her bare neck, the hair lifted from the nape with delicate strands escaping from the clasp. His hand rose, perhaps with the intention of touching, feeling the softness. He quickly changed it to a gesture of welcome.

"This way." He indicated the open-plan living room on the left. "Sit down, please. Would you like a cool drink?" He looked from one to the other, but Chloe shook her head for them both and remained standing.

She met his eye with a firm, direct gaze. Her eyes really were beautiful. Deep green with golden brown flecks. The lashes were dark, which contrasted stunningly with the blond hair. Natural blond, he'd bet. She had no artifice about her.

"No, thank you. We don't want to intrude. Sebastian has something to say to you."

Alex tore his attention from the fascinating aspects of Chloe's hair and eyes. He studied Sebastian. Just a kid. A pimply-faced, frightened boy. Despite the stance and the attitude, the blue eyes weren't those of a hardened thug. Fourteen, the police had told him. Trying out his wings and getting into more trouble than he'd dreamed existed. One stupid action and *wham!* Alex knew all about the injustice of that.

Some kids got away with murder over and over again. Others do something foolhardy once, and they're caught. First go. He and Sebastian. Lucky, really, although Sebastian wouldn't see it that way for many years to come.

He watched the boy working out how to start his little speech. He would've prepared something — Chloe would've seen to that. And Grandma. People who cared were this boy's saviors.

"Thanks for not, you know, um, charging me with, um, trespassing and that." Sebastian's face was deep rose pink. He glanced at his sister, and she nodded encouragingly. He looked back at Alex, met his gaze briefly, then lost courage and spoke to his top button instead. "And for not sending me to court."

"All right." Alex waited.

Chloe frowned at Sebastian and murmured, "Go on." She flicked an anxious glance at Alex, and he raised an eyebrow slightly.

"I'm sorry about what we — I mean, what I did. Breaking the lights and stuff. Sorry." He subsided into silence.

"Thank you for coming to see me," said Alex. "I appreciate it. It's not easy to own up to something you've done wrong. Shows courage and character."

Two pairs of eyes regarded him intently, expecting more. An outburst perhaps. A tirade about the inconsiderate selfishness of today's youth and the path to ruin. He said nothing. Chloe's whole body relaxed as she realized he'd finished. The tension left her shoulders, and she suddenly looked incredibly tired.

Alex impulsively extended his hand to Sebastian, and as he shook it, a tentative smile crept across the boy's lips.

"I thought you'd be really mad."

"I am," Alex replied, and the smile disappeared in a flash. "But you've apologized, and I accept your apology."

"So what happens now?" Sebastian's gaze swung to Chloe, then back again, clearly bewildered.

Chloe grasped his arm. "We leave Mr. Bergman in peace and don't bother him again. Ever. Thank you for seeing us, Mr. Bergman." She edged her brother toward the door.

Never see her again. Ever? Her perfume danced in his nostrils as she moved.

"Wait a moment," he said quickly. They paused. Alarm registered on her face for an instant, but Alex smiled gently. "You mentioned some form of recompense?"

"Oh, yes. I'm sorry. You didn't sound very keen." She gathered herself together and faced him squarely. "What did you have in mind?"

Alex shoved his brain into gear, top gear. Overdrive. He hadn't thought at all. He hadn't wanted the boy here. Did he want him here? What about Steffie? But he could organize it so that Sebastian didn't come on her weekends. He seemed a nice enough kid, deserved a second chance. Do him good to work off his debt. Those sensor lights weren't cheap to replace. And scrubbing the concrete would be a good lesson.

A horrible job.

"He can clean the graffiti off my driveway for a start. And next door's. They've got young children, and that language is downright offensive. There's gardening, the gutters need cleaning, and some painting needs to be done."

Chloe jumped in with, "He can't do gutters. He's not good with heights."

"Chloe!" The cheeks went red again. Sebastian met his gaze, and Alex spontaneously found himself sharing a man-to-man glance. A mother hen. That could become claustrophobic for a teenager. Had it? Had this been Sebastian's clumsy form of breaking out?

He said dryly, "Not a good idea from a safety point of view anyway. Don't want you to sue me if he fell off the ladder."

"I wouldn't!"

Alex kept his expression neutral at the horrified look on her face. Crazily he wanted to laugh. He wanted to see her smile. She hadn't since he'd met her. Not once. Did she ever have reason to smile, or was her life too fraught with worry and responsibility?

He turned to Sebastian, who was trying to hide a grin. "How about you come for a couple of hours every day? If we calculate you'd earn fifteen dollars an hour, it would take you about forty hours to pay off the cost of repairing the damage. Or, alternatively, you could just pay me in one go."

"Six hundred dollars?" gasped Sebastian. No sign of the grin now. His cheeks had gone white. He gulped.

Chloe firmed her mouth. Alex Bergman was deadly serious, his eyes hard and calculating. He was still angry with Seb. Very angry, and he wanted compensation despite his gracious acceptance of the apology. How could he possibly think she'd sue him if Seb hurt himself?

Now came Seb's moment of truth. Paying for his sins. He had seventy-three dollars in his savings account from his milk run and delivering papers. Julian, more frugal, had one hundred and two, but he wouldn't be coughing up for this. Brotherly love extended only so far when you were saving for a computer upgrade. She deliberately kept her expression blank.

Alex regarded him steadily. "Those lights were the best quality. I had ten, and some had to be installed by an electrician. Electricians charge a fortune to walk in the door. There's also the letter box and removing the graffiti."

"But six hundred?" groaned Seb.

"Don't argue," said Chloe firmly. She turned to Alex. "When would you like him to start? He has two more weeks of holidays, but he can come after school for an hour when term starts and maybe on weekends."

"Tomorrow at eight-thirty. Before it gets too hot."

"Eight-thirty?" Sebastian groaned again, but Chloe jabbed him in the ribs with her elbow. "You don't get a say in this."

"All right."

"You can ride your bike over." Deal done, Chloe nudged her brother toward the entry foyer.

Alex held the door open for them. "See you tomorrow, Sebastian."

"See ya," the boy called. He jumped down the two steps and sauntered toward the dark red sedan parked in the street, big T-shirt hanging loosely from his thin frame.

"Thank you, Mr. Bergman." Chloe stood uncertainly on the porch while he held the screen door. He stepped outside and let it close behind him.

"Please call me Alex." He smiled. "You make me sound ancient." Maybe she thought he *was* ancient. A grumpy old man. He couldn't be more than seven or eight years older than she.

She looked up at him. Still no smile but

no fear now. That, at least, was progress. "Seb will work hard for you, I know. He's a good boy. Really he is."

"I can see that, or I wouldn't have suggested he come to my house."

"I'll make sure he does what you want."

"Stop worrying, Chloe." He smiled again, trying for reassurance without being patronizing.

"I'm not worrying. Not really. I just — this whole thing is so . . ." She stopped. The pink tip of her tongue ran across her lower lip. He watched, fascinated. She swallowed, raised her face. A shaft of the setting sun caught her hair in a glow of gold.

"It's not your fault," he said gently. The green eyes gazed into his, hypnotizing him. The possibility of unshed tears was there. Unmistakable, the moistness at the corners of her eyes. She was fragile, this girl. Strung taut, near to breaking. "I'm really sorry about what I said to you at the police station. I hope you've forgiven me."

"Yes." She swallowed. "Yes, I know. We were all — it was all wrong. And you were worried about your family. It's natural to be angry under those circumstances."

"Maybe," he said slowly. "But it's not a good enough excuse to attack you." He couldn't stop staring into her eyes.

"Well." Chloe suddenly averted her gaze. She shifted her purse to her other hand and jingled her car keys. "I'd better go. Your wife will be wanting you to have dinner. Thanks again. I'll make sure Seb comes right on time. Eight-thirty on the dot. Thank you."

Before he could say a word, she was down the steps and heading for the car. *I live alone,* he wanted to tell her, but he couldn't yell that down the driveway with Jeannie next door watering her petunias and casting curious glances their way.

"Good-bye," he called.

Chloe turned and waved briefly. The skirt of the sundress swished about her bare legs. Chloe Gardiner was a peach. Sweet and utterly tempting. But too young, too complicated, too inexperienced. And the last thing Alex wanted was an entanglement with another woman after the mess of the divorce and the complication of Steffie's visits. More children would mean more responsibility. He was too busy for extras. He'd help these kids, especially the boy, because they'd had a tough life, but when Seb's hours were up, he was on his own. Alex's civic duty would be done.

Chloe drove home in a daze of unidentifiable emotions. Relief was in there somewhere. Surprise too. She'd been totally wrong about the man. He was nothing like the monster she'd met that night. He was kind, and he seemed to understand about Seb. They'd shared a masculine comprehension of . . . something, an innate bond of which she was only dimly aware but sensed. And it left her apart in her femaleness.

Yes, Alex Bergman had been polite and friendly. He hadn't made it any harder for Seb than it already was. He'd kept it between them, which was good, not dragging in his wife and child to complicate matters with an audience. And he really seemed to feel bad about his attack on her, kept apologizing. Needn't have worried at all.

Unless he had a hidden, violent temper such as he'd displayed that night. A temper that could resurface at any moment. If Seb annoyed him inadvertently. What if he let fly with a fist occasionally? What if he drank? Or worse? Would Seb be safe there with him? Should she have checked with Constable Burrows if this was a good plan?

"Will you be all right, Seb? If he does anything the slightest bit off, get out of there." She could call the constable and ask. Tonight.

Seb stared at her with his face screwed into an expression of complete disbelief. "What are you going on about? Do you think the guy's a child molester?"

Chloe changed gears as they approached a yield sign.

"No!" She'd scoffed at Simone's notion that Alex was a wife beater, and instinct told her he indulged in none of those other evils, but a child was involved, and she couldn't figure out if he was still angry or if he'd really forgiven Seb. His face and his manner could be so stern.

But then there was the completely different expression he'd worn when he made his apology just now. As if he was truly concerned that she understood how sorry he was. His eyes had pierced her. Just the memory of that look generated heat in her cheeks.

"If he tries anything, I'll kick him where he'll feel it most." Seb snorted with laughter, and she smiled reluctantly. Seb was right — she was paranoid.

"Make sure you stay outside."

"What if I want to use the toilet?"

"You can wait till you get home."

"Chloeeee." Seb sighed ostentatiously. He tapped his fingers on his thigh.

"We don't know him at all," she retorted.

"Exactly. Doesn't mean he's some kind of pervert. Why do you always think the worst of people?"

72

"He has a bad temper, so watch out." It was a last resort. The attraction that hovered in the background didn't bear any form of scrutiny whatsoever. She wouldn't give it brain space.

"I think it's a very good idea," said Constable Brent Burrows that night. "It'll make him realize the consequences of what he's done and look good in court. Shows remorse and a desire to make recompense."

"I just realized we don't know anything about Alex Bergman. And Seb's very young."

"His name would have popped up if he had a record of anything along the lines you're thinking, Chloe." He laughed that nice, friendly, reassuring laugh. "Don't worry."

"I'm sorry I bothered you."

"Don't be. That's what we're here for."

"Well, thanks again." Chloe waited for him to say good night before she hung up, but instead he said, "I was going to call you."

"Were you?" Her hand froze on the receiver. "Is something else wrong? Another complaint?"

He laughed. "No. This is purely personal. I wondered if you'd like to go out. Dinner, something, anything?"

"Oooohhh." The sound rushed out in a whoosh of relief. A date. He wanted to go out on a date. Nice Constable Brent. Why not? Simone would be pleased. So would Katy. What would a date with Alex Bergman — shut up, he's married. "That would be lovely. Thank you. When?"

"I finish at six in the morning. We could do breakfast." His voice was light, joking.

Chloe laughed. "That'd be a first, but I couldn't leave the kids at that hour."

"I'm not always on night duty, but I have another three weeks of it." His disappointment was clearly evident. "What about lunch? I don't sleep well in this heat anyway."

"I can take an hour at twelve-thirty. Is that all right?"

"Fine. Great. What about tomorrow?"

So soon? "All right. Can you come to the shop?"

"I'll be there," he promised. "Good night, Chloe. I'm glad you called."

Chloe replaced the receiver carefully on its cradle. This would be her first proper date for — how long? She frowned. Five years? No! Impossible. Was it? Since the Lachlan disaster. They'd been together exclusively for nearly eight months. After that experience she wasn't in a hurry to hook up with anyone.

She'd gone out with friends over the years but always in groups, and she never lingered the way the others did, because the baby-sitter was always waiting at home. Then her contemporaries in the music course had graduated and moved out into the world while she stayed on. Teaching music privately was a solitary occupation.

It was hard to meet anyone interesting, and now that she thought about it, she hadn't been invited out, one on one, for a long, long time. The other problem, of course, was that at her age, when an interesting man did cross her path — in the shop or as a prospective student — he was already taken.

Alex Bergman, for example. Objectively speaking, purely as an example, he was interesting. Handsome and smart but, typically, married. And even if he wasn't, if he was divorced or separated as many were at his age, he had at least one small child in tow, and the last thing Chloe needed or wanted was to take on more children. Especially a spoiled, grumpy little one even younger than Katy.

When the front doorbell shrilled, Alex was sitting on the rear terrace under the shade umbrella, lingering over the word puzzles in the paper and his second cup of tea. Sebastian was prompt. A good start.

He sent the boy to the back garden via the side gate rather than let him walk through the house. When he regained the terrace, Sebastian had propped his bike against a birch tree and stood waiting, stretching first one arm, then the other, across his chest.

His expression displayed neither resentment nor anger at having to work off his crime. He watched with an alert intelligence, and his blue eyes took in the garden and the pertinent details as Alex explained his chores to him.

"You can start by raking up all the leaf litter and fallen twigs and stuff. The rake's leaning against the shed, and there's a wheelbarrow if you need it."

"Fine." Sebastian sauntered over to collect the rake and began scraping at the grass with practiced ease. Of course those kids would have to maintain their own house. No parents to do the gardening and take the garbage out, prepare meals and clean the house. They'd all have to chip in.

Alex returned to the paper and the puzzles, watching his worker surreptitiously while trying to come up with a nine-letter word from the letters *NPDOLUSEU.* This Focus puzzle was a challenge. One nine-letter word and varying quantities of four-letter words and above, all including a designated letter. Today he'd reached the Very Good level, but that nine-letter word eluded him.

He glanced at his watch after a time. Eight-fifty. He'd have to afford the kid a measure of trust; he couldn't sit here like a guard dog all morning. Time to get to work. The phone rang inside. Should be the plasterer. He'd better have a good reason for not turning up at the site yesterday, and for having his phone turned off.

"I'll be in my office," he called to Sebastian. "Bang on the door if you need anything."

Half an hour later the wheelbarrow began trundling between the front and back gardens, and the gate clicked and banged occasionally. From his office window Alex caught glimpses. The boy worked steadily, not fast but consistently. Must be heating up out there.

At ten-fifteen Alex took a jug of iced water and a glass out to the table where he'd had breakfast. Sebastian was emptying the wheelbarrow. He glanced up but didn't stop what he was doing.

"Like a drink?" called Alex.

"Thanks." Sebastian threw the last armful of debris into a bag. "It's hot now."

"Don't want your sister to think I'm treating you like a slave."

Sebastian plopped down on a chair in the shade of the umbrella. He drained the glass in one long gulp and refilled it, emptying that almost as quickly.

"Forgot to bring my water bottle." He wiped his mouth with the back of one hand.

Alex surveyed the garden. Not a stray leaf or twig to be seen. "You've done a good job."

"Front's almost done." Sebastian looked at the paper, picked up the pencil Alex had left on the table, and wrote *PENDULOUS*.

"Drat it." Alex stared at the word that was so glaringly obvious now.

Sebastian dropped the pencil and stood up quickly. His eyes opened wide in alarm. "Sorry, I thought you'd finished."

"Hey, relax, mate. Sit down." The boy looked ready to run. Did he terrify the whole Gardiner clan? "I sat there for ages trying to get that rotten word and couldn't for the life of me. It was driving me nuts." He laughed. "Took you half a second."

"Usually does." Sebastian sat down again with a cautious smile.

"Do you do those puzzles every day?" Alex pulled up a chair, although he'd only meant to bring the water and leave it on the table.

"Yeah. We all do them over breakfast. I get the Focus word first, but Chloe's best at the crosswords. Especially the cryptic ones. I'm not so good at those yet. Katy's the math genius. And Julian's pretty smart."

"Good heavens." Alex tried to assimilate this picture of an orderly hive of intellectual activity with the image he'd had in his head of their house — chaotic and frantic at best. "How many of you are there?"

"Chloe. Me and Julian, we're twins. And Katy. She's eleven."

"Identical twin?"

"Yep."

"But Julian didn't get involved with those same kids you did?"

"No." Sebastian frowned. "He likes computers, and he plays the flute."

"What do you like?"

"Sports."

"I swim a couple of mornings a week and play basketball on Thursdays. Season starts again soon. What do you do?"

"Cricket. I do volleyball in winter at school."

Alex nodded. "I played cricket at school and university. Wicket keeper."

"Bowler," said Sebastian. "Spin."

"Cool. Most young bowlers want to be pace. Been following the Tests?"

Sebastian nodded eagerly. "The Aussies are doing well. I'd love to wear the baggy green."

"So would I. Won't now, of course. But you could."

"Doubt it."

Alex stood up. "Keep at it, and you never know. If you finish up the front, that'll do you for today. Tomorrow you can tackle that graffiti."

"How was it?" asked Chloe when she entered the house after work and found Seb sprawled on his bed in his room.

He lifted his face from the cricket magazine he was reading. "Okay." His gaze dropped to the article.

"Was he pleased with you?"

"Yeah."

"What's he like?"

"Okay."

"Not angry?"

"No. Why would he be angry? I'm there working for him, aren't I?" His expression clearly announced, *Stop with the dumb questions.*

She withdrew and went to find Simone

80

and Katy.

Later that evening the phone rang. Chloe, yawning in front of the TV, thinking about bed, picked up.

"Hello."

"Hello, Chloe. Hope I'm not calling too late."

The sound of his voice, so unexpected and warm in her ear, jolted through her body, snapping her to attention. She jerked up straight on the couch. Her hand, unaccountably, had begun to shake. She opened her mouth to reply, but nothing emerged.

"Chloe? Are you there?"

"Yes." She coughed and cleared her throat.

"Were you asleep?"

"No." She glanced at the clock.

"I thought I should report on Sebastian."

"Did he do a good job?" Her hand clutched the receiver as though it were a life preserver.

"Excellent."

"Oh, thank goodness," emerged on a pent-up lungful of air. "What did he do? I couldn't get much more than a grunt out of him."

Alex laughed softly and didn't reply for a moment. "I had him tidy up the front and back lawns. There's not so much as a blade of grass on the loose there now."

"He does our garden. Takes turns with Julian. We all have chores to do. It wouldn't work otherwise." The stiffness melted from her spine, and Chloe lounged back into the cushions and swung her bare feet up, wrapping her free hand around her bent knees.

"It must have been impossibly difficult for you," Alex said. "At the time."

"Yes." Chloe swallowed. "It was hard. But we're all right now." She felt her cheeks warming uncomfortably. What on earth would he think about that remark? How could Seb's turning into a juvenile delinquent possibly classify as "all right"? Especially by the man whose property he'd vandalized? She straightened her legs and sat up. What a total idiot she was, sitting here like a teenager talking to her boyfriend. Thank goodness he couldn't see her. "I mean, until recently," she said stiffly.

"I don't think Sebastian is heading for a life of crime, Chloe. He made a mistake, he's owned up, and now he's doing his best to pay for it. He's too smart to do it again."

"Do you think so?"

"Yes." The firmness of his reply was reassuring. "But he has a lot more hours to do for me, so we'll see if he can keep it up." The stern man reemerged, the real one. The one who had a family and property to protect. The virtual stranger doing Seb a favor.

"Yes, of course." Chloe bit her lip. Alex was right. Seb might not think this such a good plan in a few weeks' time, when school was back in session and all his other commitments kicked in.

"Tomorrow I'm making him clean the graffiti off the driveway here and next door. There are four neighbors he'll have to visit too. Send him along with some rubber gloves. Mine will be too big."

"What can he use to remove it?" Wasn't spray paint really tough to get off? How much would paint remover cost, or had Alex already factored that in? Probably. He was very organized.

"I've bought some stuff. I'll give him a mask to wear — the fumes are pretty toxic."

"Is it safe?" she demanded swiftly.

"Yes. Trust me, Chloe. I know about these things. I have a builder's license."

"Sorry." The man was a professional — highly qualified, educated, and busy. Very soon he'd cut off this meandering conversation to do something more important.

"Not at all. You're right to be concerned. I'm quite paranoid where my daughter's health and safety are involved."

Apart from letting her overeat and spoiling

83

her. Chloe stifled her grin in case her jangly nerves made her laugh out loud. "How old is she?"

"Six going on seventeen." He laughed with all the proud love of a doting dad. "I suppose all fathers say that about their daughters. Can't bear to see them growing up."

"Bevan used to say that about Katy," said Chloe. How he'd adored his little girl. But she *was* an adorable child. Still was. They all loved her fiercely.

"Bevan?" Now his voice was subdued, as if felt guilty for mentioning fathers and daughters and guilty for having an unimpaired, close relationship with his. Such talk didn't bother any of the children now. They'd long ago worked through the grief and the associated traumas. Counseling had been provided, and someone was always available if any of them needed help in that way.

"Bevan was my stepfather. Mum married him when I was ten and my sister Terry was twelve. He was a fantastic dad to all of us. He wanted as many children as he could convince Mum to produce." She smiled at the memory. "But Mum thought five was plenty. Especially if more twins were likely."

Alex chuckled softly. "I don't blame her.

He sounds very special."

"He was."

"What about your real father?"

"He wasn't special. He cleared out when Terry was eighteen months old and Mum was pregnant with me."

"You've never met him?"

"Never laid eyes on him. Never even heard a peep out of him when Mum and Terry were killed."

"What a miserable wretch of a man," Alex said with a snort of disbelief.

"I never think about him. Bevan was my dad, even though he came along a bit late. Good thing he did. He restored my faith in the male of the species." Chloe gave a little laugh.

"I'm glad. We're not all stinkers," retorted Alex.

"I know."

"I'd better say good night." He sounded reluctant. "I have to go to a building site early tomorrow. Check on a delivery. The whole thing's becoming a gigantic headache."

"Do you want Seb to come later?"

"No. I should be back by eight."

She glanced at the clock. They'd been chatting for nearly ten minutes. Friendly chat, sharing information. At least she'd

85

been sharing information. She didn't know anything more about Alex Bergman other than he was pleased with Seb and thought he was a smart boy, which anyone with half a brain would discover in a second. And he worked hard and doted on his daughter, which she already knew.

"Good night. Thanks for calling."

"My pleasure."

What on earth would his wife be thinking?

CHAPTER FOUR

Sebastian and Alex sat on the terrace under the shade umbrella again the next morning. The boy had scrubbed and scrubbed until the foul words had completely disappeared. The driveway had a very clean patch, which contrasted strangely with the surrounding grayed concrete. It had taken him two solid hours and then some.

"Should I do next door's now?" Sebastian asked.

"Do you want to?" Jeannie would be pleased. Four-year-old Kenneth had taken to announcing the spray-painted phrase at all sorts of inopportune moments.

"Might as well, while I've got the stuff."

"All right, but have a break and a drink first."

"Did you get the word?" Sebastian peered at the paper, opened to the puzzle page.

"Yes, I did." Alex smirked. He poured water into a tall glass. Ice cubes tinkled against the sides.

"How long did it take you?" Sebastian grinned.

"Not long."

Sebastian drained the glass and refilled it. "Did you watch the one-day game yesterday?"

"Only caught bits on the car radio between appointments. Close one, huh?"

Sebastian embarked on an analysis of the Australian bowling attack and the weakness of the South African batting lineup, which lead to an in-depth discussion lasting at least half an hour.

Alex finally looked at his watch and stifled a gasp of annoyance. Half the morning gone, and the Robertson bathroom renovation quote still not typed up, plus Smythe's kitchen. Too much work. Not for the first time the thought crossed his mind that he needed a partner. Or at least a secretary. When he set himself up solo, he'd had no idea just how busy he'd become. "Listen, mate. It's probably too hot to be using that stuff on the driveway now. How about you do it first thing tomorrow?"

Sebastian nodded and got up to put the equipment away in the shed. "See ya," he said.

Alex waved and went inside. A part-time

secretary — that's what he needed. Someone to take care of the reams of paperwork. The phone rang stridently. And to answer the phone.

"Bergman Design."

"Is Seb still with you?" asked a desperate voice. A secretary to answer the phone unless *she* was on the other end.

"He's just wheeling his bike out the gate."

"Thank goodness. I thought he must have . . . I don't know," she finished pathetically.

Alex grimaced with a belated realization of the situation, her natural, albeit panicky, assumption that the boy had nicked off somewhere. "I'm sorry. I should have phoned to let you know he'd be late. He worked overtime, and then we had a drink."

"A drink?" interrupted Chloe in a squeak.

"Iced water," said Alex. "Then we talked about cricket."

"Oh."

Silence. How did she know Sebastian wasn't at home? Grandma must have reported in.

"Are you at work?"

"Not today. I have Wednesdays off."

"He might be late again tomorrow. He's doing the same thing at the neighbors.' "

"I'll tell Simone."

"He should be home soon."

"Thanks. Sorry to disturb you. Bye."

Click in his ear. Alex shook his head, smiling. Chloe was a case, all right. Worse than any mother. She needed a focus in her life other than all those children. Did she go out? Did she have friends? A boyfriend? He'd ask Sebastian tomorrow.

Alex posed his query idly over their morning drink the next day. He justified the break to himself — he'd started very early, and Sebastian had worked slavishly on Jeannie's driveway, with Kenneth supervising and asking questions in a piping voice Alex could hear from his office.

"Yeah, Chloe's got friends," Sebastian said. "Although most of them have left town now. They were mainly her friends from Uni and school. She had a boyfriend, but he dropped her after the bombing."

"Really?" Just when she'd need the guy most.

"He was a loser."

"What did she study?" Chloe had a degree? What in, and why was she working in a shop if she was qualified in some other profession?

"Jazz guitar at the ANU, but she didn't finish."

Alex swallowed his surprise. *A jazz guitarist?* "How much had she completed?" No need to ask why. She was a musician, a performing artist. How that must hurt. A surge of rage almost choked him at the senselessness of the terrorists who had created this vast wave of destruction stretching on into the future. Multiply Chloe's story by hundreds, no doubt.

"Two years and part of the third. She says she can't even think about finishing now."

"She could still go back, couldn't she?"

Sebastian shrugged. "I suppose."

"Does she still play?"

"Yeah, she teaches. She plays classical guitar too. And sings."

So talented. Wasted. "As well as working in that shop?"

"She only does that part-time and during the school holidays when students don't come for lessons and she can't go to the schools."

"I see."

"She does gigs sometimes. Not much, though." He sucked in the last ice cube from his glass and rolled it about in his mouth. "She went on a date with that cop," he said through a watery slurp.

"Which cop?"

"The one who called her about me."

"Burrows?" Tall, dark-haired, a protective arm around her shoulders, stern expression in the face of Alex's fury that night. Someone she could trust in a time of trouble. A little squirm of envy coiled deep in his gut. And guilt.

"Yeah. He's cool."

He had to ask. Casually. "Does she like him?"

"Dunno."

"How would you feel about having a cop in the family?" Alex raised an eyebrow.

Sebastian pulled a face, and Alex grinned.

"She won't marry him," said Sebastian. "She's not going to marry anyone. Not until we've left home." Was that relief swamping the envy? Ridiculous. Why should he care who Chloe Gardiner dated? He barely knew her.

"Why not?"

"She said she wouldn't leave us until we could support ourselves."

"Really? How long will that be?"

"Ages. Katy's eleven."

"What if she falls in love with someone?"

"Who'd take on all of us?" asked Sebastian with startling insight. He stood up. "I'd better go, in case she has a fit again. Gran has to call her if I'm not home by eleven-forty-five."

"Okay, mate. You can do the place on the other side of Jeannie's tomorrow."

"Fine. Thanks for the drink. See ya."

Alex smiled as he collected the pitcher and the glasses and took them indoors. Nice boy. Smart as a whip and very caring of his sister. Fully aware of her devotion.

But did she really need to sacrifice her own life for the children's upbringing? Alex emptied the dregs of the iced water into a potted fern. Did she have any real choice? Although . . . surely a man who truly fell in love with her would be happy to act as big brother and guide to the young ones. It wouldn't be forever, just a few years until the littlest one reached eighteen. What was that? Seven years at most?

Big ask, though. Wow. He'd have to be some big-hearted guy. Like the stepfather. Or love Chloe to distraction. He couldn't do it. Take on three kids when — let's face it — he could barely fit his own daughter into his schedule.

Alex went to his office and attempted to concentrate on kitchen plans. When had Chloe had time to go on a date with Burrows? Not at night. Must have been lunch.

On the following Monday just before twelve, Alex walked into The Music Room. Chloe, stacking new releases into a display stand, saw him enter. The sight of the man — tall, confident, relaxed in blue jeans and white shirt — sent a familiar shiver through her body. Not fear, not apprehension now, because she knew he wasn't angry anymore — something else, unsettling and uncomfortable. Her breath tightened in her chest. The CD she was holding slipped from her hand and clunked into the rack. He spotted her immediately and came straight toward her, smiling.

"Hello, Chloe."

"Hello." She clutched the armful of CDs to her chest and stared up at him. He had a lovely smile. His teeth were even and white, and the little lines creasing the sides of his mouth did odd things to her knees. "Is something wrong? Did Seb turn up?"

"He's fine." Honey-smooth voice, cheerful, friendly.

"Is there something else?" she asked tentatively. Alex's gaze remained disconcertingly fixed on hers. Too intimate again. She looked away, back to the CDs, and resumed placing them on the rack.

"I want to buy a CD," he said. "What have you got there?"

His hand reached across in front of her and took the next case from between her

94

clammy fingers. His wrist brushed her forearm, and his fingers closed on hers briefly. Chloe's heart stopped. Thudded. Restarted.

"Beethoven," she blurted. "A new recording of the piano sonatas by a young German woman, Bettina Hauptmann. Nineteen. Brilliant, apparently. I haven't heard it, but the reviews have been excellent." She stopped, breathing heavily. Swallowed.

He stood close beside her, reading the cover notes. A crisp, clean fragrance intermingled with another male aroma danced in her nostrils. His own individual smell. Chloe breathed more deeply. Her mind stopped for a second, then cranked back into action. Sluggish and scattered. She stuck another CD into the rack. Alex replaced the Beethoven.

"I'm after Vivaldi," he said. "Violin concertos."

"Any one in particular?" He was still very close, peering over her shoulder at the titles as she arranged them. Her whole body vibrated like a guitar string while her brain fired into overdrive.

"No. I just like that Baroque stuff while I'm working. It's very soothing."

"We have the complete violin works. He wrote hundreds of pieces."

"I know. Very prolific." He still hadn't moved. Chloe had run out of CDs. If she turned, she'd be face-to-face with him. She sidled along the row toward VIOLIN CONCERTOS. He followed.

"Violin concertos." She indicated the section with a jerky movement of her hand. "Do you have *The Four Seasons*?"

"Yes. Thanks."

"I'll leave you to it." She escaped to the counter.

"What's up?" asked Tran.

"Nothing."

"Your face is all red," he said.

"It's hot in here." Chloe grabbed a flyer for a jazz festival and fanned herself ostentatiously. Trust Tran to blurt out the obvious. He had all the tact of a carrot.

"No, it's not."

"Shut up," she muttered, and she punched his arm gently.

"Someone special?" He grinned and raised his eyebrows in the direction of Alex, who stood with his back to them on the far side of the shop. Chloe pretended she didn't see his inquiring, teasing look.

Alex couldn't have heard that exchange, not with John Coltrane wailing on the sax through the sound system. Would he have noticed her heated exterior? How embar-

96

rassing if he had.

The phone rang, and she snatched it up before Tran could lay a hand on it. Alex turned as the caller began asking about an obscure early jazz release. He had two CDs in his hand.

"I think my colleague can help you better," she said into the phone. "Tran, take this. He's after Emmett Miller."

Tran's expression switched from annoyance — when he assumed she was fobbing off one of their regular, chronic bores — to extreme interest. Alex reached the counter and laid the two CDs side by side.

"Did you find what you wanted?" *He's another customer, just another customer. Don't look into his eyes.*

"I can't decide. Which would you recommend?"

Chloe assessed the two titles. "Zukerman playing Bach and Vivaldi," she said without hesitation. "He's wonderful."

"Done."

Chloe found the disc and inserted it into the cover while Alex pulled cash from his wallet. She rang up the sale.

"Thank you." He took the bag. His fingers slipped briefly over hers. Burning. "Any chance of having lunch with me?"

Chloe's mouth dropped open. "Lunch?"

97

she echoed faintly.

Alex nodded. "Won't you be free soon? I can wait."

"I can't," blurted Chloe. "I'm sorry. I have an appointment."

"No problem. See you later." And he was gone, swinging the small bag casually as he sauntered from the shop.

Chloe bit her lip, frowning in dismay and unexpected disappointment. Taking Katy to the orthodontist — that was the appointment. Alex couldn't have been very interested in her company; he hadn't waited for an explanation. He wouldn't care anyway. He was just being friendly, now that they had a kind of bond through Seb. Filling in time. And there was a wife. What would she think of her husband idly inviting a woman out for lunch?

"Alex is a finalist for some award," announced Seb at dinner on Friday.

"What award?" asked Chloe. He must be very talented. No wonder he was so focused on his work.

Seb said dismissively, "Some architecture thing. He wants me to help him build a frame for an awning over his back terrace this weekend. He's only got an umbrella at the moment. There are other projects he wants me to help him with too."

"You'll do your time in no time," observed Julian. He wound spaghetti onto his fork in a large untidy bundle.

"You've done twenty-three hours," said Katy. "I've kept count."

"Do you want to spend your weekend there?" asked Chloe. "It's your last one before school starts."

A chorus of groans greeted that remark.

"Alex is cool." Seb put down his fork and pushed his empty plate away.

"Can I come?" asked Julian.

"This is supposed to be punishment for Seb, not fun," protested Chloe.

"I guess," said Seb, ignoring her and speaking directly to his brother. "I'll ask him."

"Sweet." Julian chewed another large mouthful, trailing pasta strands from his mouth. Red sauce dripped down his chin.

Chloe tried again. "He won't want a whole tribe of you invading."

What was happening over there each day? Seb stayed longer and longer and came home as cheerful as could be. Not the punishment she'd envisioned.

"Alex won't mind," said Seb with supreme teenage confidence.

"His wife might," Chloe replied tartly.

"He hasn't got a wife."

"But he has a daughter. Stephanie. I've met her, and she was there when you tried to break in!" Chloe cried.

"I didn't try to break in." Seb rolled his eyes. "His wife is married to someone else," he explained as though Chloe were a complete idiot. "I haven't seen any little kid."

Katy giggled. "That's silly."

"What?" Seb glared at her.

"You said Alex's wife is married to someone else. She can't be his wife if she's married to someone else."

"They're divorced, dopey," put in Julian.

"Then she's still not his wife, is she?" insisted Katy.

"No," interrupted Chloe before the row escalated and food was thrown. "She's his ex-wife. How do you know, Seb?"

"He told me."

"Do you two talk a lot?" Chloe fingered her water glass casually.

"Course we do. He doesn't treat me like a criminal. He likes me."

"What do you talk about?"

He shrugged. "Stuff. Cricket. He said he'd come to watch one of my games when we play at the local oval."

Chloe frowned. What did the man think he was doing by befriending Seb? Making rash promises. Playing at being a big brother? How long would that last before Seb became a nuisance? It wouldn't cost him anything at the moment, this emotional largesse, but when Seb had worked off his debt, what would happen?

"Don't get too attached to him," she murmured.

"What does that mean? 'Attached to him'?" demanded Seb. Two red spots fired in his cheeks. His Bolognese-stained mouth took on an angry tightness.

"He might not want to be your friend after you've finished your time." The explanation sounded far crueler spoken out loud than muddling around in her head.

Seb flung his chair away from the table and leaped to his feet, knocking over Katy's glass of water as he did. "You always say things like that, Chloe. You're such a cow sometimes." He crashed from the room.

"Look what he did!" Katy shrieked.

Julian began clearing the dirty plates. "Get over it, Katy."

Chloe righted the glass. "Get a sponge and mop it up." Just what she needed — two outraged, screaming children.

"Seb should. It's his fault."

"Just do it."

Katy slid off her chair and flounced to the

kitchen. Chloe exhaled heavily. She leaned her elbows on the table and covered her face with her hands. This was too much, too complicated. She did her best. She tried to protect them and nurture them, and what happened? Seb accused her of being a cow, when the whole situation was his fault in the first place.

But she had to prepare him for the fact that Alex's friendship might be short-lived. He was a busy man, and he certainly wouldn't want a teenage boy hanging around all the time. Seb would feel discarded and unwanted, and what would he do then? Alex felt sorry for them, that was all. He was doing his charitable deed for the year — helping Seb, inviting her for lunch. Plenty of people helped them in all sorts of little ways. All their neighbors were very supportive, but they didn't offer charity, and the Gardiner family didn't need it anymore. Do-gooders had been rife immediately after the tragedy, but now only the genuine, caring friends remained. As it should be.

Alex Bergman wasn't one of those. Seb mustn't think he could rely on him. None of them should. The only people they could rely on were one another. The only adult they had to rely on was her. She wouldn't let them down. Never, ever.

A pair of arms slid awkwardly around her shoulders. "Are you crying, Chloe?" asked Katy softly.

Chloe smiled and shook her head. She wiped her eyes quickly with the backs of her hands, discovering that a few tears had escaped unnoticed. "No." She slipped her arm around the slim body and squeezed. Katy climbed into her lap for a cuddle, and Chloe rested her head against the smooth cap of hair.

"Do you think Simba will ever come home?" Katy asked.

"She might. Cats sometimes get into the storm drains and lose their way." Chloe pressed a gentle kiss onto Katy's head.

"She might find another family."

"I think she'd want to come back to us. She's never lived anywhere else."

The boys were convinced she'd been run over. Katy was adamant she was alive. Chloe was unsure but secretly and reluctantly assumed the boys were right. Thinking about the missing Simba didn't relieve the teariness one bit. She sniffed.

"Alex wants to speak to you." Seb's voice startled her. He stood beside her, holding out the phone.

"Chloe can't talk now. She's crying," said Katy with fierce protectiveness.

"No, I'm not." Chloe grabbed the receiver, covering the mouthpiece with one hand. "What does he want?" she hissed over Katy's shoulder to Seb.

Seb shrugged with sullen disdain. He turned away. Chloe eased Katy gently off her lap and stood up.

"Hello."

"Are you all right? Why are you crying?" She sat down again immediately because her legs totally gave way. No strength, no bones, as feeble as the spaghetti they'd eaten for dinner. His voice poured into her ear like melted chocolate. Sweet, rich-toned, full of care. No wife.

"I'm not crying." But the way the words jerked from her mouth and the spontaneous gasp of air negated the statement.

Katy said, "You were."

Chloe strode from the room, heading for her bedroom and privacy while Alex said into her ear, "Must be tough at times being a mum."

"It's impossible at times. Especially when people interfere. They think they're helping, but they're not." She stopped abruptly, drawing in ragged breaths, her heart pounding.

"Anything or anyone in particular?" Now his voice was cool, bland.

Chloe hesitated. She couldn't attack him over something that hadn't happened yet. At the moment Seb was fulfilling his part of the deal, and so was Alex. *Leave it. But monitor it. Keep a wide, businesslike distance between them.*

"Not really. I'm . . . Katy's upset because the cat's missing. What did you want to say to me?"

"I wanted to check that you approved of Seb and Julian coming over tomorrow to help with the awning. Seb works like a demon. I'm very impressed."

"Good." So it was *Seb* now rather than *Sebastian.* Sounded like mates.

"So? Can they come?"

"You make me sound like a dragon," she said in a strained voice. And *he* sounded like one of their friends asking if they could come out to play. Boys together.

"I don't mean to. I thought I was doing the right thing by asking." Now he sounded bewildered.

"Yes, thank you for asking. They seem pretty keen."

"But you don't." It was a statement rather than a question.

Chloe licked her lips. "I wanted this to be a punishment for Seb. I thought you did too."

105

"I do. It is. But?"

"It seems like he's having too much fun." Silence. She thought he was going to laugh — it sounded so ridiculous even to her — but he must have been considering his reply.

"I don't think they should be mutually exclusive, necessarily," he said eventually. "We want Seb to compensate me for the damage, but we also want to steer him onto another course. Actually, back on course, because he's by no means a hardened thug. If we achieve that by occupying him and teaching him other skills he happens to enjoy, what's the problem?"

Chloe pursed her lips as she listened. Every word was true, and she agreed one hundred percent. The lawyer had said the same thing. It was afterward that worried her. "You're right about all of that."

"But you're still worried about something."

"We."

"Pardon?

"You say 'we' all the time, but it's not 'we,' is it? It's me. Just me. When Seb finishes his hours, your involvement is finished."

"In a way, yes." He was obviously still confused, bewildered. Why couldn't he understand without her having to spell it out so baldly?

"You'll have helped him, I don't deny that, but you're not his father or his brother. You have no connection with us other than this. You'll continue with your own life and your own family. And forget about Seb."

"You think I won't want Seb to drop in after he's done his hours? Is that what you're saying?" Alex's voice had risen as he spoke. Indignation verged on anger. "You think I'll just cast him aside like some old shoe? Is that what you think of me?"

"I don't know!" cried Chloe. "I don't know anything about you. How would I know? I can only go on experience, and this is what experience tells me. People get tired of doing charitable deeds."

"This isn't charity," he said loudly.

"Isn't it? Aren't you getting a kick out of doing something for the poor orphans? Why did your attitude change so drastically when you found out our history? When you thought I was an irresponsible, single, prob-ably junkie, on-the-dole mother, you weren't so keen to help. Quite the opposite."

Alex was silent.

"And inviting me to lunch the other day. What was that if not charity? Take poor Chloe to lunch because she never has any dates?"

That must have stung in exactly a tender,

guilty spot, because he stated too defiantly and loudly, "I invited you to lunch because I thought you might like to have lunch with me. I would have enjoyed it, but you obviously didn't want to."

"I had to take Katy to the orthodontist," cried Chloe.

"Why didn't you say so?" he demanded, angry frustration evident in his rising intonation. Quick temper, just as she'd thought.

"You walked out before I could say anything." Plus he'd totally dumbfounded her, and she couldn't think, let alone speak.

"Would you have come if you hadn't had that appointment?" He was almost shouting now.

"Yes!" she yelled without thinking.

"Right. Thursday. Same time. Same place." It sounded like a dare. A challenge.

"Right." Still riding the crest of her anger.

"Good-bye."

"Good-bye." Chloe slammed down the phone. And froze.

CHAPTER FIVE

What had she done, accepting an invitation to lunch with Alex when she'd emphasized to Seb not to get too friendly? He'd virtually forced her into saying yes, railroaded her into making the date before she could think straight.

If she'd had time to think, she would have said, "No, thank you." Not without regret, but it was much safer to keep to the line she'd drawn in the sand. He stayed on his side. Gardiners stayed on theirs.

And on top of that she wouldn't be at The Music Room on Thursday. She began her regular teaching schedule next week.

Now what? Call him back and explain? Chloe sank onto the bed, her burst of adrenaline-fueled energy dissipating like air from a leaky balloon. Her whole body was shaking from the stress of that exchange. She needed a moment to regroup before tackling another session with him.

She sat up suddenly. Why had she agreed to lunch, even in anger, when she didn't want to encourage him to become closer to the family? How would Seb interpret that mixed message? *Alex is okay for you to socialize with but not for me?* He'd be even more furious and rightly so. She had to decline, somehow gracefully back out.

If she waited too long, she wouldn't have the nerve. Or the inclination. Chloe snatched up the phone and pressed redial.

Busy signal. She tossed the phone onto the bed and lay down. Her pulse was resuming its normal rate, the shakes gone. She sat up again. What was happening to her? Bobbing up and down like a yo-yo. Was she having a mental breakdown? Everything was spinning out of control. First Seb with the police, now this thing with Alex and Seb, then Julian wanting to get in on the act and hang out with the man. That use of *we* when it quite patently wasn't *we* — or wouldn't be for more than a few weeks. Inviting her to lunch. All part of his guilt-fueled enthusiasm to help the orphans. He was driving a wedge down the center of the family unit.

Chloe picked up the phone again. Alex had probably reconsidered his invitation too after the display she'd put on. He'd be regretting the impulsive gesture made in residual anger at her initial refusal. She'd probably insulted his masculinity by not accepting the way he'd expected. Why, and how, did these things become so complicated?

This time he answered.

"It's Chloe," she said coolly. "I'm sorry, I forgot I won't be at the shop next week. I start teaching again, so my timetable is quite different."

Alex said nothing for a moment, possibly considering whether to take the out she'd offered him. The easy option of, "We'll do it some other time." Then he said, "Does your new timetable have Thursday lunch scheduled at all?"

"I finish at two, but I have to be home for Katy at three."

"Any other day better?"

"I have lunchtime students every day."

"Are you saying you can't have lunch?"

"I think so."

"What do you mean, you think so? Are you really saying you don't want to have lunch with me?"

Chloe blanched at the baldness of the statement, and a tiny part of her knew it wasn't true. She did want to have lunch with Alex, but she wouldn't. The situation would became way too complicated if she opened that door even the tiniest crack. She'd decided that long ago. "I don't think it's a good idea."

"Why not?"

"I don't think we should get too friendly."

"What?" He gave a disbelieving, astonished laugh.

"Seb would get the wrong idea."

"Two adults having lunch is a 'wrong idea'?"

"No, that I . . . that I don't want him to think of you as a family friend. You're not."

"All right, Chloe. I understand." His voice nearly pinged, taut as wire. "I apologize for putting you in a difficult situation. I won't do it again. Thank you for calling and explaining."

The line clicked in her ear.

She should be pleased he hadn't pressured her for a better explanation. She wasn't. He thought she didn't like him, which wasn't true. It had been at first. But not now. His invitation had set a door ajar, and what she sensed through that doorway was bigger and more overwhelmingly frightening, more indescribably tempting than she dared consider possible. And she hadn't congratulated him on finaling in the awards.

Simone arrived on Saturday afternoon to

take Katy out for a sleepover at her town house.

"Chloe went on a date," announced Katy almost as soon as Simone entered the house. She dropped her overnight bag onto the floor to give Simone a kiss and be smothered in a hug redolent of L'Air du Temps.

"Who with?" Simone sprang instantly to alert, letting Katy go but accompanying the question with a conspiratorial stare.

"Brent Burrows, the policeman who arrested Seb. They had lunch together."

"Ooh." Simone giggled and nudged Katy. "Is he handsome?"

"I haven't seen him."

Chloe sent a smiling glare at the pair of them. "He's tall and skinny with dark hair."

Simone pulled a face. "Doesn't sound too attractive. I like something to get a grip on."

"He's very nice," protested Chloe.

Simone shook her head. " 'Nice' doesn't cut the mustard, lovey. Does he make your knees tremble?" she demanded. Katy laughed with delight.

"No." Brent had been good company, polite and safe.

"Does your breathing stop and your mouth go dry?"

"No, thank goodness — that sounds awful." She pulled an alarmed face at Katy, who was giggling uncontrollably.

"Not when you're in love. It's the most marvelous feeling." Simone sighed and clasped her hands. "But I've had my turn. What about Chloe? That's our question. Is anyone else on the radar other than nice Constable Plod?"

"Yes. Alex called her last night."

"Seb called him," corrected Chloe.

"But he wanted to talk to you. And she took the phone to her bedroom and shut the door," Katy announced to Simone, whose razor-thin eyebrows shot toward her bouffant cloud of platinum hair.

"The man Seb vandalized?" she asked Chloe directly. "I thought he was bad-tempered and rude despite his sexy phone voice."

"Seb thinks he's cool," interjected Katy. "Julian's gone with him today to help build something."

"Julian as well?"

"Yes," said Chloe. "Katy, go and put your bag into Gran's car." She waited until Katy had disappeared out the front door, frowning as she considered how to address the subject. "I'm a bit worried, Simone. Seb really loves going there, and now Julian's gone with him. This whole thing was sup-

114

posed to be a punishment, but it's turned into something else entirely."

Again the eyebrows shot skyward, resembling two alarmed worms. "Are you worried about the man himself? He's not likely to be violent, is he? Or a drinker?"

"Heavens, no!" Chloe grimaced.

"You never can tell. I was reading just the other day how —"

Chloe leaped in before she got right off track. "No, definitely nothing like that. I think he genuinely likes having Seb there. Seb says they talk a lot."

"What about?"

"I don't know."

"Hmm. How much longer has Seb got?"

"After today, about fourteen hours."

"He'll be finished soon. Don't worry. When he gets back to school and sees his friends again, he won't be so keen on visiting the man."

"I hope not. I'd like it to ease off naturally, but I don't want him hanging around there all the time."

"No, I can see that could be a nuisance. Does this Alex see it as a problem?"

"No, and that's part of the problem. I don't want Seb to get too attached to him, because Alex isn't going to want Seb coming around indefinitely, is he? I mean, they can hardly be proper friends. The age difference is enormous."

"I wouldn't worry about it too much. Maybe they talk boy stuff. Seb can't get that from you, you know."

"But he has Julian," said Chloe. "And there's Frank next door. He likes the boys and is happy to help out when the mower breaks down or something."

"He must be nearly eighty!"

"Come on, Gran," came a wail from outside.

"He's seventy-three," said Chloe. Just a few years older than Simone but, admittedly, not nearly as well preserved.

"Hardly a spring chicken. I'd better get a move on before Katy blows a gasket. Ask this Alex what he thinks. He might simply like Seb. We do." She laughed and patted Chloe's arm. "You worry too much. And you never know, he could be interested in you, not Seb at all."

"I doubt it. I hardly see him." Was he? Sometimes he'd looked at her a certain way. Not the appraisal of a disinterested man. But no. Sophisticated Alex Bergman would not be interested in ordinary Chloe Gardiner. Too much imagination could be a dangerous thing.

"Graaaan!"

"Coming," trilled Simone. "I'll bring her home tomorrow afternoon about four. Go over there if you're worried. Observe them in action. Make sure you wear something nice. You look good in pastels. White is always fresh and pretty too, especially around the face."

Chloe stood on the front path and waved as Simone backed her yellow hatchback carefully down the driveway and onto the street. She turned inside and closed the door. *Drop in and see how they're doing? Impossible. Seb would kill her. Alex would . . . what?* She had no idea how Alex would react. He'd think she was paranoid and suspicious. A loony.

The big, roomy house was unnaturally quiet after the chaos of the long summer holidays. She wandered into the kitchen and began stacking the dishwasher. The boys had rushed off early this morning, eager to get started on the project. Julian's interest had surprised her. He was usually loath to tackle anything connected with outdoor work. He did his share of the gardening chores grudgingly and always tried to do a trade-off with Seb when it came to lawn mowing or, worse still, pool cleaning.

Seb must have told him things in private. Shared secrets the way they always did.

Maybe Simone was right, and the boys craved youthful adult masculine company. Both of them. She didn't know. How could she? She was a girl. She'd only had a sister. Darling Terry. They'd been as close as only sisters can be. The dish in her hand blurred briefly. She shoved it into the rack, wiped her eyes, slammed the door, and pressed the start button.

Chloe changed into her bikini for the luxury of a peaceful swim in the deserted pool. She floated on her back, eyes closed, and allowed the heat of the sun to bathe her face and chest. Couldn't stay too long; the late-summer sun was vicious. She flipped over and stroked languidly up and down a couple of laps, then hauled herself out and lay on the banana lounge in the shade of the wide verandah.

Wear something nice? Didn't she always wear decent clothes? Simone had made her sound like some sort of unwashed hippie in ill-fitting hand-me-downs. Chloe shifted her damp bottom and eased the straps of her bikini off her shoulders. She closed her eyes. A couple of galahs squawked loudly from their perch in next door's towering gum tree. Cicadas whirred. The sound of a hot, dry Australian summer. She drifted in and out of sleep . . . such rare peace. The boys

118

would be hungry after their day as labor-
ers . . . they were always hungry . . . maybe
order pizza.

The clang of the side gate accompanied
by boisterous voices startled her awake. Seb
and Julian were home. Her eyes flicked
open. She was dry-mouthed, heavy-headed,
and blinking in the sudden glare. The
shadows had lengthened across the patch of
lawn. Chloe stretched her legs and toes,
reached her arms over her head, and
yawned. The bikini top slid precariously,
but she grabbed it with one hand and retied
the straps.

"Hi, Chloe." Julian was first to appear
around the corner of the house, wearing a
grin from ear to ear.

"How was it?" She sat up straight, swinging her legs to the smooth wooden planks
of the verandah, moistening her sleep-dry
lips with her tongue.

"Fine. We're on our way to the shops."

"Why? I thought we'd order pizza." She
yawned again, still muzzy-headed from
daytime sleep in the heat.

"Alex is doing a barbie for dinner, so we
came home to get changed and pick you
up." He didn't stop to discuss it, just kept
walking toward the sliding door to the
house.

"A barbie?" She stood up to follow him and ask for details, but Seb and Alex appeared as Julian bounced up the verandah steps and disappeared inside.

"Hi," said Seb, eyes averted. He followed Julian swiftly, leaving Chloe with a smiling Alex unashamedly taking in generous eyefuls of her bikini-clad body.

"Hello." He strolled closer and leaned against one of the verandah posts. His gaze traveled leisurely up from pink-painted toenails to arrive finally at her hot face. "We finished the awning, so I thought that, seeing as we were all starving, we could christen it with a barbecue."

Chloe gulped. She groped for her towel and dragged it hastily over her shoulders, watching him watch her. He had on leather sandals, baggy khaki shorts, and a navy T-shirt that displayed tanned, muscular legs and arms. He was also wearing the smile that created havoc with her innards. Her right knee began trembling, so she shifted her weight onto that leg in case he saw.

The weakness of her body infuriated her. It wasn't fair. This man knew she wanted to keep the relationship with Seb on a certain level, and here he was, inviting them for a barbecue. Inviting her when she'd told him how she felt. How she ought to feel. The extreme physical reaction to him was not part of the plan — the incapacitation of her limbs, the raging heat of her blood, the soaring, crashing tumble of her heart. Did he realize? If he did notice, he'd probably exploit it.

He said cheerfully, "Julian said you were here by yourself, so would you like to join us?"

"Join you? I haven't said *they* could go yet." Didn't he get it? Even after the conversation last night?

Alex drew in air and firmed his mouth while he considered his reply. "Chloe, it's just a barbecue. They worked hard, and I'd like to thank them by feeding them. We all have to eat," he added.

"You should have asked me first before you suggested it." How surly she sounded. Dragon lady.

He pushed away from the post. "Maybe I should have. I'm sorry. But for heaven's sake." He raised one arm and let it fall. "Aren't they allowed to have some fun?"

Chloe stared at him in shock as his offhand remark hit home. She bit her lip and dropped her gaze to her feet. The anger died, extinguished in an instant by guilt. Her mouth opened and closed, but no words came out. Instead, her lips trembled,

121

and she had the most horrible feeling she was about to cry. Why, she had no idea, but his words had cut the ground from beneath her feet.

She clutched the towel around her upper body as a kind of armor against his prying eyes and his unfairly harsh, penetrating remark. "Of course they're allowed to have fun. You make me sound as though I lock them up and don't let them out. I do want them to have fun. They do. Far more than me. The house is always full of their friends." Her voice nearly broke on the last words. She summoned enough strength to finish. "I just want to protect them, that's all. I don't want them to be hurt. But look what happened — Seb . . ."

Alex took the two steps in one stride but at the last second stopped short of touching her. He gazed down at the distraught face so close to tears and so deeply worried, and he longed to wrap her in his arms and hold her tightly, protect her. Standing there trembling in her hot-pink bikini, clutching that towel over her beautiful body, she was sexy and desirable but so overwhelmingly vulnerable, he couldn't possibly act on any baser instincts.

What on earth was she so terrified of? That he was a child abuser? A slave trader?

Surely not. He was a father himself; the idea of harming a child was abhorrent.

"I'd never hurt them," he whispered through a throat choked tightly shut.

Chloe raised her head and looked into his eyes. Her expression softened. The eyes blurred by unshed tears seemed larger, more luminous. Lovely beyond belief.

"I'm sorry." She spoke so softly, he barely heard her. "I know you wouldn't. I think you're a good man."

Never in his life had he wanted to hold a woman more. Never had he wanted to kiss a mouth more. But he wouldn't. Couldn't. Not when she was so fragile, so confused.

Instead, he lifted a strand of damp hair and gently eased it from her cheek. She didn't shrink from his touch. Her lips trembled slightly; the depth of her eyes was hypnotic. Her warm, tanned skin exuded an odor faintly reminiscent of coconut oil and chlorine. A summer smell. Bikinis and sexy bodies. Boys and girls flirting and making out. Too tempting. But off-limits. Chloe wasn't the girl for a sexy summer fling. Chloe was a woman who deserved forever. And he'd already done forever.

He swallowed, then smiled into those eyes with what he hoped was a friendly, non-threatening grin. "Go and change. Come with us. I do a great barbecue."

She nodded once and slipped away from the fingers he hadn't realized were still resting gently against her cheek. When she moved, the space she left was vast.

Just a barbecue. That's all. Just a barbecue. Chloe stepped into the shower with the mantra spinning in her head. The boys deserved a small treat at the end of the school holidays. Julian did, anyway. They didn't socialize as a family much. None of them went away from home very often. There was the odd school camp excursion. They didn't go on family holidays. Couldn't afford to. Sometimes someone would be invited down to the coast with a friend or for the occasional sleepover. Katy stayed with Simone now and again. Mostly the friends came here.

The family had been the focus for all of them. They preferred to stay together. Perhaps it was a residual fear that if they split up, they might never see each other again. Chloe had voiced that fear once in a therapy session, and Ruth had replied that it was a perfectly natural reaction and would fade with time. Only if they became obsessive about staying together might problems arise.

Was she obsessive? Is that what was happening now? To her? Alex obviously thought so. And Simone, in a loving way. Although it was difficult to tell with Simone. She wanted Chloe to have a boyfriend, but she wouldn't want her to walk away from the children. Simone couldn't see the inherent contradiction in her scenario. What twenty-something young man would take on a girl with three children? He'd want her to be free to go out spontaneously at night, stay out late, go away for the occasional weekend. All the things she'd done as a student. Hopeless now.

Chloe turned off the taps with a vicious twist. Yep, this would be just another barbecue with a well-meaning friend. Might even be fun, and at least they wouldn't have to worry about what to have for dinner.

Alex sprawled on the banana lounge Chloe had been using, while he waited for the crew to assemble. He folded his arms behind his head and enjoyed the rest after a day of hard labor. The sparkling blue water of that pool looked inviting. Very tempting to strip and jump in. Just imagine what Chloe would do if she found him swimming naked in her pool. Attack him with that straw broom propped against the wall, probably. He chuckled. She was so sweet. Trying so hard to be a good mother to them all. And succeeding.

Those two boys were amazingly identical. Seb had a slightly larger frame and more muscles from his sporting activities, but their voices, expressions, and faces were so similar as to be indistinguishable. Great senses of humor. Especially Julian with his dry wit and knack for impersonations and accents.

The inclusion of Julian in the project had been a mystery, but Alex figured it was curiosity rather than a desire to get his hands dirty that had lured him away from his more cerebral pursuits. Like Seb, Julian hadn't shirked his jobs. The whole activity had been fun and taken half the time it would have on his own. In fact, unbeknownst to Chloe, they'd finished just after lunch and spent the bulk of the afternoon listening to music and talking under the new awning. A rare afternoon of relaxation for him. He'd even turned his answering machine on and his cell phone off.

A barbecue seemed a natural conclusion to a pleasant day. And the boys thought it natural to include Chloe. Katy, whom he was yet to meet, was sleeping over at the grandma's, apparently, or she would have come along too. How many fourteen-year-olds automatically included their eleven-year-old sisters in social get-togethers? Extraordinary how comfortable he felt with them, when children weren't his thing at all.

The sliding door scraped. Alex sat up as the boys reappeared. They'd changed their shirts in his honor. He grinned.

"Pool looks good."

"Come 'round for a swim if you'd like," offered Seb. "Everyone else does."

"Thanks. Might take you up on that one day. Have to ask Chloe, though."

"She doesn't mind our other mates coming 'round," said Julian.

"I'm not really your mate, though." Alex pointed at Seb, whose expression had sagged with disappointment. "I'm his jailer."

"What does that make me?" cried Julian over Seb's crow of relieved laughter.

"The condemned man's visitor," said Alex.

Chloe stepped onto the verandah amid the laughter. She'd changed into a short white skirt and a blue tank top that showed off the honey gold of her skin. Did she realize how attractive she was? Alex doubted it very much. She didn't spare much thought for herself, or if she did, it was only in relation to the kids.

"Ready?"

"Did you check the windows?" she asked the boys.

"Yes." Seb sighed ostentatiously and glanced at Julian.

Julian explained to Alex, "When we all go out, we each have a job. Ours is closing all the windows. Katy makes sure the cat is out and the cat flap is locked, or at least she did until the cat ran away."

"It's dead," put in Seb.

"She might not be," said Chloe. "Simba disappeared," she added, sending Alex a quick, meaningful glance.

"Cats sometimes come back after being away for months," he offered, hoping he'd interpreted her look correctly.

He must have, because she said, "That's right."

"I bet it's been run over," said Seb. "It's been gone a month already."

"Don't you dare say that to Katy any-more." Chloe cut the obviously well-worn argument short by looking at Alex. "Shall we take our car?"

"No need. I can drive you home after-ward."

"We can walk home," said Seb. "It's not far." He jumped off the verandah and headed for the gate. Julian sprinted after him and jostled his way past to be first to the car.

"They're good kids," Alex said softly as he followed beside Chloe. "You've done well."

"Hardly." But he could tell she was pleased, because the edge had left her voice, to be replaced by a dry skepticism.

"They are," he insisted. "I enjoyed hanging out with them today."

She glanced at him as he held the gate open for her to pass through. " 'Hanging out'? I thought you were all working."

"We were," he said hastily. "But we had to have a rest now and again."

He pointed the automatic opener at the BMW. Seb and Julian piled into the backseat. They'd been mightily impressed with his choice of vehicle. Their own car was an aging Holden with no chance of an upgrade until it completely collapsed. Alex opened Chloe's door for her and tried not to ogle her legs as she sat down.

"We'll nip down to Jamison first. Pick up some sausages and drinks."

"What about salad?" Chloe asked. *Typical female.* Lucy was the same. Or had been until she married Derek. Derek was a take-out kind of guy. The greasier and easier his food, the better.

"Relax. I've got plenty at home. We can pick up some tabouleh or coleslaw, if you'd like. And we'll need bread. What do you guys like to drink?" He flicked a glance at Julian in the rearview mirror as he pulled up at the traffic light on Bindubi Street.

"Beer," said Seb, and he laughed.

"No way," declared Chloe right on cue.

"Juice or water will do," said Julian. "Thanks, Alex."

"My pleasure." Alex smiled across at Chloe, who wore her perpetually worried face. "I have a very nice Hunter Valley Riesling in the fridge at home for us."

"Oh." Her cheeks turned a delicious pink.

"Good thing you're not driving, Chloe. You can get plastered," said Seb with a convulsive snort from the backseat.

Alex caught her eye and grinned. To his amazement, she returned his smile. A sweet, intimate, private smile just for him. A moment shared and made all the more special because it was the first time he'd seen her mouth curve just that way to reveal a single dimple in her cheek. The first time he'd seen her eyes sparkle with genuine amusement. She'd been pretty and attractive and sexy before; now she was deeply beautiful.

Alex's breath caught somewhere deep in his lungs. Something shifted. Maybe it was the earth. Maybe it was the planets realigning. Whatever it was, Chloe Gardiner smiled, and he fell in love.

"Light's green, Alex," called Seb.

"Earth to Alex, Earth to Alex," said Julian in his Texan Mission Control voice. "Engage gears, depress the lever directly beneath your right foot, and release the manual retardation system with your left hand."

Chloe's smile widened before she looked away. Alex jammed the gearshift into first and roared across the intersection, catching a glimpse of Julian's grinning face in the mirror.

CHAPTER SIX

Alex swung into the parking area and stopped the BMW with a jaunty flourish. The world dazzled him with its clarity and brightness. The sky was suddenly bluer than before, the puffy white clouds whiter and puffier than they'd ever been. The Saturday-evening shoppers were his friends, even the ones he didn't know.

He waited for Chloe while the boys piled out of the car and headed for the entrance. He didn't dare touch her, though his fingers longed to slide down her bare arm to take her hand and hold it securely in his. Instead, he walked close enough for his arm to brush hers and send a shudder of electricity through his body. She edged away, and he smiled to himself. His secret.

With that one smile Chloe had told him many things. Things Alex was positive she didn't realize she'd revealed. She'd relaxed, decided to enjoy their evening together, regarded him as a friend despite her protestations to the contrary, accepted his friendship with the twins, wasn't frightened of him, and he wasn't the ogre in the story anymore. With that came his own realization — he wanted to be the hero. Her hero.

He glanced at her face in profile. She was gorgeous. She attracted him like no other woman, including Lucy at the height of their romance. That had been an immature attraction based on the overenthusiastic hormones of a couple of twenty-year-olds and fueled in part by his father's disapproval. At thirty-one he was wiser, experienced, and infinitely more cautious if not downright cynical about the existence of true and lasting love.

This fledgling love exploding upon him in a sunburst was so totally unexpected and so totally out of character, he needed time to examine it. Time to hold it in the palm of his hand, turn it this way and that and study all the ins and outs of its new, exciting shape. He couldn't possibly tell Chloe. He couldn't even hint at it, or she'd run so far and so fast, he'd never get near her again. Look how she'd reacted to the innocuous suggestion that they be friends.

This passion, while it lasted, was doomed to secrecy. But that was all right. Alex grinned. He could enjoy her company, enjoy seeing her open like a flower, seeing her smile, and perhaps even hearing her laugh. He could enjoy learning about her. He wasn't in a hurry to develop a relationship with anyone, and Chloe Gardiner with all her responsibilities was the least suitable woman to fall for he could possibly have found.

"What are you laughing at?" she asked. Way ahead the boys had already grabbed a basket and were heading for the meat section.

He smiled into her eyes, reveling in the soft acceptance of his presence he saw there. "I'm happy."

"That's nice." She preceded him through the turnstile.

"Aren't you happy?" Her tone had made him frown. "I mean . . ." He gestured vaguely. It was a stupid question, really, all things considered. "The kids are healthy, they're smart, and . . ."

"In trouble with the police," she finished for him.

"But apart from that. Anyway, it's not all of them."

She shot him a wry look. "I've never thought about whether I'm happy or not. Haven't had time, I suppose. I think more about whether the kids are happy."

"I think they are. From what I can tell." He couldn't help himself, couldn't resist gazing into those gorgeous eyes. "I want to know about you."

"What sausages are we getting?" Chloe cut him off briskly and deliberately. "And bread, you said. I'll get that while you and the boys organize the meat."

She strode away, leaving him with his unrequited love and his unanswered questions and wondering what it would take to release her from her self-imposed martyrdom to the family. Pondering the problem, Alex joined the boys, who were busily discussing the merits of various flavored sausages.

Chloe sat under the new awning and watched Alex and Seb concentrating on the barbecue. Secret men's business — and they took it so seriously. Julian, having arranged plates and cutlery on the wooden table, wandered about the garden. From over the fence occasional bursts of childish laughter mingled with adult voices in the warm evening air.

Alex glanced across and caught her eye. He smiled, and she grinned back and raised her glass to him. Juice. She'd declined the

Riesling. She liked wine but rarely drank these days. Seb was right about getting plastered. She mustn't.

"Are you sure I can't do anything?" she called. "I feel guilty doing nothing."

"There's nothing to do," said Alex. "Enjoy your drink."

"And shut up," added Seb.

"Bit of respect, if you don't mind." Alex clicked the barbecue tongs in Seb's direction. "Julian, nip in and get the salads from the kitchen, please, mate. We're ready to go here."

Julian hurried across the lawn and bounded up the terrace steps.

Chloe fingered her glass thoughtfully. Both boys seemed very much at home in Alex's house, and he seemed very comfortable with them. In control but not like Attila the Hun — more like friends. She was the outsider, the guest. It was an odd experience, being waited on like this by Seb and Julian in a house that wasn't their own.

She looked up idly at the cream-colored awning. It was a good idea. It stretched overhead between two newly erected corner posts and the house, shielding the terrace from the midday and afternoon sun but allowing any cooling breeze to waft over the recliners and diners. Seb and Julian had proudly shown her the concreting they'd done to anchor the posts while Alex had used the electric drill on the brick house wall to secure the other two corners. The whole area smelled of newness — freshly turned earth, newly sawed wood, cement, and paint. Jasmine or maybe a grapevine was going to be trained up the wooden poles to hide the bareness, Seb said.

She'd hadn't seen him so enthused about anything except sports for ages. And Julian too. Perhaps Simone was right, and they needed a masculine role model. If that was the case, who was she to prevent them from getting to know Alex? Unless it was just a novelty for them all. School began on Wednesday. Life would return to normal for the boys, and then she'd be able to judge more accurately the depth of this relationship.

Julian placed two bowls in front of her. One overflowed with lettuce, tomato, cucumber, and olives. The other held potato salad, lightly mixed with mayonnaise and a garnish of fresh parsley. The fresh rolls they'd bought were already in a basket on the table covered by a tea towel.

"Who made the salads?"

"Alex, before we came to pick you up. I peeled the spuds, though."

"Don't you think I can cook?" asked Alex, setting a platter of sizzling sausages on the table. The hot-off-the-barbecue aroma set her mouth watering in anticipation. "Help yourself, Chloe. Dig in, guys."

Seb and Julian pounced on the food. Chloe speared a fat sausage with her fork and ferried it to her plate. "I haven't thought about it at all. But now that I do, I suppose if you live alone, you'd have to learn to cook something."

Alex smiled. "Steffie stays with me on alternate weekends, but she has a very limited menu."

"Where does she live the rest of the time?" asked Julian.

"With her mother and stepfather in Giralang."

"Pretty close."

"Yes."

"How long have you been divorced?"

"Seb!"

"What?" He looked at Chloe blankly.

She frowned. "Alex might not want to discuss his private life with us."

"It's fine, Chloe. There's no secret. Lucy and I split up four years ago, when Steffie was two. It was pretty much a disaster from the start, and we never should have gotten married. She's happy now. Derek's not a bad bloke. He loves Steffie, which is the main thing."

"Half the kids in my class last year were from divorced families," said Julian.

"It's sad," said Chloe.

"You are too," pointed out Seb. "Dad was your stepfather."

"But my real father never married Mum, so it's different. Bevan was the only dad I ever had." She smiled at the boys, and they returned her smile briefly before turning their attention to their food.

Alex watched the brief interaction. How did a man like Bevan learn to be such a good father? By example? His own father hadn't set up any guidelines he'd want to follow. Was that why he struggled with parenting?

"Steffie's coming tomorrow," he said. "Just for the day. She's been with her aunt in Sydney for the last ten days."

"You must miss her," said Chloe.

"Yes." Her sympathetic tone encouraged him to say, "But it's not easy coping with a little girl. I don't really understand small children — wasn't ever very keen on them, to be honest. It's a bit better now that she's older, but she's definitely better off with her mother. Every now and then she says she wants to live with me, but — I don't know."

"Bring her over for a swim in our pool," said Seb.

Alex looked swiftly at Chloe for her reaction. She was in mid-swallow but didn't choke or gag in disgust. "Thanks, Seb. That's very kind. I'll see what she wants to do. She's having swimming lessons, so she needs as much practice as she can get."

Chloe said nothing. She sipped her drink and placed the glass precisely on the table before serving herself more green salad.

"Would you mind?" he asked.

She shook her head slowly. "Half the neighborhood's in our pool most of the time. Two more won't matter."

"Come anytime," said Seb.

"Thanks. I'll ring you to confirm."

"Congratulations on being a finalist for an award," said Chloe suddenly.

"Thanks. I'm pretty pleased. It's real recognition." Alex refilled her glass. She'd relaxed. The worried frown had left her face, and she smiled readily when he offered her more food.

"What's it for?"

"Housing Industry Awards. I'm up for best private house extension."

It was all he could do not to touch her at every opportunity. The random, accidental contacts became amazingly monumental in significance. When he reached for the sauce or she leaned across to replace the salad bowl and their arms brushed. When he extended his left leg under the table and discovered her right foot next to his. Incredible how such slight brushes of bare skin against bare skin could spark such longing. Incredible how during the meal he'd begun to manufacture innocent-seeming ways of making contact.

"We forgot dessert," cried Seb through a mouthful of sausage.

"Watermelon all right?" asked Alex.

Julian said, "Great, thanks."

Alex pushed his chair back. Chloe sprang to her feet. "At least let me help with that."

"Follow me." Alex led her inside with a suddenly pounding heart. Did the boys suspect anything? They were very sharp, that pair. Would they see and interpret? Would they tell Chloe? But no, they were talking about someone called Nicola they'd run into at Jamison.

He opened the fridge and removed the half watermelon. Chloe pulled a knife from the knife block on the counter.

"This one?" she asked, holding it up.

"Yep." He undid the plastic wrap. She rinsed her hands in the sink and dried them on the towel hanging on the oven door handle. Alex followed suit. This relaxed Chloe was the real one, the one the boys loved and the grandma so staunchly protected. This was the woman he needed to explore, the one she'd kept hidden from him. The one he'd scared off with his anger.

He took a platter from the cupboard and set it next to Chloe, then paused by her side, watching her slice the sharp blade into the thick green rind of the melon. Juice flowed across the white chopping board in a sweet pink flood and cascaded onto the granite countertop.

"Gosh, I'm making a mess," she said with a childish giggle. She reached for the sponge and caught several drips before they reached the edge and plummeted to the floor.

"I'm so glad you came."

Chloe didn't turn her head from her task, but the cheek he could see turned a deeper pink. She resumed chopping.

"Thank you for the invitation." Very stiff. Very formal.

"The boys said you were home alone. You should have come over earlier."

She glanced at him very briefly. A quick snatch of hazel eyes and luscious lips before her face was in profile again. "Seb would think I was checking up on him." She severed another slice from the melon.

"Anyway, I rarely have time to myself."

Alex smiled. "I have plenty."

"Does that worry you?" Still she focused on the fruit, deftly trimming the rind from the crisp flesh. Alex laid the slices on the platter, the refrigerated chill contrasting sharply with the heat of his fingers, his body. Far hotter than the warmth of the day warranted. His arm brushed hers.

"No. I prefer working from home. I like being my own boss. It's not as if I go for weeks without seeing anyone. I see clients and tradesmen on building sites all the time. I play basketball with friends once a week. It's not the same as having family, though."

"I spend most of my time with children. I have way more young students than adults." She laughed a self-conscious little laugh. "I have my fill of kids. Sometimes I crave adult conversation."

"Come and visit me. I'll do my best to oblige."

Chloe paused to flash him a smile. "I wouldn't do that. You'd be too busy. I'd interrupt something important." She cut the last slice into smaller pieces.

Alex laid a hand on her arm, forcing her to stop what she was doing and look up into his face. He edged closer. "No. You wouldn't."

She half turned. Her eyes met his. The smile faded from her mouth, to be replaced by uncertainty. Her lips parted, and she drew in a small gasp of air.

"I mean it," he said softly. Her mouth was mere inches from his. All he needed to do was bend his head, slip an arm around her waist, and draw her against his body, a fragrant, delicious armful. All he needed to do was place his lips against hers. Softly, so as not to alarm her. Slowly, to give her time to refuse. Gently, to revel in the delight of a first kiss. He could almost feel the softness of her mouth, taste the sweetness. Her perfume intoxicated him, drew him to her. He was incapable of resisting.

She turned her head. "The boys love watermelon," she said shakily. She put down the knife.

"Good," he muttered through a throat thick with desire. "Chloe?"

Her head remained bowed, face hidden. Her fingers remained pressed on the counter amid the juice and the discarded watermelon rind. She breathed deeply. He longed to press his lips against the soft skin of her neck.

"Chloe?" With one gentle finger under her chin, he turned her face toward his. She wasn't ready; he saw it instantly. He'd alarmed her with this sudden advance into intimacy.

He smiled, leaned forward slowly, and kissed her cheek, closing his eyes to better absorb and savor the brief contact, allowing his cheek to rest against hers for a moment. A light floral perfume mixed with barbecue smoke. Skin warm, softer than silk. Her breath held a hint of orange juice. When he drew back, he saw that her eyes were open, watching. She blinked, staring straight into his own eyes with a cool awareness that stopped his breathing. It was his turn to feel the prickling heat of embarrassment.

He never should have touched her. He couldn't hide the feeling behind his kiss, and he'd as good as made a declaration of his infatuation. By the expression on her face, she didn't welcome it. Or it amused her. He couldn't tell. Emotional floundering. A very uncomfortable and unfamiliar sensation.

Taking refuge in action, he opened the cupboard beneath the sink. "How come you never have any dates?" he asked in a louder, teasing voice.

"What?" She frowned in bewilderment, but he could see relief behind the confusion. Relief that he hadn't turned that moment into something truly awkward.

"You said on the phone, and I quote, 'Take poor Chloe to lunch because she never has any dates.' " He dropped the melon rinds into the rubbish bin.

"I had a date last week," she retorted.

"I know."

"How do you know?" She shook her head. "Don't tell me. Seb. And men accuse women of being gossips. Sheesh!"

"Did you enjoy yourself?"

She looked him straight in the eye then. "Yes, very much."

He returned the gaze, unflinching, although the firmness of her reply was like a punch in the gut. "Good. I'm glad."

She actually laughed in his face. "You don't sound it."

"I am glad. I'd hardly want you to go out and have a rotten time, would I?"

She shrugged, the light still dancing in her eyes. "I don't know," she said. "You might."

And the woman he'd assumed was an innocent — vulnerable, fragile — picked up the platter of melon, raised her eyebrows saucily, and sashayed out to the terrace, swaying her sexy behind for his benefit as she went.

A grin slowly spread across his face as he watched her go. He shook his head and finished tidying the mess she'd made. The more he discovered about her, the more he realized he didn't know her at all. But he'd sure enjoy finding out. He'd have more opportunity for skirmishing tomorrow. They'd all be swimming. She'd wear her bikini.

"Don't want to go swimming." The lower lip pouted; the eyes glowered threateningly. The red-shorts-clad bottom wriggled itself more firmly into the sofa cushions. "I want to watch my Barbie movie."

Alex studied his six-year-old party pooper. He'd looked forward to introducing her to Chloe and the twins, convinced they'd find her as lovable as he did. But not the way she looked at the moment.

"You met Chloe at the music shop. She's nice."

"No, she's not." Two arms folded defiantly across the chest. "I don't like her. She's a pooey-poo."

"That's ridiculous." Alex flung his arms wide in exasperation. What had happened to his sweet, biddable baby girl? "Come on, honey."

"No."

Alex squatted in front of the sofa. "You need swimming practice. Mum said she thought it was a good idea."

"I don't care. Swimming's pooey."

"You'll enjoy it. It's so hot today. Perfect for a swim. You can watch TV when we come home."

"Don't want to."

"Steffie, we're going, and that's that. You need the exercise, and you need the practice."

"Do not."

"Don't you want to be a good swimmer?"

"No."

Time for a change of attack. "If we stay home, you're not watching TV. We'll do something else instead."

"What?"

"I need to go to the vegetable markets." Guaranteed to horrify her.

"I hate the vegetable markets." The pouting face wrinkled in disgust.

"I know, but we need fresh fruit and vegetables."

"I hate vegetables. If I go swimming, may I have an ice cream on the way home?"

Alex sighed. "Steffie, you know I don't like you eating too many sweets. I'd much rather you had a banana."

"Derek lets me eat whatever I like." She stared at him, daring him to bite. "So does Mummy."

Alex stood up. He wasn't getting into that discussion. He'd already mentioned Steffie's diet to Lucy and been subjected to a run-down of Lucy's busy schedule: caring for Steffie and baby Mark, who suffered from allergies; work; husband; mortgage; car trouble; Derek's hernia; his own idle selfish-ness in suggesting she wasn't a good mother; and why couldn't he take Steffie more often?

"We'll stop at the markets after we visit Chloe. Go and put your swimsuit on." He held out a hand, and she hung on as he pulled her off the sofa and into his arms for a hug and a kiss.

When she'd disappeared, stomping into her room to change, Alex picked up the phone and dialed Chloe's number. Julian answered.

"Is it all right if I bring Steffie over for a swim?"

"Sure."

"In about ten minutes?"

"Fine. We're all just hanging out by the pool anyway."

"Chloe too?" An image of her smiling at him in the car flashed before his eyes. Sweet dimple, sparkling eyes. Gorgeous.

"Yeah, she's here."

Silly how her heart beat faster when Julian said Alex was coming over with his daugh-ter. Ridiculous how, when he kissed her on

149

the cheek, she'd nearly gone into cardiac arrest. Stupid to lie awake half the night thinking about every nuance of that kiss, how his cheek had felt against hers — slightly rough from beard stubble — his skin smelling of the barbecue and his breath of sausages — and that other scent that was peculiarly his.

Thinking how surprised she'd been. How she didn't know how to react when he said in a voice quite unlike his usual one that he'd like her to visit. She'd really thought he was about to kiss her. Such a shock. And then he'd turned her face toward his, placed a finger so gently under her chin. *Stunned* was the only word for her reaction.

Lying awake at three in the morning, she'd considered the motivation for such an intimate gesture. Or was it as intimate as she'd thought? Was it simply a friendly kiss such as friends or relatives would exchange? How could she tell? She barely knew Alex. She didn't know what sort of person he was. He might be one of those kissy people who hardly need any excuse to plant one.

If that was the case, what had been his reaction to her little display as she left the kitchen? Had he fallen on the floor laughing at her clumsy attempt at being sexy? Or was he horrified at her complete misinterpretation of what he'd meant as a gesture of friendship? He'd almost immediately begun teasing her about her dates, showing her he wasn't serious. *Too long between kisses, Chloe.* Too long since a man had paid her that type of attention. She'd lost her judgment, and she hadn't even realized she'd become desperate.

Whatever he thought, she wouldn't make the same mistake again. When he brought his daughter around, she'd be distant politeness personified. Chloe dropped her library book onto the verandah, pried herself off the banana lounge, and went to change out of her bikini and into something less revealing.

They arrived shortly after she sat back down, clad now in mint green shorts and a sleeveless white T-shirt. The boys were leaping in and out of the pool, trying to see who could jump the farthest and creating tidal waves in the process. For once there were no hangers-on.

Alex opened the gate and ushered his daughter in ahead of him. "Hello," he called. Shorts. He had on baggy khaki board shorts again. He carried a blue bag with a yellow and orange towel dangling from the open top.

Chloe stood up. "Hi. Hello, Stephanie."

151

The child was staring at the boys through the safety fence. She had on a red T-shirt and shorts outfit, which made her look exactly like a little, round, overripe tomato. White zinc cream had been smeared across her nose and cheeks. She tore her attention away from the rowdy antics in the water and stared at Chloe instead. Alex nudged her and murmured something Chloe couldn't hear.

"Hello, Chloe," she said, but no smile struggled to the surface. The whole sulky demeanor screamed, *I don't want to be here.*

"Thanks for inviting us." Alex smiled down at the sullen lump beside him. "Steffie needs lots of practice swimming, don't you, hon?"

"I hate swimming." She bent and scratched one leg ostentatiously.

"The water's really warm," Chloe said. "Come and put your things down on the verandah. Do you need to change?"

"No, we've got our swimsuits on underneath." Alex waved to the boys, who yelled greetings before resuming the leaping and splashing. He mounted the verandah steps. "Aren't you swimming?"

His eyes took in her shorts and top, then bored into hers for a moment. He smiled, and a spark of something crackled between

152

them. What was he thinking? Was he wondering what she'd been on yesterday?

Chloe shook her head, knowing her cheeks had turned pinker than could be explained by the sun. "I'm reading."

"Daddy, I'm thirsty. I want a drink." Stephanie yanked at his arm.

"Water's in the bag, hon." Alex put the bag on the verandah, where it fell over and spilled out the brightly striped beach towel.

"I don't want water." Two gray eyes stared at Chloe. "I want something else."

"We have milk, orange juice, or cordial," Chloe replied. Not a *please* in sight. Surely Alex didn't approve of this behavior, especially when visiting. He'd been quick enough to criticize her own parenting skills when Seb was involved.

"Steffie, we brought our water bottles. We don't need to bother Chloe." Alex grinned at Chloe with a quick lift of the eyebrows as if to say, *Isn't she a cute little thing?*

"I want a Coke." The familiar whine entered her voice.

"We don't have any soft drinks in the house." And even if they did, this kid would need to improve her attitude dramatically to get any.

"Mummy always has Coke at home."

Alex cut in swiftly. "Steffie, you can drink

153

water." At last a firm tone that she must have recognized as final, because Stephanie began rummaging in the bag, strewing a cloth hat, a plastic bottle of sunblock, and a second towel over the immediate vicinity.

"I'm sorry," Alex said over her head. He grimaced. "Lucy and I have different ideas on most things."

"Must make it difficult." *For everyone, Stephanie included.* Tough to be six and shunted between two people you love, not quite sure where you fit. No wonder she demanded attention from her dad. Sympathy overcame annoyance as Chloe watched the little girl find her water and gulp down several mouthfuls.

Alex sighed. "Sure does."

He took off his shirt, revealing a broad, tanned chest covered in tightly curled dark hair. Chloe looked away quickly. Stephanie, standing in the midst of the mess, was eyeing her curiously. That child would be sure to make some sort of comment if she thought Chloe was taking an inordinate interest in her father's body. Alex shoved the fallout from her search back into the bag along with his clothes.

"Where's the girl?" asked Stephanie suddenly. "You said there was a girl here for me to play with."

"Katy's visiting her gran, but she'll be home very soon. Have you got brothers or sisters?"

"A brother. Mark's a baby, and he needs lots of attention. He cries all the time. He gets sick a lot. I have to be very quiet."

Chloe smiled and nodded in understanding but was met with another of Steffie's trademark stares.

Alex said with cheerful enthusiasm, "C'mon, Steffie. Get your clothes off."

The scowl returned. "Don't want to."

"Come on, hon." He squatted to look into the sullen face. "You'll enjoy it. It's so hot today."

"It's not."

"But that's why we came." He stood up, clearly at a loss and embarrassed with it.

"You go in with the boys, Alex," Chloe said hastily, keeping her eyes and her mind away from the way the muscles rippled in the tanned thighs as he straightened. "Steffie and I can watch for a bit. They're too rowdy, aren't they?"

Steffie stared. When she did that, she had the blankest, most expressionless face Chloe had ever seen. And she did it often. In between whines. The burst of sympathy faltered slightly under that pudding-faced gaze.

"All right. Thanks, Chloe. But then it's your turn, Steffie." Alex gave her a stern frown before dashing across the lawn to the pool gate to be greeted by cries of delight from the inmates.

Chloe sat down on the lounger. She indicated the second one. "Sit down."

Stephanie scrambled onto it with a surprising turn of speed and lay back like a Hollywood starlet with one knee bent and an arm draped over her head.

"What do you like to do best?" Chloe asked.

"I like TV."

"Do you read books?

"Sometimes."

"Do you play sports?"

"No, I don't like sports. I hate swimming. I didn't want to come." Even if she hadn't so blatantly stated the fact, no one could possibly be left in any doubt. Stephanie wasn't one to suffer in silence.

"It's important to learn how to swim, though."

"That's what Mummy and Daddy say. And Derek."

"They're right."

"I hate it. I hate the swimming teacher. She gets cross when I won't put my head under the water. She's a pooey-poo."

Chloe bit the inside of her cheek to stop herself from grinning. "Maybe you'd like it better with a different teacher."

"No."

"Do you like music?"

"I don't know. Daddy plays music in his house, but Derek doesn't."

"None at all?" Inconceivable to live a life devoid of music.

"Only sometimes. Mummy says she likes quiet. Except Mark cries, and she gets upset."

"Must be fun having a baby brother."

"A bit. I'm hungry."

"Would you like an apple?"

"Apples are pooey. I want an ice cream."

"We only have ice cream in a tub. Would your daddy let you have a bowl of ice cream?"

Stephanie nodded enthusiastically. "He said I could have ice cream if I came swimming."

Chloe hesitated. Was this a delicate subject? "Maybe you should have a swim first."

"I don't want to go in with those big boys. They're too rowdy." She glanced at Chloe with an ingratiating little smile. "I could have ice cream first and then go into the pool."

"All right. Come inside."

While Chloe spooned two scoops of vanilla ice cream into a bowl, Stephanie prowled about the kitchen. She pulled a leaf off the poinsettia that one of Chloe's students had given her for Christmas, then spilled some of the dirt by tilting the pot. Having exhausted the possibilities of the countertop, her attention moved to the fridge, where she peered and poked at the postcards and notes stuck to the surface with magnets. When Chloe said the ice cream was ready, Steffie knocked several pieces of paper and postcards to the floor in her haste to eat, treading on two as she stepped forward with hands outstretched.

"Would you pick those up, please, Stephanie?" Chloe said casually, replacing the lid on the tub.

"After I have my ice cream."

Chloe's eyes widened. The cheeky little so-and-so! "I don't think so," she said firmly. "Pick them up, please."

Stephanie glowered. Chloe slid the bowl farther back on the counter behind her and folded her arms.

"I don't want to pick them up."

Chloe waited silently.

"I hate you. You're a pooey-poo, and I won't do anything for you. Pooey-pooey-poo."

Chloe removed the lid of the ice cream, scraped the contents of the bowl back into the tub, strode to the fridge, and replaced the whole thing in the freezer.

Stephanie stamped both her feet. "You said I could have ice cream. You're a liar, and I hate you. I hate you!" she yelled.

"I think you should go outside if you're going to speak like that."

Stephanie darted for the sliding screen door. Chloe hurried after and dragged it open in case she jammed her fingers and caused even more of a scene. Or, in her rage, punched a hole in the mesh. The red tornado barreled outside and raced across the verandah, yelling. "Daddy, Daddy, I want to go home. I hate her. I hate it here."

Three startled faces turned their way from the pool. Alex wiped both palms over his hair, flicking water from his eyes with a blink and shake of his head. He waded to the edge and pulled himself out to meet Stephanie as she fumbled with the child-proof catch on the gate.

"What's the matter?"

The wail doubled in intensity when she discovered she couldn't open the gate, and the words fell out between deep gasps and sobs of rage. "I hate it here. She's mean to me."

159

Alex flung the gate open and cradled her in his arms, hugging and soothing and murmuring in her ear. She clung to his neck and sobbed bitterly. Chloe stood on the verandah and watched the performance with her arms folded. Seb and Julian climbed out of the pool and stared in amazement. Julian's face had the intense, tight look it wore when he was trying hard not to laugh.

Seb called to Chloe, "What did you do to her?"

"I didn't do anything!"

"Why's she crying, then?"

"Goodness me! What's going on here?" Simone's amused voice cut through the wails. "World War Three's broken out, Katy."

The shrieks of outrage ceased for a moment as Stephanie paused to assess the newcomers. Katy, wide-eyed, stood next to Simone, clutching her overnight bag. Both had their eyes fixed on the pair by the pool gate.

Alex released his hold on Stephanie and stood up. She clutched his hand with both of hers, still sobbing in chest-heaving gasps, face now as tomato red as her clothes.

Chloe stepped down from the verandah and approached them. "Simone, this is Alex

160

Bergman and his daughter, Stephanie. Katy and Simone, Alex."

"Hello." Alex held out his hand.

Simone shook it firmly, a multitude of silver bangles jingling on her arm. "Very nice to meet you," she said, giving his bare body a comprehensive stare. "I've heard quite a lot about you. Hello, Stephanie."

Stephanie didn't deign to acknowledge the greeting, keeping her head averted and her reddened eyes on the ground. The sobs decreased in volume and number, but shuddery intakes of air erupted noisily like the toxic gas from bubbling mud.

"Hello, Katy. Stephanie's been looking forward to meeting you." Alex smiled and shook hands with Katy.

"Hello." Katy stepped closer to Stephanie, bending to peer up at her hidden face. "Would you like to come and see my room?"

The dark head shook twice.

"Steffie's a bit upset at the moment. Thanks, Katy. I think perhaps we should go home."

"You don't have to go because of a little tantrum." Simone flapped one hand airily. "She'll be over it in five minutes. Children that age are very fickle."

"It's a bit more than a tantrum," said Alex with a tight smile. "Something upset her very badly." He glanced at Chloe. Unblinking, Chloe returned his gaze. No way was she apologizing for her part in that obnoxious child's behavior. If he couldn't see what a problem daughter he was raising, then tough.

"What did you do to her?" The belligerence in Seb's tone was unmistakable. Chloe glared at him. He knew the child even less than she did.

All eyes except Stephanie's turned to Chloe. She kept her tone even, nonjudgmental. *Stick to the facts. Don't get emotionally involved.* She'd had plenty of experience dealing with the overprotective, irrational parents of the world's next musical geniuses.

"She said she was hungry. I offered her an apple. But Stephanie doesn't like apples. She wanted ice cream." Chloe looked at Alex. "We don't have ice cream during the day usually, only after dinner. She said you'd let her have it because she came swimming."

"But then you lied — you said I couldn't!" came a sulphuric burst from Stephanie. "She said I could, then she put it back in the freezer."

"It's important to keep your promises with children, Chloe," said Alex. "I don't like Steffie eating ice cream instead of an apple either, but if you'd said she could have some, you can't then say no. It confuses her."

From the corner of her eye Chloe could see the round face staring up at her from the protection of her father's side. If she looked directly at that child, the expression of smug satisfaction she was positive would be there would completely blow her self-control. She kept her eyes on Alex. He, at least, should understand the situation if she explained exactly what had happened. He wouldn't think she was a liar. He must know how spoiled and demanding the kid was.

"I can if she's rude."

"Were you rude to Chloe?" Alex asked.

"No."

"Did you say please and thank you?"

"Yes. I always do. It's rude not to." The gray eyes opened, wide and innocent.

"That's right. Good girl." Alex's chilly gaze returned to Chloe. "What was the problem, then?"

Chloe's mouth opened and closed in amazement. The stern man from the police station had suddenly reappeared, studying her as if she were some slimy subspecies of pond life. Any sense of intimacy between them, real or imagined in the darkness of her sleepless night, had been rapidly dispelled. Alex and his daughter were on one side of a chasm, and she was on the other.

She shook her head with a wry smile. "I'm not getting into an 'I said, you said' with a six-year-old. If you don't trust my judgment as to what constitutes rudeness from a child, then there's absolutely no point saying anything else."

"Chloe." Alex's frown darkened.

Simone said to Katy, "Take your bag inside, sweetheart." Katy didn't need a second prompting.

"I believe you, Chloe," she whispered as she passed. Chloe flashed her a smile. What a sweet six-year-old Katy had been. She'd no sooner act the way this red monster did than fly to the moon.

Alex turned to the twins, who were leaning on the pool fence watching the proceedings with casually amused interest. They had no idea of the trials of parenting yet. "Thanks for the swim, guys."

Simone was watching him with her violently plucked eyebrows raised almost to the level of that improbably blond stack of hair. Dolly Parton sprang irrelevantly to mind — minus the curves and face-lifts. He managed a tight smile. "Nice to meet you, Simone and Katy."

He strode toward the verandah and his

bag. What on earth had happened in there? Sure, Steffie could be difficult, but all kids were, and Chloe, with her experience, should be able to handle a child better than that. He was no expert, but he'd never seen his baby so upset. His heart broke to hear her cry that way. The sooner he got her home and calmed down, the better.

"Let's go, hon. Good-bye, Chloe." He took Steffie's hot, sticky palm in his. The little fingers clung tightly.

Chloe observed him through blank eyes. She didn't say a word. She didn't need to. Her whole demeanor told him exactly what she thought. Impotent rage welled again, surprising him with its intensity. This was his child! She needed him. Rarely before had he experienced such a surge of parental emotion. It was a rage fueled by disappointment. In the situation. In Chloe. What did she expect? That he'd take her side against his daughter? A defenseless six-year-old? She, of all people, should understand the overwhelming urge to protect. Witness her leap to defend Seb against his anger in the police station that morning.

"Daddy, I want to go with that girl." Stephanie pulled at Alex's arm. He tore his gaze away from Chloe and looked down into her upturned face.

"Her name is Katy. No, I think we'd better leave."

"But I want to staaaay." She released her grip and moved closer to Katy, who'd stopped to glance back at Chloe uncertainly. Chloe's eyes narrowed slightly, but she remained eloquently silent.

Simone said, "Why don't you let the girls get to know each other while we have a cool drink on the verandah? Your little one's calmed down now."

"I want a cool drink too, Daddy." Steffie ran to him. He squatted down. Her face had resumed its normal color, and she'd stopped the heart-wrenching sobbing.

"Do you really want to stay?" he asked softly, searching her eyes anxiously. She nodded with vigorous enthusiasm.

"That's settled, then. You go with Katy, Stephanie. Come inside, lovey." Simone slipped her arm around Chloe's waist as she passed and drew her along. Their heads bent close as they stepped up onto the verandah. Alex couldn't hear what they said. His once near-hysterical daughter darted past him and followed Katy inside without a backward glance in his direction. He sighed heavily. *Women.*

"Coming in again, Alex?" Seb's voice startled him.

"No, mate, don't think so." He looked toward the house, where Chloe was sliding the screen door closed behind her with a stiff, jerky movement. Her head was tilted at an unnatural angle, and she didn't glance his way at all. He bit his lip. Had he been too hasty in condemning her? But Steffie was a relative baby still; she didn't understand how to adapt to new people's rules. And she had the added confusion of two households — Lucy's and his.

"She'll be all right with Katy," said Julian. "Everybody gets on well with Katy."

Alex firmed his mouth into a straight line as he considered the implications of Julian's comment. Did he mean that Steffie was awkward to get on with, or Chloe?

Alex turned. Julian and Seb were watching him expectantly. Both sets of blue eyes almost implored him.

"Come on, you only just got in," said Seb. "It's too hot to stand around."

Seb turned and took two running steps before launching himself into the water, tucking his knees up to create the biggest splash possible. A shower of cool drops reminded Alex just how hot his skin had become, exposed as it was in the afternoon sun. Julian followed Seb in with a whoop of glee, and more water cascaded over Alex.

"Right, you asked for it." He sprinted to the gate, flung it open, and leaped in after the boys.

CHAPTER SEVEN

In the kitchen, Simone dropped her straw tote bag onto a stool and opened the fridge, carefully avoiding the postcards and paper strewn on the floor. "I'll do the drinks. You sit down and compose yourself." She removed the lemon cordial and the jug of iced water.

Chloe perched on a stool. "That child is the most obnoxious little barefaced liar I've ever met," she hissed, conscious that the girls were in Katy's room just along the corridor. "She knocked all that stuff to the floor and point-blank refused to pick it up when I asked her to. And I asked nicely."

"I'm sure you did, lovey."

"She never said one please or thank you. I don't think she even knows the words, and if she does, she's never in her whole, spoiled-rotten life used them. She's the Red Terror — like a plague or an invading horde of barbarians."

Simone put glasses on the counter. "Children that age can be truly horrible if they put their minds to it."

"Katy was never like that. Neither were any of her friends." Chloe sniffed. She reached for a tissue. "I can't believe I let her upset me so much." She blew her nose and laughed self-consciously. "She's a little kid, for heaven's sake."

"She's *his* kid." Simone took the ice tray from the freezer and began emptying ice cubes into each glass.

"So?" demanded Chloe.

"So you're extra sensitive. You want to like her, he wants you to like her, and she isn't very likable at the moment, poor little thing. It makes a difference, I think." Simone was wearing her inscrutable sphinx face as she concentrated on her task.

"Who to?"

"Him, you, definitely to Stephanie."

"You think I'm overreacting."

"Yes. But it's not about Stephanie. You'd normally handle her behavior without any problems. It's about Alex."

Alex? He wasn't showing much in the way of parenting skills. Stephanie, despite her outrageous carrying on, was only a small child. A father should know how capable she was of getting her own way, and her methods. Maybe he didn't know her as well as he thought.

"She didn't want to come swimming. She told me straight out she didn't want to come at all. I actually felt sorry for her — for about two minutes."

"Like I said, children that age can be impossible even without their parents being divorced. Does she see him much? I expect she just wants her dad all to herself."

"She can have him. I certainly don't want to take him away from her." Chloe sniffed into her tissue.

"My daddy doesn't want to be with you, anyway." Stephanie, with Katy close behind, appeared in the doorway. Her round little face had twisted into a grimace of disdain. Chloe gripped the tissue in tense fingers. Simone was right. Stephanie was a child, a child with problems much too big for her to cope with and none of them her fault. Alex needed to spend more time with her.

"You don't need to worry about that, Stephanie," said Simone. "Now, how about picking up these cards you knocked onto the floor?"

"They're my postcards from when my friend Estelle went to Fiji," cried Katy. "Did you throw them on the floor?" She glared at Stephanie.

Stephanie looked from one distraught face to the other stern one and must have decided she was outnumbered. She hastily bent to pick up the postcards. "I was going to before, but she was mean to me," she said.

Katy took them from her fingers and studied them carefully. "One of them's got a dirty mark." Her face drooped in dismay. "Did you step on it?"

Stephanie peered at the offending card. "Sorry, Katy. I didn't mean to drop them. I bumped them when I was just looking."

Chloe and Simone exchanged a glance. "Maybe Chloe deserves an apology from you as well," suggested Simone.

"Sorry, Chloe." The singsong tone would convince no one.

"Thank you, Stephanie." Chloe couldn't bring herself to smile at the smug face. She looked at Katy instead. "Would you girls like lemon cordial?"

"Yes, please." Katy replaced the postcards carefully on the fridge.

"I like lemonade better," said Stephanie.

"We don't have lemonade, Stephanie." Chloe poured cordial and iced water into a glass for Katy. "Would you like cordial, iced water, or nothing?" *Or perhaps a session in the Gardiners' long-unused "naughty corner"?*

Katy took a big gulp of her drink and tinkled the ice cubes against the sides of the glass. Stephanie watched. "I want cordial," she said suddenly.

"I thought I heard you tell your daddy you had good manners." Simone stood with hands on hips, face stern.

"I'd like cordial, please."

"That's better. Shall we take this outside to the verandah, Chloe?"

Chloe handed Stephanie the full glass, staring at her so she was in no doubt as to what was expected.

"Thank you." The fingers closed around the glass. She took several large gulps and put the tumbler on the counter. "Katy, I want to go to your room again." Stephanie barely waited for a response from Katy, who hastily followed her as she ran from the kitchen.

Poor Katy deserved a special treat after this solo barbarian invasion. Maybe they could all go and pick out another kitten from the desperados at the RSPCA shelter. Chloe slid off the stool. "I'll bring the lemon, lime, and bitters for the adults."

"Pity we don't have any vodka to go with it. It's getting to be about that time. Where's a tray?"

"Beside the oven. I could sure do with a

173

shot, and I don't even drink." Chloe opened the fridge.

Simone arranged the remaining glasses, the iced water, and the cordial on the tray. "How often is she with him?"

"Fortnightly, I think." The chill of the bottle clutched to her chest helped cool her blood as the mention of Alex in connection with that child sent another hot surge of rage through her body.

"So you won't cross paths much at all."

"Never, if I can help it."

Simone nudged Chloe's arm with her elbow as they headed for the door. "He's very handsome. I've always gone for that dark-haired, blue-eyed look. Good body too. You should work on him, Chloe."

"Simone, for heaven's sake! The man's not interested in me, I'm not interested in him, and even if I was, he's got Stephanie for a daughter, and she's guaranteed to put off any prospective girlfriend. No thank you!"

Simone waited while Chloe slid the screen door open. "Yes, yes, yes," she said. "But he's handsome, single, and he likes the boys — Katy goes without saying — and he *is* interested in you, despite what you say."

"He is not." But was he? She'd thought so yesterday and most of last night. Deep down inside she did, despite all her cogitations and prevarications and thoughts that she was kidding herself. Was Simone's assessment accurate? She often made pronouncements on subjects she didn't know much about, and Chloe usually dismissed her opinion as a sort of over-the-top rant. But this time she wasn't sure.

Simone knew a lot about falling in love. She'd had two husbands and, if her stories were true, many affairs. She was more experienced with men than Chloe, that was for certain. On the other hand, she'd been angling for Chloe to find a man, any man, for ages. Maybe she based her opinion that Alex was interested in her on one aspect only — he was there, and he was available.

"You'll see." Simone began unloading the tray onto the wooden table. "You wouldn't mind if he was, would you?" She grinned shrewdly at Chloe.

"Did you see his face when he looked at me after that Oscar-winning performance by his child?" Chloe snorted derisively. "Believe me, any interest he may have had was flushed straight down the gurgler."

"Oh, Chloe." Simone flapped a hand. "That won't put him off."

"It put *me* off." Chloe plopped down onto the nearest chair. "When Katy's old enough, I want my life back. I don't want to be continually skirmishing with that little horror, or one like her."

Simone cupped her hands to her mouth and called to the boys. "Drinks!"

The three swimmers hauled themselves out of the water, tanned bodies sleek and shining, hair plastered to their heads, faces alight with laughter.

"Tell me you don't think that's worth fighting for," said Simone, staring blatantly as Alex walked around the edge of the pool to the gate.

If physical attraction was the only issue, they wouldn't be having this conversation at all. What woman could deny that Alex had a very sexy pair of legs beneath slim hips, an even sexier flat stomach and broad chest? And there was something about the way his cheeks crinkled when he smiled, and the way his eyes bored into hers, as though he could see right into her mind.

Except attraction *wasn't* the only issue, and if he could see into her mind, he would have seen the truth about the showdown with his daughter instead of automatically assuming she'd been deliberately nasty to his precious. She couldn't afford to let her thoughts veer that way at all. That way lay heartache. That way lay shoals and rocks for the unwary traveler.

"Here be dragons," she murmured.

"Pardon?"

"Nothing." Chloe grabbed the cordial and poured measures for the boys, topping the glasses with ice and chilled water.

Alex walked slowly toward the verandah where Chloe sat with Simone, pouring drinks. He dried himself as he walked and wrapped the towel around his waist before he sat down on the steps.

"Sit here, Alex." Simone indicated the empty chair between Seb and Chloe.

"I'm all wet."

"So are we. Who cares? You'll be dry in a minute." Seb yanked the chair away from the table. Chloe kept her face averted and appeared to take no interest at all in the seating arrangements.

"Where's Steffie?" he asked.

Simone answered him with calm assurance. "With Katy in her room. They're fine. I told you, these little storms pass quickly. Doesn't do to make too much of them."

Alex heard the veiled rebuke. Had he overreacted? Judging by that comment and Chloe's manner, he had. "I'm not sure how to handle her sometimes. She's growing up so fast."

"You need to lay some ground rules and stick to them."

"It's difficult when there are two households with different ideas involved."

"True."

"And I only see her on alternate weekends." At least Simone was sympathetic. Chloe still hadn't made any sort of conciliatory gesture. Surely she wasn't that upset by the incident. Even Steffie appeared to have gotten over it.

"Cricket starts next Saturday, Alex," Seb interrupted. "You said you'd come and watch."

"Where are you playing?"

"The primary school ovals at nine."

"I might come. Can't promise."

"Cool." Seb grinned happily.

"Are you going, Julian?"

"No. Orchestra starts again on Saturday morning."

"Really?" What a talented and energetic bunch they were.

"Julian's a very good player." Simone smiled proudly. "Isn't he, Chloe? He must have gotten that from your mum's side of the family. My lot can't sing a note in tune."

"He's doing well." At last the glimmer of a smile reached the surface as Chloe glanced at Julian.

"I want Steffie to learn an instrument. What would you suggest, Chloe?"

"The recorder," she said bluntly. "She's too young for anything else except the violin." Still she wouldn't meet his eye.

"I thought perhaps the piano."

"Waste of time until they're old enough to concentrate for more than five minutes. Plus their fingers are too small. Wait till she's about seven or even eight."

"Unless she's the new Mozart," Julian put in.

"I don't think I have another Mozart." Alex laughed.

"No point forcing her if she shows no interest. The best thing you can do is sing and dance and encourage her to join in. Fill your house with music, so it's a natural part of her life. Some people expect music teachers to teach their kids to appreciate music but never listen to anything at home." Chloe's face had become increasingly animated as she expounded on a subject so obviously important to her. "Music is a life thing."

Seb groaned. "Stop her, someone."

"No, it's interesting," said Alex. "Do you perform much?"

"I do occasional gigs with a band when they need a sub. Not as much as I'd like."

"Chloe plays beautifully and sings very well too," said Simone. "She plays jazz and classical guitar."

"Will you play for me?" Alex leaned forward to emphasize the earnestness of his request. Did she register the *me?* More important, would that affect her decision?

"Now?" Chloe stared at him, brow wrinkled, a half smile hovering. Pleased? Hazel eyes met his, locked in for a moment, assessing. Yes, tempted.

"Why not?" He didn't set her free, kept her captive with his gaze, but Simone broke the spell.

"Go on. I haven't heard you play for ages." Chloe shook her head, but Julian was already on his feet. "I'll get your guitar."

"I'll call Steffie to come and listen." Alex grinned at Seb, who raised his eyes skyward. He pushed his chair back and scooped up the bag with his clothes as he went. Might as well change.

"They're in Katy's room." Simone followed him into the house.

Chloe met Seb's glum gaze. "I didn't offer. He asked."

"You didn't have to agree."

"What's your problem?"

"You always take over. Why can't we do anything without your being the center of attention?"

"Me?" It emerged as an outraged squeak.

Seb folded his arms. "Alex came around to let his daughter practice swimming, but you wrecked that."

"You heard her. She didn't want to! I tried to entertain her."

"Yeah." His lip curled. "Alex is *my* friend. You don't have to like him."

Chloe shook her head. She gave up. If they wanted to hang out together, so be it. They both knew how she felt and ignored her. "You can have him, Seb, complete with his daughter. You'll have to fight her for him, though."

"That's your opinion. You obviously upset her."

"You obviously haven't had anything to do with her."

The sliding door rasped. Julian carried Chloe's guitar case. Alex and Stephanie followed, he clothed in shorts and T-shirt, she with a sulky scowl. Katy and Simone brought up the rear, both smiling.

"Play the one I like," said Katy, skipping a couple of steps.

Chloe sent her a special smile. Julian handed her the guitar, which she rested on her knee, using the case as a footrest.

Alex resumed his seat. Steffie climbed onto his knee. He put his arms around her, cuddled. She wriggled. "I don't want to

181

listen, Daddy, I want to play with Katy."

"Shh, hon. Chloe's going to play for us."

"I don't care. I don't want to listen."

Little brat. Chloe strummed a chord, adjusted the tuning carefully, strummed another. Put the image of strong brown arms and bare chest out of her head.

"Daaaddeeee."

"I want to dance," said Katy. "Chloe's playing my favorite tune, Stephanie. We'll play after."

To Alex's surprise, Katy stepped across to the little patch of grass and struck a ballet-like pose. Steffie stopped squirming in his lap and stared. Chloe sent a smile across to Katy so full of love, his heart contracted with a sharp pang of envy for the rapport between them, instantly dismissed as unfair but with a lingering bruise all the same. Would Chloe ever smile that way at him? How could he earn her love? He wasn't doing well so far. And Steffie sure wasn't helping.

Chloe bent her head over the guitar and began.

A shimmery melody poured from her fingers, at once sad and beautiful. Simple. Exquisite. Spanish without a doubt. He had no idea what it was, but it touched that place already tender in his soul, his already yearning heart. He wanted it to go on forever. He wanted to sit spellbound with his daughter on his knee, watching Chloe consumed by the music, her brow creased gently in concentration, her slender fingers plucking expertly at the strings. The guitar came alive in her hands. He'd never personally known anyone so proficient on an instrument, never seen anyone perform so professionally and yet so casually.

Katy began moving, waving her arms softly, graceful as a butterfly as she improvised her dance, stepping and bowing, floating with the music. Quite lovely. The mesmerizing performance drew to a gentle close, the last notes soaring up and away on the warm evening air. Katy fluttered to a halt.

Alex and Simone clapped loudly. "Brava," he cried, forcing his stupefied, lovelorn mind into a semblance of coherency. "What a lovely piece. What is it?"

Chloe smiled. " 'Lecuerdos de la Alhambra.' "

Simone blew Katy a kiss. "You were wonderful, my darling."

"Thanks, Gran. Play rock 'n' roll, Chloe. Come and dance, Steffie." Katy held out her hands.

Chloe launched into a funky blues riff.

Alex pushed Steffie off his lap. "Go on, hon."

"Don't want to."

Katy capered about the lawn. Simone leaped to her feet and joined her, laughing and springing like a child, clapping her hands over her head. Steffie stared, goggle-eyed. The boys writhed in their chairs from laughter. "Go, Gran!" called Julian.

"Come on, Steffie." Alex stood and grasped her hand, but she resisted, pulling back so he had no choice but to sit again. She clambered onto his knee and gripped his neck with both hands.

"I want to go home," she said loudly.

"When this tune is finished." Alex lowered his voice, frowned, and glanced at Chloe. "We have to say thank you first."

"Then can we go?" Steffie grabbed his face between her palms and held him captive, staring into his eyes. Such a sweet face. He dropped a kiss on her cheek and smiled.

"Yes."

"Good."

Chloe, bent over her guitar, gave no indication she'd heard the exchange, but she must have, sitting, as she was, so close. Steffie slid off his lap and stalked across to their bag. She zipped the top closed and dragged it over the verandah to his chair, bumping Chloe's guitar case on the way. Chloe's foot slipped, the guitar lurched, and the music stopped abruptly.

"Can we go now, Daddy?" Steffie leaned on his knee, gazing into his face.

"You bumped Chloe's case," Alex said. "I'm sorry, Chloe. It didn't damage anything, did it?"

"No." Her blank face gave no indication what she thought.

Time to go.

Steffie grabbed the strap of the bag. "Come on, Daddy. You promised."

Alex grimaced at Chloe. "Sorry. I'd better take her home. Thank you for the swim and the music. You play wonderfully well. Thank you." He tried to tell her with his eyes and his expression how sorry he was to interrupt her playing, how impressed he'd been, how amazing her little family was. Each of them a tribute to her integrity and values.

"Thanks." Chloe bent and opened the case, slipped the guitar inside, and clipped it shut. She stood up. "Good-bye." She'd withdrawn. No longer the laughing, happy woman from the barbecue yesterday, she was now the stiffly proper one. The one he'd thought was frightened of him but, at this moment, suspected in some way he'd disappointed.

185

Simone and Katy, giggling and puffing, joined them on the verandah. "Bye-bye, Stephanie," said Katy.

"Bye-bye, Katy." Alex nudged her. "What do you say, hon?"

She glanced up at him, then at the ground. "Thank you for playing with me, Katy."

"And Chloe, for inviting us over," he prompted.

"No." She kicked at the ground with one foot.

"Don't bother, Alex." Chloe's eyes met his briefly before flicking to his daughter. "Good-bye, Stephanie."

Better quit right now. Alex stuck out his hand. "Nice to meet you, Simone. Bye, Katy. See you later, boys." He grabbed Steffie with one hand and their bag with the other. His towel had jammed in the zipper, but it could stay there until he reached his car. He had to get his daughter away before she embarrassed and humiliated him even more. What on earth had got into her? The gate clanged shut behind them.

Alex unlocked the car and tossed the bag onto the backseat. Steffie climbed in and clicked her seat belt, cooperative and smiling now. He slammed the driver's door and started the engine, glancing in the rearview mirror at her face. She was looking out the window, a little smile on her lips.

"That was very rude of you, Stephanie. I'm disappointed."

Silence. He glanced in the mirror again. She'd closed her eyes. "Steffie?" Silence. "Why were you so rude to Chloe?"

"I hate her." She began kicking her feet up and down against the back of his seat.

"That's no excuse. You mustn't be rude to people." He clamped his mouth shut. Hadn't he been guilty of exactly the same behavior when he first met Chloe? "Stop kicking the seat, please."

"Can I have pizza for dinner?"

"We're not having dinner together. Mummy wanted you home early so you could get ready for school."

"Are we going there now?"

"Yes."

"Daddy, I don't want to go home. I want to stay with you." The face in the mirror stared back at him earnestly.

All his frustrated anger and disappointment melted away. She really was a sweet child, but he couldn't provide the care she needed, and he hadn't had a clue how to deal with her behavior this afternoon. She was far better off with her mother and baby brother in a stable home environment. "I'd love to have you stay, hon, but we can't."

"Why not?"

"Mummy loves you too, and she wants you with her and Derek and Mark."

"I still want to live with you."

"We'll see." But it wouldn't happen. Lucy would never agree, despite her ravings that he shirked his responsibility. He just couldn't see himself as a full-time father.

"I want to live with you *and* Mummy."

And *that* definitely was never going to happen.

CHAPTER EIGHT

Alex remembered Seb's cricket match mid-morning on Saturday. He pulled off the yellow rubber gloves he'd donned to scrub the shower and looked at his watch. Ten forty-five. He could cycle to the oval and continue to the shops. After that he should do some work.

Ten minutes later he wheeled down the street. Not so hot today. Clouds were piling up on the southwesterly horizon under the influence of a stiffish breeze. Storms had been forecast, but everyone had given up on rain ever arriving as promised. He should cycle more often. He always enjoyed it when he did, despite Aranda's being full of hills.

Saturday-morning traffic was sparse, allowing him to spin straight through the yield sign and turn right. Minutes later the ovals were in sight. Two games were in progress on opposite sides of the playing fields. He squinted at the nearest players.

Too young for Seb.

A ragged line of spectators lounged on the boundary of the far game. Alex scanned the white-clad boys sitting waiting to bat, wheeling his bike across the grass. No Seb. Perhaps he was batting. Couldn't really tell from this distance, with all players wearing white trousers, shirts, and broad-brimmed sun hats. Nor could he recognize any of the fielding team.

"Hi, guys," he said. "Is Sebastian Gardiner on your team?"

A couple of faces glanced up at him. "Nah."

"Ask the scorers." One boy pointed to a man and a woman sitting on folding chairs several meters away. Both had clipboards in their laps. Both wore straw sun hats. Both stared intently at the game. The woman was Chloe.

"Thanks." Alex removed his cycling helmet and hung it on the handlebars. Chloe had no idea he was here. How would she react? The thought of her possible displeasure made him ridiculously nervous. He wheeled his bike to a position a few meters behind and to the side of the scorers and sat on the grass to watch the game. He'd come to watch Seb. He'd promised. It was a public oval.

A boy resembling Seb was fielding in slips. The batsman whacked a ball to the boundary, and the small crowd of spectators clapped. His teammates roared their approval. Chloe said clearly, "Nice shot."

The over finished, and the boy Alex thought was Seb took the ball. He gave the umpire his hat, measured out his run-up, and whirled his bowling arm several times to loosen up. Definitely Seb. Alex realized he was leaning forward, clasping his hands tightly together in anticipation. He relaxed his grip. The other boy was on strike now. He hadn't had much of a go since Alex arrived; the first boy was the danger for Seb's team.

Seb ran in to deliver his first ball. Wide. The umpire's arm went out. Alex frowned. Chloe groaned audibly, and her companion said something. She laughed. The second ball was a beauty, cutting back in and completely bamboozling the batsman. Pure luck he wasn't clean bowled.

"Do that again," Alex murmured, staring hard at Seb as he walked back to his mark. The kid had a terrific style. A natural. This time the ball was straighter, but the batsman slashed wildly, only succeeding in looping an easy catch for the wicket keeper. Seb's team cheered.

"Well done, Seb!" shouted Alex, clapping vigorously. Chloe spun around in her seat, spilling her clipboard to the grass and nearly upending her folding chair.

"Hello." Alex grinned at her astounded face. "Great ball, wasn't it?"

She nodded and scrambled to collect her score pad. Seb squinted across toward them, shading his eyes with one hand. He waved suddenly. Alex lifted his hand in return. Seb's teeth flashed in a wide smile, and then he turned to study the new batsman, tossing the ball casually from hand to hand. Could he remove this one too? The way he'd delivered that second ball, he most likely could.

But the batsman doggedly blocked the rest of Seb's over. As the fielding side changed ends for the new bowler, Alex walked to Chloe's side and squatted down.

"How are they doing?" The cheek he could see turned rose pink under the wide brim of the straw hat. She studied the score sheet on her lap.

"Grammar has sixty-three off twenty-two overs. Six wickets down."

"Not bad," said her companion, a round-faced fellow with an English accent. "Who's bowling now?"

"Peter Hammond. Sorry," Chloe said to

Alex. "We have to concentrate."

"Okay. I'll see you after."

"Thanks for coming. Seb was hoping you'd remember." Chloe flashed him a smile. He'd never thought to see one of those sent his way again. Ridiculous how that imagined loss had pained him all week. Even more ridiculous how the small show of warmth lightened his heart.

"I said I would."

"I know but . . . you know." The smile faded.

"Dot ball," said her companion.

She turned away, eyes focused intently on the action in the middle. The sun hat obscured her face.

Alex walked back to where he'd propped his bike and sat down, arms resting on bent knees. She'd thought he wouldn't keep his promise. She didn't have much of an opinion of him. Or his daughter.

He needed to explain to her about Steffie, how difficult it was and how Lucy sometimes threatened to minimize his involvement with her even to the point of changing her name, something he'd never agree to. She was *his* daughter, not Derek Dwyer's. He met his financial obligation with meticulous precision. Lucy had no cause for complaint there. Admittedly he didn't spend as much time with Steffie as any of them would like, but it was difficult. He tried, but he was busy. He couldn't possibly have her live with him, but Chloe must see how he loved his little girl despite her failings.

He wanted Chloe to know, wanted her to understand. If she didn't, the misunderstanding would gape like a chasm between them. He stared at her white-clad back. The sun hat obscured her lovely hair, but her bare legs were visible — a smooth, elegant line of calf, neat ankle, sandals revealing feet with pink polish on the toes. She was perfect. Falling for her was a torture of denial. Every now and again she turned her head toward the Englishman, and Alex caught a glimpse of cheek and mouth, smiling. Lovely. Kissable.

Seb didn't bowl again. When the innings finished, he jogged across to Alex and threw himself down onto the grass beside him.

"Hi."

"G'day, mate. Great wicket. You nearly had him with the ball before too."

"I took another wicket earlier, but you missed it. Clean bowled."

"Excellent! Sorry, had some things to do at home."

"That's all right. Glad you came. Thanks." Seb grinned with unashamed delight.

Thank goodness he'd looked at his watch when he did this morning. Such a simple way of pleasing the boy.

Chloe heard them chatting behind her but couldn't quite catch the words. Seb sounded excited about something. She toted up the bowling figures for Seb's team and compared them with Hugo's from the opposition, on scoring duty with her. Hugo headed toward a group of parents equipped with Thermos flasks and cookies.

Chloe pulled a banana and her water from the bag at her feet. Seb's drink was in there still. She glanced across to the pair sprawled on the grass and nattering like crazy. A gust of wind threatened to whip her hat away. The sun went behind a cloud. Piles of dark, stormy bundles had built up without her noticing. She stuffed her hat into the bag.

"Seb." She held up his drink. He scrambled to his feet and beckoned her over.

Alex straightened up as she approached, smiling. "Hello."

"Hi. You finished with two wickets for eleven runs, Seb."

Alex nodded his approval. "Well done!"

"What did they get?"

"Eighty-nine."

"Hopeless! We should beat that."

"If it doesn't rain." Chloe indicated the

buildup of storm clouds. A low grumble rolled around the distant Brindabella Mountains.

Alex stood up and brushed wisps of grass from his jeans. "I'd better head home. Don't want to get caught."

"Can't you stay for a couple of overs? I don't go in till number six."

"Seb, Alex wants to leave." Chloe frowned a warning.

"We can give him a ride home if it rains. His bike will fit in the boot."

"Seb." Chloe sighed. She looked to Alex for help, but he seemed to be wavering. She shrugged. "Whatever. You're a big boy."

Alex laughed. "Okay, mate. I reckon we'll all get wet if that breaks. Wish it would — we sure need it."

"We're on again," said Chloe. Hugo had returned to his chair. "My brain can't take too much of this level of concentration. Math isn't my strong point." She grinned.

"Just make it up," said Alex. "They won't know."

"Hey!" Seb threw a pretend punch at Alex's shoulder, and they proceeded to shadowbox, laughing and jostling.

Chloe turned away. She'd been wrong, Simone right. There were things Alex could offer Seb — male things. The boys needed that contact. Instinctively they both gravitated toward Alex. And he obviously enjoyed their company.

Chloe picked up her scoring papers and clipboard. The two parents doing umpire duty walked onto the field, followed by the players.

Maybe Alex needed the boys as much as they needed him. Maybe he was lonely in that house all by himself, separated from his daughter — pain though she was. Maybe he missed having a family. She'd never considered that aspect.

"Hey, Chloe. Concentrate." Hugo's jovial voice cut through the haze.

Twenty minutes later the warm, frolicking wind became a serious gale-force blast. The gathering clouds combined into a solid wall of bruised gray, the light dimmed dramatically, and the temperature plummeted. Several large raindrops landed on Chloe's score sheet, smudging her neat figures.

"Time to leave, methinks," announced Hugo. "Don't want to be struck by lightning."

Chloe jumped to her feet.

Players and spectators bolted for cover as thunder crashed overhead. There was no pavilion for shelter. Cars or trees were the only option. Chloe thrust the score sheets

197

at the coach, who was standing nearby yelling instructions to his scattering team to collect the stumps and ball. She grabbed the folding chair and her bag and sprinted for the Holden parked fifty meters away. Seb, lugging his kit bag, and Alex, wheeling his bike, followed, laughing like idiots.

Chloe tossed her gear onto the backseat and flung herself into the front. Let them manhandle the bike into the boot. Water dripped down her face from her sodden hair. She was absolutely soaked through, and talk about wet T-shirt contests! The waterlogged fabric had become virtually transparent.

Chloe pulled the clinging garment away from her body and attempted to wring out some of the excess water. As soon as she let it go, the fabric molded itself firmly around her again. Thumps and scraping noises came from the back of the car. They'd never get that bike in properly.

The passenger door opened, and Alex jumped in beside her, bringing a cool, wet gust of wind. The nearness of him, so large, so male, so attractive . . . Chloe gulped and swallowed. She concentrated on guiding the key into the ignition with a clammy hand.

Seb slammed the back door. "Drive slowly."

"Did you fit it in?"

"Not really." Alex grinned. He dragged a hand through his hair. Drops of water ran down his arm and dripped onto his jeans, the denim plastered firmly around his thigh, inches from her own knee. "But we don't have far to go."

"Our place is closest," said Seb. "Alex can come with us and ride home later."

Right. Chloe dragged her fascinated gaze away from damp, shiny skin and the way Alex's shirt as well as his jeans displayed the contours of a body her fingers itched to touch. She reversed carefully out of the parking spot. Rain thundered harder on the roof, drowning out conversation. The road ahead had disappeared, obscured by the gray sheets plummeting to earth. Plus the windshield had begun to mist up.

"I can't see a thing."

Alex wiped a hand across the glass to clear her vision. "Put the air conditioner on."

"It doesn't work," Seb said from the back-seat. "We've got manual air-conditioning — as in, open the windows."

Alex snorted with laughter. He wiped the windshield again, leaning across so his shoulder brushed Chloe's. She gripped the steering wheel tightly to stop herself from running her left hand over his extended arm. Something had happened to all the air in the car — she could barely suck in a breath.

Chloe crawled to the main intersection, judging distance by the red dots of light from the rear of the car in front of her. Another turn, follow the curve of the street, splash through a newly formed lake on the corner, and they were home. She drove straight into the open garage, and the roar on the roof ceased abruptly. Seb flung the door open and jumped out to retrieve Alex's bike.

"Goodness." Chloe sat momentarily stunned, sucking in huge lungfuls of air. "What a cloudburst."

"Hope it keeps raining. A few days' worth would be good." Alex didn't move to get out. Instead, he touched gentle fingers to her cheek, smoothing away wet hair. "You're soaked."

"I know." *The T-shirt!* How could he not notice, with her chest heaving like a bellows? She glanced at him to ascertain where his eyes were directed.

Right at her. Right into her eyes. His eyes were dark and intense. And he'd moved nearer. The fingers slipped farther around her neck. Chloe held her breath against the warmth and mind-blowing intimacy of his touch. So firm, so wonderful. In the next moment he pulled her close and brushed his lips against hers. Gently. Then again. More firmly. Fire leaped in her belly. Her mouth opened, and a small sigh escaped. The boot slammed shut.

Chloe bounced away. Alex sat back with an inscrutable, sphinxlike expression, half smiling, half considering. Her face was so hot, her hair would be dry in no time. Steaming. She groped for the door handle and almost fell out when the door sprang open. *Inside.* She had to get inside, fast. What a reaction! What a kiss!

She wanted more.

Behind her the car door slammed. Alex and Seb began discussing the abandoned game. Chloe wrenched open the connecting door to the house, shivering despite her overheated skin and racing pulse. She headed straight for her bedroom, passing a startled Katy and Julian in the kitchen with a brief hello thrown their way.

"Gosh, you're wet," floated down the hall after her.

"Yes, I'm soaked."

Just before she closed her door, Seb's voice in the kitchen said, "You can wear some of my clothes, Alex."

Chloe stopped in the center of her room,

breath coming hard and fast. Alex had slipped into the family circle as easily as could be. Wearing Seb's clothes, including Julian in the building thing, kissing her. Right now he was probably charming Katy. And the worst thing about it was, he fit perfectly. Could it be that Alex wouldn't mind a girlfriend with massive responsibilities? Did she dare hope? Did that kiss mean something?

She yanked her wet shorts off. He certainly knew what he was getting into. She went to the bathroom, dumped the wet garments into the hamper, and grabbed her towel. Why else would he kiss her that way? He was attracted to her the same way she was to him.

Clean, dry, long-sleeved T-shirt. Jeans. Chloe stared at herself in the mirror as she wielded the hairdryer. What on earth could Alex Bergman possibly see in Chloe Gardiner? *Don't get carried away. Maybe Alex Bergman is a flirt with a roving eye.*

And — Chloe lowered the dryer and glared at herself — *do not, on any account, forget the Red Terror!* What a shocker. What sort of relationship would that be, constantly going ten rounds with Stephanie? Especially since Alex wouldn't even consider that his darling might lie.

When she entered the kitchen, the kids and Alex were engrossed in lunch preparation. She paused in the doorway to observe the peaceful, domestic scene. Katy was pulling a lettuce apart, Julian had mugs ready on the counter for coffee, and Seb was assembling his special, monster-sized salad rolls.

Alex glanced up from slicing a tomato and smiled. A spark of something leaped from his eyes to hers. An awareness, a new intimacy. He thought he belonged here. He assumed too much. *Cool. Be cool. This mustn't take off.*

"Like your shirt." Chloe joined the workers. "Didn't know you were into AC/DC."

"I don't mind them, as a matter of fact." He looked down at the shorts, which were baggy on Seb but just about right on Alex. "Good thing Seb wears his clothes several sizes too big."

"I don't!"

"Yes, you do," said Katy. "They're always nearly falling off."

"How was orchestra, Julian?" Chloe asked.

"Fine. We're doing Beethoven's Sixth and a trumpet concerto with some dude from the School of Music."

"I like the trumpet," said Alex. "When's

203

the concert? I'll come along and bring Steffie."

Now, that was something to look forward
to. Stephanie whining and wriggling her way
through an orchestral concert.

"June."

"Great."

"I'm invited to Jenny's birthday," said
Katy.

"When?" Katy always had heaps of party
invitations. If they were obliged to recipro-
cate for Katy's birthday, they'd need to rent
a stadium.

"Saturday after next. We're going to the
movies and then dinner at her house."

"Sounds fun."

"How many of you?" asked Alex.

"Five."

"I don't know much about girls' parties.
Steffie's mum organizes hers."

"Do you get to go?" Katy gazed up at him
with a sympathetic expression.

"Yes, but as a visitor."

"When's her birthday?"

"In November. When's yours?"

"September the seventh. Chloe's is in
April." Katy's eyes sparkled, and the expression on her face was exactly the same as
Simone's in matchmaking mode. That pair
would have to be kept away from each other.

"Is it?" Alex paused in slicing the tomato to raise his eyebrows.

"Yes, and she'll be twenty-seven."

"We'll have to do something to celebrate." Alex grinned at Katy, and she nodded vigorously. His gaze caught Chloe's and held it for an instant. The back of her neck tingled where his fingers had caressed. She ran her tongue over her lips, tasted his kiss.

"Depends." Chloe glanced at Seb. "On what happens to him. His court appearance is soon. I might not feel like celebrating anything."

"Will you be a character witness for me?" Seb asked Alex. "My lawyer said I should have character witnesses. Frank from next door will. He's known me all my life."

"Sure, mate." He landed a light, affectionate punch on Seb's upper arm. Seb beamed.

"Really?" asked Chloe.

His gaze swung from Seb to her. The shadow of a frown passed across his face. "Of course I will. Why would you be surprised?"

Chloe shrugged. She couldn't answer. Her reaction had been spontaneous. Any doubts she had were deeply embedded, stemming from her original, less than perfect impression of Alex and the fact that Seb's transgression had been against him in the first place.

"Seb has repaid his debt to me, and he's done it with style. I reckon that should carry a bit of weight with the judge. Seb won't do anything like that again."

Four pairs of eyes bored into her. Seb and Alex's were particularly critical. Julian and Katy's were plain surprised.

Chloe nodded. "He'd better not, or Children's Services might interfere and split us up," she said, and immediately regretted stating something that had never been mentioned by anyone but had always lurked nastily in the back of her mind.

"Would they?" Katy's face had gone pale with fright.

"No," said Alex with great firmness. "They'd have absolutely no reason to. You're all doing extremely well, and I'll make that quite clear in my statement."

"Thanks." Chloe turned away to hide the burning red of her face and began taking plates from the shelf.

"I already set the table, Chloe," said Julian.

The rain didn't stop, so after lunch Chloe drove Alex home. He sat beside her wearing Seb's clothes and holding his own in a plastic bag. They didn't speak during the short trip. Chloe drove up the driveway as close to the front door as possible. She didn't turn off the engine, just sat and waited for him to get out — or for whatever happened next.

"Come in," he said.

If she faced him, she'd be lost. Instead, she stared through the rain-spattered windshield at the heavily drooping branches of the bushes by the fence. "I shouldn't."

"Why?" His voice caressed her. Inviting, tempting, seducing.

"I should get back. Seb . . ."

"He won't go running off anywhere. Come in. Just for a minute or two. I want to talk to you."

"Talk?" Chloe turned her head to meet his gaze. He was watching her, his eyes full, darker blue, the way they'd looked before he kissed her. Her lips remembered. Her skin remembered. Her breath raced in shallow bursts from her lungs. A curious heaviness suffused her limbs.

He said, "I never get a moment alone with you."

"That's what comes with raising three kids." But she switched off the engine.

Alex grinned, his hand on the door latch. "I'll go first."

She watched him bound up the couple of steps to the front door, his figure blurred by the wet glass. The porch afforded minimal shelter, because the wind blew the rain in under the portico. He was getting wet again, fumbling with the key. Should she leave? Her brain said yes; her body screamed no. Her hands lay inert in her lap.

The door swung open. Alex turned toward the car and beckoned, his face pale in the gloom of the afternoon. Ridiculous, in Seb's teenager clothes. But he'd accepted them with no hesitation and no fuss. Amazing for a man with such style and sense of himself. He'd surprised her again and shown once more how wrong she'd been.

Did he want to talk? Or did he want something else? Chloe pulled the key from the ignition, leaped from the car, and sprinted to the house. Alex closed the door behind her. It was done. The decision made.

"I'll change. Just be a minute. Sit down."

He disappeared down the hall to the right. Chloe wandered into the living room where she and Seb had stood so uncomfortably that day. Then, she'd been so nervous, she could barely talk. Still angry both with Seb and with the man who had attacked her — unfairly, viciously, when she was at her most vulnerable. Hard to reconcile that man with

the one who'd kissed her, whose kiss she —
Stop!

The room was the same — quiet, tasteful, spacious. The atmosphere was completely different. Strange, how time altered perceptions. Time and knowledge deepened understanding — for both herself and Alex.

CDs lined a large cabinet. Chloe tilted her head to squint at the narrow spines. He had wide-ranging tastes — from Miles Davis to Sinatra. From Vivaldi to Van Morrison. Photos stood on a low bookcase by the wall. Chloe crossed the polished floor for a better look.

Family photos. Stephanie, developing from a sweet, chubby, laughing baby into the difficult little girl she was now. The most recent was the ubiquitous school photo. Taken last year, probably. She picked it up. A kindergarten child. Head and shoulders of a round, unsmiling face wearing a slightly bewildered expression. She stared straight at the camera with wide eyes under a severely cut fringe — sad, almost frightened eyes. Way too much so for a little girl. The thought stabbed Chloe's mind, sharp-edged and penetrating. She put the photo down quickly.

An elderly couple smiled in the next frame. Alex's parents? The man had a similarly shaped face and brow line. The woman was slim and attractive. Alex's confidence, Alex's direct gaze. The next was a family group in a garden. The same couple with a younger Alex, a brother, and a sister.

Chloe held the photo, unseeing. They had a similar photo at home. Mum and Bevan with herself and Terry. Before the younger ones were born. The girls and Mum were laughing like loons because Bevan had set the timer on the camera, tripped on his way back, and scrambled madly into position. In the photo he was the only one posing with a serious expression, pretending the others were mad.

"My parents." Alex's breath came warm on her cheek, and his body touched hers gently as he stood close to look over her shoulder. "And Charlie and Lauren."

"How old are you there?"

"Fifteen. Charlie's seventeen, Lauren's thirteen."

"Your mum is lovely."

"She was. She died three years ago." He moved away.

"I'm so sorry." Chloe put the photo carefully back in its place.

"Thank you. She had cancer."

"How is your father coping?"

"He travels the world. We think it's a kind

of avoidance technique — so he doesn't have to stay home all alone." His expression was blank.

Chloe nodded. Constant reminders. She knew all about those. In her case the sight of blood or bodily injuries brought up images of how the bombing victims must have looked — her imagination far too graphic, based as it was on news footage and media photos. She'd identified the bodies from photographs, although their identities were clear from their possessions. The faces were unmarked and familiar, their ruined bodies unshown. Yes. She knew all about avoidance techniques.

She looked at the photo again. Something about the dynamic, a tension — the father's face. "Did you have a happy childhood?"

Alex hesitated. "My father has very high standards," he said eventually. "I disappoint him constantly. Marrying Lucy was a low point."

"Didn't he like her?"

"Yes, but he thought we were too young and accused me of marrying to spite him. Maybe I did. He kind of washed his hands of me after that." His lips twisted in a bitter attempt at a smile, as if it were a joke for a son to be cast off by a father. "He doesn't think running my own company is much either, no matter how well I'm doing. I gave up a job with a big firm to go it alone. He said I was stupid."

"That's awful. Does he know about the award?"

"I haven't told him." He shrugged. "He actually said 'Told you so' when we divorced." He smiled suddenly. "Neither of us scored very well with our birth fathers."

Chloe grinned. "No. Where is he at the moment?"

"Heading for Rio."

"I've always wanted to go to Brazil." The burst of enthusiasm lit her whole face.

Alex laughed. "Why?"

"I don't know. It's just one of those dreams. Plus I love the music."

His turn to nod. "I've always wanted to see the pyramids."

"Me too."

"We could go together."

He was joking, but the way Chloe's smile faded, Alex knew he'd overstepped some mark. The way he'd done when he kissed her in the car. But that was completely spontaneous. She was irresistible, and he'd wanted to for so long. And she'd responded. For a fleeting second or two she'd returned his kiss. Bliss. Gave hope to his heart in "this astounding, lucid confusion" that was falling in love.

She sat down on the nearest chair, avoiding his eyes. "What did you want to talk about?"

"This."

"What?" Her head jerked up in surprise.

He waved an arm vaguely. "About anything, everything. I want to talk to you. The Chloe away from the children, away from her responsibilities. I want to get to know *you*."

"There isn't a me away from my responsibilities."

"There is. You just keep her locked up."

"I don't. This is all there is." She clapped a hand to her chest.

Alex stepped forward and squatted down before her. He clasped her hands in both of his, and his own earnestness amazed him as much as it did her. Throat clogged, he felt he spoke through cotton wool. "Yes, you do, Chloe. You sacrifice yourself to the kids' lives, which is natural and commendable, but you don't need to. They're growing up. You need to find yourself again. Give yourself a life. You're young, you're beautiful."

"And what are you recommending I do, Alex?" Now her eyes met his, and the gaze was icy, reserved, distant. But she didn't pull her hands from his, and they were warm against his palms. "Should I let the kids fend for themselves and go out whenever I feel like it? Should I get myself a boyfriend and bring him home for sleepovers?"

She stood up so abruptly, Alex nearly toppled backward to sprawl at her feet on the floor. He saved himself by flinging his arms back. He jumped upright. "No! Not that!"

"Not what?" Chloe glared at him.

"Don't get yourself a boyfriend."

"You just told me I should."

"I didn't say that."

"What, then?"

What *was* he saying? He didn't have any solutions to give her. He only knew he couldn't bear the thought of her with another man. He also knew he wanted to kiss her so badly, he'd do himself an injury if he restrained himself much longer.

"It's not as simple as you seem to think." The fierceness had left her voice.

He started again. Gently. "You could have any man you wanted."

She cut him off. "*Any* man I wanted?" The ice had melted. This was a challenge. His chance.

His voice dropped. He stepped closer. "Yes."

"You?" Her gaze never wavered. She was daring him to put his feelings on the line, to expose his innermost secret. His desire for her. His burgeoning love.

"If you'll have me." He touched gentle fingers to the curve of her cheek, couldn't believe the softness of her skin. Luscious lips parted, moist. Eyes wide and wonderful. The delirious realization flooded his brain at the same moment his control collapsed and he reached for her — she felt the same; she really felt the same.

"Yes," she might have murmured, but the word was smothered by his mouth on hers, and all sound and awareness of the outside world ceased. Her arms stole around his neck; his wrapped themselves around her slender body. Nirvana.

Chloe floated. She hadn't been kissed before. Not like this. All other kisses became instantly invalid. This kiss exploded in her body like fireworks, cascading through the nerve endings, flowing through her veins, flooding her organs and her heart, filling her mind and her body to overflowing. Luckily his arms supported her, or she would have sunk to the floor, a boneless doll.

His lips eased away from hers, and her eyes flickered open in startled dismay. He smiled, and she saw her own smile mirrored in his eyes. The arms holding her remained firmly in position.

"Is that a yes?" he whispered, and he kissed her again so she couldn't reply except in kind. Kiss for kiss, lips for lips, caress for caress.

"Yes," she gasped when next he released her.

"Good," he murmured. Another kiss, another hiatus in the time/space continuum. Eons later she opened her eyes again to find those gentle blue seas smiling into hers, soft and loving now, not harsh, not piercing. How could she have thought him fierce and arrogant? He squeezed her tightly before lifting her off the floor and swinging her around.

"Alex!" Chloe squeaked as the breath was forced from her lungs and her feet left solid ground. But his arms supported her, and his body was firm beneath her clinging hands. He set her down and pulled her closer for another kiss.

"This is going to be difficult, you know," she said, placing her fingers as a barrier against his lips.

"Why?" He nibbled her fingertips, and she giggled.

"Children."

"They're no problem," he murmured as he explored her throat and neck. "They're great kids. They like me. I like them."

"But yours doesn't like me." Chloe steeled herself against the desire rushing through her body. Every inch of skin his lips caressed tingled and burned with an exhilarating fire, but she had to keep her head. She couldn't abandon herself to his touch the way she longed to. There was too much at stake and too much to consider.

Alex raised his head. He studied her face. "You hardly know each other." He kissed her nose, kept his tone light. "You didn't give her much of a chance, you know, Chloe." She stiffened in his embrace. "That was one of the things I really did want to talk to you about."

"To give me a dressing-down for the way I treated your daughter?" She raised an eyebrow, and her voice was dangerously cool all of a sudden. She slipped from between his arms like an ice cube and sat on the couch, bottom perched on the edge, spine straight. "Go ahead."

He ran a hand through his hair, still damp from the sprint between car and house. This would be easier if she was in his arms. Everything would be easier if she was in his arms. "Steffie behaved badly, I know. I apologize. But you must understand, she's going through a tough time at the moment. Lucy thinks she's jealous of the new baby — which is understandable."

Chloe nodded. "Having been number one all her life." The way she said it didn't bode well, but she offered no further comment.

"Yes, plus the fact that she's been teased at school."

Chloe's expression changed instantly. "Oh, poor little girl. How horrible."

Encouraged by the sympathy in her face, Alex sat beside her and took her hand in his. "It started late last year at kindergarten, and this year the same nasty little pieces have been at it again. She doesn't say much to me, but Lucy said it's getting to the point where she doesn't want to go to school at all."

"I thought the schools dealt with that sort of thing. Katy's does."

"They do have a system, but little girls can be very cunning in their nastiness, apparently."

"Have you thought of moving her?"

"Lucy and Derek think she should ride it out. I tend to agree, to a point. Quite honestly I think they're more interested in the baby. Lucy's gone back to work full-time, and her life is jam-packed. She doesn't need, or won't acknowledge, any extra stresses."

"Poor Stephanie."

He squeezed her hand and brought her fingers to his mouth to kiss one by one. "Sheltering her from these things isn't going to prepare her for life."

"But she's only six." Chloe frowned uneasily. "Can't you do something about it?"

"She wants to live with me, but it can't happen. Not yet anyway. Maybe when she's older."

"I'm sorry, Alex. I had no idea she had those problems."

"Perhaps I should have told you, but —"

"You didn't."

He slipped an arm around her shoulders, pulling her hard against his chest. "I was hoping you'd see what a sweet child she really is." He was gazing so earnestly into her eyes as he spoke, Chloe could do nothing other than nod and murmur, "I see," before his lips landed on hers once again. Rational thought ceased for long minutes.

Eventually Chloe pried herself away from the magnet that was his body and the delights his mouth bestowed.

"I should go home."

This time he didn't argue. He released her reluctantly, trailing his hands down her arms to her fingertips.

"You'd probably better. If you stay any longer, you'll never get away."

"I don't think I'd want to." Chloe stood up on legs wobbly with desire and happiness and, as near as possible, requited passion. He stood and threw an arm around her shoulders to escort her to the door.

"You haven't even gone, and I miss you already."

They stopped in the foyer for another kiss. Alex opened the door. "Rain's stopped."

Hand in hand they walked to her car. A gust of wind shook the branches of the birches by the path, showering them with chill drops of water.

"Yikes." Chloe laughed. "That's cold."

Alex scanned the sky. "Seems to be clearing. Pity."

Chloe said slowly, the idea only half-formed in her mind, "Maybe we should do something all together when Stephanie visits you next." For Alex's sake she should give the girl another chance. "A picnic next Sunday?"

"Good idea. We could meet you somewhere — we won't all fit in one car." He smiled with such pleasure, she stretched up to kiss his cheek.

"How about Pine Island? The kids can

swim in the river."

"We could swing by your place and go in convoy. Seb might like to come in my car."

"Probably."

"See, Chloe?" he said. "This will work just fine."

He spoke so confidently, she believed him. Anything seemed possible when Alex was involved. Even making peace with the Red Terror.

CHAPTER NINE

Of course, he couldn't wait a whole week to hear her voice. He could barely wait a decent interval — like overnight. He wanted to run inside, give her time to drive home, and phone her right away. He didn't. Instead, he discovered the cleaning gear he'd discarded in the bathroom that morning and threw himself into scrubbing the loo. Amazing how the whole world could turn inside out in such a short space of time.

Cleaning the bathroom was a chore, but now he didn't care because he wasn't with Chloe, and if he wasn't with Chloe, it didn't matter what he did. He had to be somewhere, and if he couldn't be with her, what did it matter where that somewhere was? He laughed out loud at the crazy delight of falling in love and being loved in return, and the sound of his laughter bounced off the smooth white and blue tiles of the bathroom.

Then he remembered he'd completely forgotten the phone calls he'd meant to make at lunchtime. Too late now. The client would be out. And probably cross. He called and left a message. The tradesmen would have stopped work when it stormed. More delays to the town houses. Alex made himself sit at his drafting table and work.

The next day Alex called Chloe midmorning after forcing himself to wait that long.

Katy answered the phone. "Simba came home," she said after he'd said who was calling and before he could ask for Chloe.

"The cat?"

"Yes, this morning. She was soaking wet and starving."

"But she's all right?"

"Yes." The word rode on a childish laugh of delight.

"That's wonderful news."

"I knew she'd come home, and you said she would too, didn't you? Chloe said."

He smiled, pleased out of all proportion she'd registered that attempt at reassurance. "I've heard of it happening."

"I have to go and look after her. I'll get Seb."

She dropped the phone without giving him a chance to explain. A couple of minutes later Seb said, "Hi, Alex."

"G'day. I hear the cat came back."

"Yeah. Looks a bit rough, though. They haven't stopped fussing over it."

"Can I have a word with Chloe, mate, please?"

"Didn't you want to talk to me?"

"Well, actually, no. Katy assumed — I wanted Chloe."

"Okay. Hang on."

Was that a touch of coolness in the boy's voice? Alex said quickly, "Seb? Want to go down to the nets this afternoon?"

"Sure. I'll get Chloe."

Dismissed. Alex sighed.

"Hello." One word of that voice and his senses were on overload.

"Hi." He pressed the phone tighter against his ear, as if that would close the distance between them. Her breath rustled against the receiver. "How are you?" he blurted. *Dumb, dumb, dumb. The conversational gambit of a tongue-tied teenager.*

"Fine. The cat came home. She was sitting on the kitchen window ledge the way she always used to. I couldn't believe it when I saw her. She needs feeding. Katy's warming milk for her, and we even went to the shops for a special treat — liver. Yucko, but she loves it."

Was she babbling from nervousness, or was she simply as excited as Katy? He interrupted the barrage of information. "Chloe?"

"Yes." Breathless now, the torrent of words screeched to a halt.

"When can I see you?"

"Next week?" It sounded tentative and very unsure.

"I need to see you before then!"

"I — I don't know. It's difficult."

"Do you have any free time tomorrow?"

"Not a lot."

"Can I see you? Even for a few minutes?"

"I suppose."

"Do you want to see me?"

The silence stretched for long seconds, almost hours. He could hear her breathing. A cold, hard lump began to form in his stomach. She didn't want to. He'd only imagined that the passion was two-way. She'd had second thoughts, and they weren't good ones.

"Chloe?" He barely breathed the word, the fear clutched so tightly at his throat.

"Of course I do, but I don't see how or when before Sunday."

"We'll find time somewhere, Chloe. Just tell me you feel the same way I do."

"I can't just walk out, Alex," she said. "It's easy for you."

"Chloe! Answer my question. Do you feel the same as I do? The rest we can sort out later."

"Yes," she whispered.

"That's all I wanted to hear."

"I have to go."

The line buzzed in his ear. He disconnected slowly. It wasn't easy for him. It wasn't easy at all. That assumption he'd made in the car on the way to the supermarket — that this passion was a crush, fleeting at best, unrequited and doomed to secrecy at worst — was ridiculous. Utter rubbish. His feeling for Chloe Gardiner had snowballed into a passion, monstrous and unstoppable.

Kissing her had become imperative. Now that he'd tasted her lips and her own desire, the monkey was on his back. He'd succumbed to the worst kind of addiction — he was enslaved to a woman.

Never again, he'd said to himself after Lucy. The occasional date — fine. Commitment? No way. Now, with Chloe's perfume in his nostrils, Chloe's voice in his ears, and Chloe's body imprinting itself on his, that position seemed inflexible, unnecessary, and downright stupid. When fate threw someone as wonderful as this woman into his path, what right had he to ignore it? He deserved

another chance at happiness. Chloe certainly did, and he could give her such happiness as she'd never known. He could.

He thumped his fist into his open palm.
With Chloe and Katy around, dealing with
a six-year-old girl would be that much
easier.

"What did Alex want?" Seb asked.

His expression bordered on jealousy. What
could she say to a resentful teenager? It was
none of his business.

"It was about next Sunday."

That was true — it was about how he
couldn't wait until next Sunday to see her.
Chloe grinned at Seb's glowering face and
went to see how Katy and Simba were
doing.

But Steffie had a party invitation for Sunday
lunch. Typically, Lucy informed Alex when
he picked her up that Friday evening.
Frazzled and with a crying baby Mark on
her hip, she glared at him when he remon-
strated about how he'd made other plans
for the weekend.

"Too bad. I did *tell* you," she snapped.
"Steffie doesn't get many invites, so you'll
have to put your social life on hold for your
daughter."

"Right." He snatched up Steffie's over-night bag. He didn't remember Lucy's saying anything about a party.

"It's dress-up," she added as she closed the door. "I haven't had time to organize anything. Marky's been sick all week." Mark let fly with an extra-loud puce-faced howl to underline her comment. The door clunked shut.

"Dress-up?" He stared down at Steffie, who stood smiling up at him.

She clutched his free hand. "Come on, Daddy. Marky's giving me a headache. He's been crying for hours."

"Where's the party?" They began walking to the car.

"At Felicity's."

"What sort of dress-up?"

"Fairies."

"Fairies!!"

"Yes. Felicity loves fairies. She wants to be one when she grows up."

"But I don't know anything about fairy suits." Lucy must have known about this for weeks. "Do we have to buy a present too?"

"Yes."

"We'll have to go tomorrow." What did other people's six-year-olds like? What did fairies wear? Chloe would know! He'd have to call and cancel out on the picnic anyway.

He phoned as soon as Steffie disappeared into her room to unpack her bag.

"That's a pity," Chloe said. "They've been looking forward to it." She added in a softer voice, "So have I."

Alex smiled. Such a sweet admission of her disappointment. "Me too. I haven't seen you for ages."

Chloe laughed, and he knew she was holding the phone tightly against her ear by the way her breath feathered into the receiver. "Five days." Her voice was husky.

"Yes, ages." Steffie emerged from her room and turned on the TV. He raised his voice to normal. "I haven't a clue about the gift or the fancy dress." He paused, grimaced. Was Chloe prepared to give up her Saturday to assist a child she didn't like? How badly had Steffie's behavior upset her? "I desperately need your help."

"Cripes. It's very short notice." She paused. An unenthusiastic pause. "Katy and I could come shopping with you tomorrow. She's an expert."

"That would be marvelous! Thank you." And Steffie liked Katy, so there shouldn't be too much friction.

"Might be fun."

Fairy shopping? Doubtful. "Glad *you* think so. We'll pick you up at ten. Thanks again."

229

"Who are we picking up?" Steffie demanded from the couch.

"Chloe and Katy are helping with your fairy stuff."

"Does pooey Chloe have to come?" The familiar whine and accompanying pout appeared.

Alex's heart sank. "Yes, she does, and I want you to be polite. Chloe is doing us a big favor. I don't know anything about presents and fairy outfits, and Mummy didn't organize anything for you."

"Marky was sick — she couldn't." Steffie glared at him. "Mummy is overworked and very stressed out."

Didn't he know it. Lucy's stress levels were constantly broadcast to anyone who'd listen. "The alternative is, you go to the party with no present and no costume because I have no idea what to do. Or you don't go at all."

"I want to go." But the situation had clearly sunk in, because after a moment's teary-eyed, silent fuming she said, "All right, we'll go with Chloe," in a drawn-out tone of vast suffering and condescension.

"Good girl." He dropped a kiss onto the top of her head. "I made macaroni and cheese for dinner."

"Yum. I love you, Daddy. I wish I could

live with you and eat macaroni cheese every night."

Chloe went to find Katy. With any luck they'd be able to do the fairy thing quickly, and she could spend the afternoon practicing. She'd picked up a gig for the following weekend with a cover band and had tunes to learn. *Kids!* Now it was Alex's little monster. Why on earth had she said yes? No brainer. Because he'd asked.

Katy sat with the cat cradled in her lap, watching TV.

"We're going shopping in the morning with Alex."

"Why?"

"We have to turn Stephanie into a fairy for a party on Sunday. And find a present. It means we can't go on our picnic."

"Never mind." Katy rubbed her cheek against Simba's head. "We can go to the Fairy Nook."

"Good idea! I'd forgotten about that place. I knew you'd be the expert." Should take an hour, tops.

The girls sat in the back of the BMW discussing fairy outfits and parties. Stephanie actually laughed once or twice and had greeted Chloe with a polite hello. No overt hostility today, thank goodness. Best behavior.

But when they arrived at their destination, the Fairy Nook was gone, replaced by a fishing-tackle shop. Alex parked in the street opposite.

"Are you sure this is the right address?" he asked.

"Daaaddee!" wailed Stephanie. "What are we going to do?"

"I'll go in and ask if they know where it moved to," Chloe said. Best behavior obviously had a time limit.

The man behind the counter produced the phone book, but no Fairy Nook was listed. Chloe returned to the car, dreading the reaction to her news.

"I'm sorry," she said as she slid into the seat beside Alex. "It doesn't exist anymore."

"Fairies must have gone out of style," he murmured, and he winked but looked decidedly concerned.

Ridiculous! The kid was six years old! Chloe grimaced. She turned to the sullen face in the backseat. "We can buy the present though, can't we? While we think about the costume. Would she like a fairy book or a poster?"

A glimmer of hope shone through the thunderclouds. She nodded.

232

"And we'll need wings and a wand," piped up Katy. "Plus some glitter."

"Now we're in business!" cried Alex. Relief radiated in waves. He eased the car away from the curb.

"But what can I wear?"

"You'll need a top and tights and a tulle skirt," pronounced Katy.

"Can we get all that?" asked Alex in a very bewildered voice.

Chloe sighed. *Good-bye, practice.* "If not, I could buy material and make it. Won't take much time." *Idiot!* What was she saying? Sewing was a tedious activity.

"That's no problem."

No problem for him, perhaps. She'd had other plans for the afternoon. Did he consider that? How to tell him tactfully that if they couldn't buy a dress, she'd changed her mind about sewing, and it *was* his problem?

"Can you really make a fairy dress?" asked a completely changed voice from the backseat. This little girl had her own worries. None of the Gardiner children ever doubted they were loved.

"I can." Chloe swiveled around to smile at Stephanie. "We'll turn you into a fairy princess." And she was rewarded by a big, wide, childish smile of delight, which

233

warmed her heart with an unexpected rush of affection. She could do her guitar practice tonight instead. Or tomorrow.

They returned home laden with fairy-creating equipment. Alex was sent away to make lunch with the boys, who had just returned, ravenous, from cricket and orchestra. Chloe unearthed the sewing machine. The girls carefully wrapped the poster and wrote the card while Chloe spread out pink taffeta and tulle on the dining table.

"I need to measure you." She stretched the tape around the chubby chest and tummy and wrote the figures down.

"Will I be too fat?" The question came completely out of the blue, tentative and worried. Little fingers stroked the pretty, silky material almost with reverence.

"No, sweetie! I'll make the dress to fit you."

"Some girls call me fatty-boom-boom," she said, gazing at Chloe with a sheen of tears in the gray eyes.

"They're meanies," said Katy. "You're not fat at all."

"Daddy says I have to be thinner."

Shades of his own demanding father? Chloe bit her lip. "He just wants you to be healthy."

"I wish I was thin like Katy."

"You needn't worry," said Chloe firmly.

"If you eat lots of fruit and veggies and run about and do your swimming, your body will adjust itself, because you're growing." She kneeled to measure the proposed skirt while Stephanie stood bright-eyed with delight and smiled and said nothing. The Red Terror had faded to a rosy pink. Maybe attention was all she needed. The right sort of attention.

Alex, slicing a tomato in the kitchen, heard the female voices in the dining room. He'd been banished — not that he could offer any assistance — but he couldn't help straining his ears for any signs of the discord that had erupted the last time Steffie had visited. The memory of those shrieks chilled him to the bone. He'd thought the expedition had crashed and burned with the demise of the Fairy Nook, and Steffie on the way to a tantrum in the backseat.

But Chloe had calmly changed course, and now Steffie was falling under her spell. As he knew she must. For the first time parenting didn't seem so bad. With Chloe as mother.

"My trial's the week after next," said Seb.

"I know, mate. I sent a statement to your lawyer."

"But aren't you coming?"

"Yes, but she wanted a statement. Are you

worried?"

"A bit."

Alex rested a hand on Seb's thin shoulder. "Just be honest."

"Have you ever been in court?" asked Julian.

"No, never." Alex returned his attention to peeling a hard-boiled egg. "I was in trouble, though, once. Big-time."

Both boys looked at him, alert and expectant, Julian ready to laugh.

"I was ten, and I really, really wanted some toy, but my parents wouldn't buy it for me." Alex laughed and raised his eyebrows at Seb. "So I nicked it."

"Hah." Seb snorted, and Julian laughed outright. "Did you get caught?"

"Yep. I wasn't very good at stealing. The shopkeeper called my parents."

"Not the cops?"

Alex frowned. "No."

"You were lucky," said Seb.

"I didn't think so. I'd never seen Dad so angry. Mum was terribly upset, and my brother and sister crept about not speaking to me, as if I was a leper." Alex looked Seb in the eye. "I've never been so ashamed in my life."

Julian punched Seb's arm. "If it all goes pear-shaped, I'll be visitin' you in jail," he said in a passable Irish accent.

"Me too." Alex placed the slippery egg into the bowl with the rest. "We ready?"

"Yeah. Lunch!" called Julian in the direction of the dining room.

They ate outside on the verandah. Alex watched his daughter chattering and giggling with Katy. He'd never seen her so animated and happy. Steffie was eating an egg sandwich — mashed with mayonnaise the way Katy liked it — with lettuce. He could never in a million years have persuaded her to eat one of those. He was better with the boys than with his own daughter. He caught Chloe's eye once or twice, and she smiled and looked away quickly. Was she thinking what he was thinking? How like one family this was?

"Have a swim after lunch, Alex?" said Seb.

"I don't have my gear."

"Only take a minute to get it," said Julian. "Or you can go nude."

"Tempting, but I'd better not. I really should nip over to Gungahlin to check one of the building sites. We've had so many delays lately." He shook his head and sighed.

"I want to swim, Daddy."

"Really?" He nearly choked on his sandwich. What had happened to his daughter? Whatever it was, it was good, and somehow

Chloe was responsible.

Steffie nodded. "Katy's going to help me."

"That's great. I'll pick up your swimsuit. Chloe, would it be all right to leave Steffie with you for an hour or so?"

"Can we come with you?" asked Seb.

"If you like. Sure." He glanced inquiringly at Chloe.

She held his gaze for a moment, then shrugged. "Fine."

CHAPTER TEN

Monday morning the phone rang. Chloe laid her guitar down reluctantly. Practice time was precious. She needed at least an hour every day but rarely managed to achieve it except on the weekends. Saturday had been a write-off with all that sewing. How she hated sewing!

A woman's voice said, "Is this Chloe Gardiner?"

"Yes." Another prospective guitar student? Better still would be someone wanting her for a gig. Teaching was fine, but playing was infinitely preferable.

"My name's Lucy Dwyer. I'm Stephanie's mother."

Stephanie? Do I have a student called Stephanie? Then it clicked. Alex's Stephanie. Alex's ex.

"I wanted to thank you for making that wonderful fairy costume. You must think I'm an awful mother. I had no idea Alex would impose on you. He's —" She sucked in a breath, hissing through her teeth. "Anyway, it was very kind of you. Steffie loves it. She wanted to wear it to bed."

"Goodness." Chloe laughed. "It really wasn't that difficult."

"For you maybe! I'm hopeless with anything remotely creative. Not that I have time, with the baby and work. I wish Alex would take more interest in Steffie."

"He loves her."

"I don't doubt that, but it's a remote-control sort of love. She absolutely adores *him*. Maybe the connection with your family will make a difference. Your Katy has inspired Steffie with her swimming."

"I'm glad. She didn't seem to be enjoying her lessons before." Understatement of the year.

"No. But what can I do about it?" She obviously didn't expect an answer. "Steffie has to learn how to swim. Anyway. I just wanted to say thanks, and I'm sorry Alex took his problem to you. He could easily have gone shopping himself. Would have done him good. He always takes the easy way out when it comes to his child. One day he'll learn that money doesn't solve everything. And the fact that he pays his child support on time doesn't absolve him from his other fatherly responsibilities. Namely, spending time with her."

"He seems very busy," Chloe put in lamely, unsure what else to say and unwilling to be involved in this character trashing. Was this really her Alex?

"Aren't we all? She's his daughter! He didn't want her in the first place — that's the real issue."

"Oh." How much of this was ex-wife bitterness?

"Still, I shouldn't be telling you all this. He'd be furious if he knew, but then, the truth always hurts, and he's very good at avoiding the truth."

Another "Oh."

"I'm sorry, Chloe. I don't mean to be such a shrew. He brings out the worst in me."

Hastily, reassuring, "It's all right."

"He spends more time with those tradesmen and his clients than with his daughter. He's still trying to prove something to his father, and that's a waste of effort — the man's a monster. Mind you, when I suggested Steffie change her name to Dwyer, he hit the roof. I didn't mean it — I wanted to shake him up a bit. He sees her as a possession." She sighed. "Sorry, Chloe. You don't need to know any of this, especially if you're . . . well . . . I don't know your relationship with Alex. Steffie's adamant that you're not his girlfriend." She laughed.

"He's a friend of my brothers," Chloe said through a strangled throat. "He's been very good to them, like a father."

"I'm so sorry. Don't get me wrong. Alex has some wonderful qualities, or I wouldn't have married him. Just don't let him use you as a babysitter." She gave a tight little laugh. "I should go."

"Thanks for calling, Lucy."

"No, thank *you*, Chloe. Maybe you can improve Alex where I couldn't."

"I don't think so. I'm not interested in a relationship right now. Like you, I have too many other things to think about."

Chloe stood holding the disconnected phone for several minutes. Some of the things Lucy had said made sense. They explained the uneasiness she'd felt about Alex's relationship with Stephanie. If he hadn't wanted a baby in the first place, on some level surely he'd resent her for the rest of her life. Or until she was big enough not to be a nuisance.

He'd made it sound as though the fortnightly visits were Lucy's doing. Lucy had made it clear she'd welcome a change. Who to believe?

And was it a good idea to become any

more involved with a man like that than she already was? A man who deep down didn't want his own child? Where did that leave any other children?

But — Alex had done the right thing by Seb, and they were developing a good relationship. Julian too. To the point where she was rethinking her opinion of his commitment. Maybe he'd changed in the years since Steffie's birth. People can and do change. She mustn't judge him purely on Lucy's necessarily biased utterances. But he had off-loaded the fairy problem and Stephanie onto her. And left to go to his building site.

Seb's case was scheduled for eleven on Wednesday morning. Julian and Katy clamored to attend, but Chloe decided against a family gallery. She, Simone, and Alex would provide enough support. Lawyer Carla was quietly confident of a good-behavior bond with perhaps a fine or community service. She met them outside the Magistrate's Court building.

"I'm glad you took my advice about the clothes," she said, eyeing Seb in his best navy blue pants and tucked-in short-sleeved white shirt.

Chloe glanced up and down the walkway

in front of them. "Is Alex here yet?"

"No," Carla said. "We should go in, Seb."

Chloe stood undecided, the morning sun beating down on her head, heat already shimmering up from the pavement. Simone hadn't arrived yet either.

"I'd better wait for Gran."

"Come in when you're ready." Carla led Seb away.

Chloe waited, staring up and down. The Court backed uncomfortably onto a busy road, screened from the hurtling traffic by shrubs. Diagonally in front was a pedestrian plaza, crisscrossed by lawyers antlike in their determined scurrying, their anxious clients, the odd, aloof policeman. To the left and forward, close to busy London Circuit, lay the City Police Station. A parking area stretched to the right. Full already. The court buildings sat squeezed in like an overweight man in a too-small chair.

Across the way lay the School of Music, where Chloe had begun her degree. In another life. Who of her friends in those heady student days could have imagined Chloe Gardiner standing outside the Children's Court, guardian to a miscreant awaiting trial, waiting for the man she probably loved?

Where was he? They'd barely spoken since

244

the fairy weekend. Alex had work; Chloe had the usual family turmoil. Private phone calls were virtually, frustratingly impossible at her end. She didn't mention Lucy's call. His voice and the sweetness of the words he spoke into her ear made those other accusations seem irrelevant and sour.

Simone came clip-clopping along, puffing and panting in the heat. Big sunglasses hid half her face.

"Am I late, lovey? I'm parked way over there." She flapped an arm vaguely.

"No, but we should go in." Chloe gazed anxiously over Simone's head. "Alex isn't here."

"He'll turn up. It's too hot standing about. I'm melting. This shirt was a mistake — polyester. Do I smell?"

"No, of course not."

"I don't want the judge to be distracted by the stench from the public gallery."

"Don't be silly."

Alex didn't arrive.

Constable Brent Burrows sat behind them, waiting to give his evidence. He leaned forward to say hello, greeted Simone, commented how well Seb had done since the incident. Reassuring.

"Thanks." Chloe managed a smile. Brent cared, and he barely knew Seb.

245

"Like to catch a movie with some friends of mine on Saturday night?" he asked, startling her with the non sequitur. "I'm on day shift now for a few weeks."

Simone nudged her in the ribs. "She'd love to," she said to Brent. "I'm more than happy to babysit."

Brent cocked an eye at Chloe. He smiled. She had to say yes. Why not? She liked Brent. Why should she turn down a date with a friend? He wasn't a prospective boyfriend — they both knew that. He'd been good to Seb. Alex kissed her and said sweet things, but Alex hadn't ever asked her out on a proper date. Just an off-the-cuff invitation to a lunch that had never happened, plus a barbecue with the boys. He only used her for help with his daughter. Lucy had told her why.

"Great. I'll call you later." He sat back.

Simone wore a self-satisfied smirk and jabbed her in the ribs again. Chloe ignored her. Where was Alex?

Expectation slowly turned to concrete in her stomach. He didn't care. He said he did, but really, when push came to shove, he didn't. All those words and kindnesses to Seb meant nothing. Did his words to her mean nothing too? His kisses? *Remote-control love* — Lucy's phrase.

Seb swiveled around several times, his face worried, confused, as he stared hopefully at the door. Chloe almost leaped from her seat to reassure him, hug him, tell him she and Gran were there for him. They loved him, regardless. Even Constable Burrows was on his side. Carla whispered into his ear and patted his arm. He leaned back in his chair and didn't turn around again.

Chloe bit her lip hard against the threatening tears. How could Alex do this to Seb? How? What could possibly be more important than standing up for a boy who admired and trusted him? He didn't care. She'd been right all along. Alex Bergman had just shown how unreliable he was.

He deserved not a moment's more thought. Not one second of her attention. How could he kiss her and hold her and make her believe that he would take on the kids, that he understood she came as part of a package deal? She, like the naive fool she was, had believed him.

And! And! She'd spent the whole of that Saturday turning his daughter into a fairy. No wonder the poor girl had problems, with Alex as a father. She'd sense his basic lack of commitment.

Gut instincts were most often right. That's what Bevan said. "Go with your guts, girls."

What had her gut told her that first day when Alex accosted her in the corridor?

But the judge had begun addressing the court. The proceedings were under way. Seb was her priority. Seb needed her. She wouldn't let him down. The way Alex Bergman had. The way she'd suspected he would all along.

"Just as I thought. Six months good behavior. And you won't be getting into any more trouble will you, Seb?" Carla glared, but a smile lurked behind the frown.

"No way. Thanks, Carla."

"Thank heaven that's over," Simone cried. "Thank you very much." She pumped the lawyer's hand up and down.

"So it didn't matter that Alex failed to show?" asked Chloe, almost but not quite succeeding in hiding the bitterness.

Seb frowned at her. "He called Carla's cell and left a message that he couldn't come."

"He didn't need to be here in person." Carla glanced at her watch. "I have to run, folks." She flashed a smile from one to the other, shook hands quickly with Chloe, and hurried away.

"Did you think Alex forgot?" asked Seb with a sly twist to his lips.

"I didn't know." Chloe started walking

toward the exit. "You have to go to school. Come on."

"You did think that, didn't you?" insisted Seb, striding beside her as they crossed the foyer. "Alex wouldn't forget to come. You should get a cell phone."

He may not have forgotten, but he obviously thought something else was more important than Seb. Work, probably. A man like Alex would always put work ahead of a child. Look at the way he treated Stephanie, only seeing her every second weekend. What sort of father agreed to those custody conditions? One who didn't want to be inconvenienced. Sure, he loved his daughter. She wouldn't dispute that, but it was a love based on not having her disrupt his life or work. As soon as she made any sort of demands, he off-loaded her as fast as possible. That's obviously why the marriage broke up. Lucy was absolutely right. He hadn't wanted a child in the first place.

A quick phone call might be enough to satisfy Seb, but Alex Bergman had better have a very good reason for not turning up this morning. A principle was at stake here, and whether he realized it or not, Alex had just failed to measure up in his first real test.

Outside, the midday sun hammered down

249

onto her head. Chloe jammed sunglasses onto her nose, but it was an ineffectual barrier against Seb's knowing look. He didn't know anything. He was far too trusting.

Simone hugged Seb. "I'll see you on Saturday. Behave yourself."

"Thanks for coming."

Another hug. "Don't be silly. Of course I'd be here."

Exactly. Of course.

Chloe and Seb turned in the opposite direction.

"What's happening on Saturday?"

"I'm going out with Brent Burrows. Gran's babysitting."

"Can we call in and tell Alex what happened?"

"No!"

"Why not?"

"You have to go to school. I've got students. Call him yourself when you get home."

"Why are you being so nasty?"

"I'm not."

"Yes, you are. Just because he didn't come. And you don't even know why."

"Drop it, Seb." Chloe increased her pace. Perspiration trickled down her sides. The heat was fierce. Not a breath of wind. Summer this year was endless. Stifling, heavy air.

"I just don't understand why you're so being so mean. It's like he can't do anything right."

"Drop it, I said. Don't you understand?" Chloe unlocked the car. Seb slammed the door and clipped his seat belt. He wound the window down with angry jerks on the handle. The interior of the car was furnace-like.

"He likes you. A lot. Can't imagine why."

"How do you know?" she snapped. Had Alex confided in the boys? Shared private things meant for the two of them?

"He looks at you all the time." Said in a tone of great disgust. "He'll learn."

Chloe backed out of the parking space in tight-lipped silence.

Back at the house, Seb raced inside. Chloe followed more slowly. Maybe she had been hasty in her condemnation. Alex might have had a car accident or a breakdown. He might even be ill. She hadn't considered any of those possibilities in her rush to think the worst of him. Why was that? Did she basically not trust him? Why did she immediately assume he didn't care? On his ex-wife's say-so.

She pushed the front door open. Seb was

already chattering into the phone. He glanced at Chloe as she walked through to the kitchen but turned his back on her to pursue his conversation.

"Don't be too long," she said, knowing her tone was unnecessarily harsh. "You can have lunch before you go to school."

"Alex wants to talk to you," he called after her.

"We don't have time."

Seb joined her in the kitchen, frowning. "He'll call you this evening."

"Eat." Chloe had plunked sandwich fixings on the counter. She would *not* ask why Alex hadn't made it to court. She wouldn't!

Seb began buttering bread. "I told him you were going out on Saturday night and he should come over."

"What?!!"

"What what?" He paused mid-buttering. "Jules and I can hang out with Alex, and Katy and Gran can do whatever."

Chloe slammed a piece of ham onto her bread and slapped mustard over the top. "Seb, Alex is a grown man. He may not want to hang out with a couple of kids on a Saturday night."

"He does. He's coming over." Seb took a huge satisfied bite from his sandwich. "So you can go out with the cop and enjoy yourself, and you won't have to put up with Alex at all."

Chloe turned her back to rinse her mustard knife in the sink and avoid Seb's grinning face with the bulging, chewing cheeks. And so he wouldn't see the flush of dismay and shock and embarrassment burning red on her own.

"Plus," he added, "you can stay out as late as you like, because Alex won't get tired like Gran does. She can go home anytime she wants. In fact, she needn't come at all."

Alex called late that evening. Chloe took the phone to her bedroom despite the fact that the others were in bed. Katy was asleep, but either of the boys could easily wander out in search of a snack or a drink. This conversation did not require eavesdroppers.

He didn't waste any time; he launched right in, forestalling her own attack.

"Why are you going out with that policeman?" he demanded.

"He's a friend. I've every right to go out with a friend, and you even told me yourself I should." She sat down on her bed.

"But I hoped you wouldn't *want* to go out with anyone else."

Chloe sprang to her feet. "Go out? I hardly ever go out. And I've never been out with you." She strode across to the window, spun around, and strode back.

"I asked you to lunch, and you refused." Righteous indignation dripped from every word.

"Only because I couldn't go." She stopped pacing. Thought. Drew a deep breath. What was happening here? Was he claiming exclusive rights? He had a nerve after what happened today. *Take her, take the rest of the family. Doesn't he understand that yet?* "I refuse to be intimidated by you, Alex. I'll go out with whoever I want, and I don't have to answer to you. I imagine you have friends, don't you?"

He sighed. "Of course I do. I play basketball with them every week."

"Any women in the group when you go out?"

"Yes."

"Right." She relented, just a tad. "It won't be just us. There are others going as well."

His relief was palpable. "All right, I'm sorry. Go out with your friends and enjoy yourself."

"I will." Now it was her turn. "And why weren't you in court?"

"One of my clients had a disaster with an electrician. I had to be there, or someone might've committed murder. Then I'd have

been in court as a different sort of witness."
He gave a short laugh, but Chloe wasn't in
the mood for jokes.

"Surely they could've sorted it out without
you."

All traces of humor vanished. "No, they
couldn't, Chloe. This is my work, my business. I have to take care of my clients, or
my reputation will be shot."

"So you chose strangers over Seb?"

"I had to. I'm sorry. I meant to be there. I
wanted to be there. *He* understands." His
voice rose on another wave of indignation.
"I couldn't even pick Steffie up from school.
She was sick, and her mother couldn't leave
work. She had to stay there in the nurse's
office."

"Is she all right?" Poor kid. Nobody had
time for her.

"Yes. They thought it might be appendici-
tis, but it turns out she has a stomach bug."

"How fortunate for you."

"Don't be like that. Can't you see how
impossible it was? What was I supposed to
do?"

"What you did, I suppose. Put your clients
above your child and your friend."

"I always put Steffie first if it's possible."

Prickling heat crawled up Chloe's back.
That was it. The lie he'd told himself for

255

years, fooling everyone but Stephanie and Lucy. The *if it's possible* gave him away. "I don't think she sees it that way, Alex. The way she behaves proves that."

"I barely see her, Chloe. I think her behavior has far more to do with the way her mother treats her. I try to show her I love her."

"Being with her and putting her first is what she needs from you. So she believes you really mean it."

"You wanted me to put Seb first a minute ago. Seb has a better grasp of this situation than you do!"

"That's because he grew up having to accept heaps of things most kids don't. Plus I tried really hard to continue the solid family base we had before. They know they can rely on me. It goes without saying. They just know I'll be there for them. And Simone."

"I know you've done all that, Chloe. I'm doing my best for Seb, but at any rate I'd have had to put Steffie first."

"Oh, of course." He wouldn't miss the sarcasm. She couldn't help it. He hadn't put Stephanie first today. If he hadn't shown up in court because he'd picked her up sick, it would've been a completely different situation. *That,* anyone would understand.

Alex started, "You're being totally unreasonable —"

But Chloe cut him off. "How can you come here next Saturday? Won't Stephanie be with you? Are you bringing her?"

"They've got something on, and Lucy wants Steffie to go. Why are you so upset about this? Is it just because I didn't make it to court for Seb? *He* understood straight-away. Why can't you?"

"He thinks the sun shines out of your behind, Alex. Just like Stephanie. I'm scared of what it'll do to him when he discovers the truth — your work will always come first with you, and then a distant second your daughter, leaving Seb where? No matter how much you say he's important to you." She was pacing again. She caught a glimpse of herself in the mirror, waving her free hand wildly, face creased, mouth distorted. She had to keep her voice down.

Alex didn't. He almost shouted. "That's unbelievable, Chloe! What you're really say-ing to me is I have to choose between work, Steffie, and Seb, isn't it? And you expect me to put Steffie or Seb first. It's ridiculous, because it depends on the situation. Can't you see that?"

"No, I can't. Seb needed you there today. He was terribly disappointed. He's pretend-ing he doesn't mind, but you should have seen his face. He trusted you, Alex. And you let him down. And Stephanie." *And me,* she added desperately in her head.

"I didn't, Chloe. I didn't let either of them down."

"Yes, you did. Sending that report in was easy. Didn't inconvenience you at all. Actually being there is another thing altogether. A crucial meeting with a client? Far more important than going to sit in the Children's Court and waste your time. Or pick up a sick little girl." A tear dropped down her cheek, followed by another. Acid tears of frustrated disappointment and rage, because she'd known all along he'd be like this but had hoped she was wrong. Had hoped Lucy was wrong. She wasn't. "And why can't Steffie live with you? She wants to, and you say you want her to, so why are you satisfied with such a lopsided arrangement? Did you choose those terms?" She scraped her palm across her eyes, furious with herself for crying. Glad he couldn't see. "Is it because you don't *really* want a child underfoot? And you can blame her mother for all the problems she has? Nice and easy for you."

"Chloe . . ."

"This relationship will never work, Alex. I can tell you that right now. I put the kids first. Always. All of them, because I love them. I even spent all of Saturday sewing for *your* daughter, and I hate sewing. You put yourself first, even though you say you love Stephanie. We'll never see eye to eye on that."

He said in a voice reminiscent of that first one in the police station, icy with rage, "I tell you what I'm not going to do, Chloe, and that's waste my time listening to this hysterical load of rubbish. Good night."

Alex slammed the phone down, fuming. His hands were clenching and unclenching involuntarily. He realized they were beginning to ache and shook them furiously. What had gotten into her? She was insane. What could he do? He didn't know how sick or not sick Steffie was. The school could cope, and, anyway, Lucy shouldn't have sent her off in the first place. Chloe didn't attack *her* for not leaving work for her daughter. Plus she'd *volunteered* to sew that dress. *Women! Impossible.*

Seb had understood his predicament. He would've been disappointed, but he hadn't carried on like a maniac about it. Everything had worked out all right. The guys were hanging out on Saturday night. No way would he break that date. Let Chloe go off gallivanting with the cop. See if he cared.

Alex concentrated on work for the remainder of the week. He didn't allow himself to dwell on Chloe. She needed time to calm down. Let her see that Seb really hadn't minded his nonappearance. Let her begin to miss him. She'd realize soon enough how much she wanted him around. It had been on the tip of his tongue to ask her to the awards dinner. Good thing he hadn't!

By Friday he'd decided to play it cool on Saturday. Be friendly. Wish Chloe a good time on her date. Leave when she came home. No hanging around just to be near her, no touching, and definitely no kisses.

CHAPTER ELEVEN

Simone arrived early to babysit, in time for a cup of afternoon tea and a chat. She eyed Chloe curiously over the rim of her teacup when Seb, on his way to the fridge, announced that Alex was coming over later, but for once in her life she said nothing. Seb finished plundering and sauntered out crunching on an apple with another in his hand for Julian.

"He looks happy. Alex has been a godsend."

"The boys like him." Chloe poured more tea with studied concentration.

"I thought you did too. He's a very handsome man." Simone leaned ever so gently on the *very*. "Especially in a bathing suit."

Chloe couldn't help it. The hot red blush started in her chest, crept up her neck, and lodged in her face. Burning, uncomfortable, and all too revealing. "Yes, he is," she muttered, avoiding Simone's eye at all costs by getting up to put the milk back into the fridge.

"He fancies you — that's blindingly obvious. The way he was ogling you that day." Simone chuckled. "Perhaps your date with Brent will give him a little prod in the right direction. Some men can't see what's staring them in the face. Or they're shy." She paused, frowned, slurped tea. "He didn't strike me as being the shy type."

Shy? Alex? "Simone, he doesn't need a prod. He's not shy."

"Whoops! You should have said something when I accepted your date for you. A polite thanks but no, thanks. Burrows wouldn't have minded. I like him, but he's no knee-trembler."

Chloe grinned and shook her head. *Knee-trembler,* of all things. "So do I like him. That's why I'm going out."

"So. Has he kissed you yet?"

No use prevaricating and asking who she meant. Simone could winkle the secret from the sphinx. "Yes."

"And did you like it?" This had a penetrating gaze attached, raising Chloe's facial temperature several degrees again.

"Yes. It all happened very suddenly, though."

"The phrase 'swept off your feet' didn't

come from nowhere. You must have swept him off his feet."

"I doubt it."

"Dear Jeff swept me right off my feet."

"But he's not — he doesn't really . . ." She gave up. Nothing was clear, and she certainly couldn't explain it. "I don't know."

"You're not playing games with him, are you? Using this date with Brent to make Alex jealous?"

"No! I'd never do that. He knows Brent's a friend."

"Good. If there's one thing I can't stand, it's a woman who manipulates her men. So what is it?"

"Alex let Seb down badly, and I can't forgive him for that. Plus he doesn't want his daughter." Chloe placed her palms flat against her cheeks, hoping they'd cool the overheated skin.

"I think that's a bit harsh, lovey, saying he doesn't want his daughter. He may not know how to handle her, but it's obvious he loves her."

"His ex-wife told me he didn't want a baby when they were married. Stephanie turned up unexpectedly, and he rejected her."

"They must have been very young. He might have changed his mind. *You* changed your mind about Stephanie."

"But he let Seb down."

"Did he? I thought he went out of his way to help. He had every right to do nothing at all. He was the victim."

Chloe sighed. Heartfelt and deep. This was a basic issue of trust. She didn't trust him, painful as that was to admit to herself. "You don't understand."

"No." Simone eased her bottom off the stool. "I don't. I'm just a silly old noodle."

Chloe sighed, smiled, shook her head. "Please don't say anything about Alex and me to the boys or Katy. I'm not sure I know what I want. It's too confusing. We have a fundamental difference of opinion about children and responsibility."

"I don't think you do, but you'll have to sort it out. Where's my Katy? You go and make yourself even more beautiful than you already are for your date."

"It's not really a date if there's a group of us."

"It's a date, and you could do with more of them. Alex might get the idea and ask you out too. Instead of stealing kisses and confusing you." And she went off to find Katy, grinning from ear to ear.

Chloe enjoyed the Thai food and the adult

company but most of all the feeling of freedom. Brent's friends weren't policemen as she'd expected. They all had wild senses of humor. She hadn't laughed so much for years.

After the movie, standing on the sidewalk in the cool of the night, someone suggested they hit a nightclub. Chloe hesitated, glanced at her watch. Just after eleven. Not late. If Alex was there with the kids, Simone could go home. If he wasn't there, she'd go to bed on the trundle in Katy's room, and they'd whisper and giggle half the night. Either way she could stay out.

Alex could babysit while she danced. Give him a taste of what having children really meant. Responsibility. Restriction.

"Sure," she said.

Alex stretched out on the couch, watching the late-night movie. After a preliminary sniff and investigation, the cat had curled up on his stomach and gone to sleep purring so loudly that he had to turn the TV up. Past midnight now. He'd sent a yawning Simone home at eleven. Katy was fast asleep by ten-thirty; the boys were finally packed off at eleven-thirty. They'd had a fun evening playing board games. Plenty of laughing, inept attempts at cheating, and general hilarity. Simone was a riot. No wonder her grandchildren adored her. He'd never heard so many crazy stories in his life. What a life she'd had if even half of them were true.

Only one thing missing. Chloe.

Was she having as good a time? Part of him hoped she was. Another part, meanly, hoped she wasn't. Hoped she couldn't fully enjoy herself without him. Was that being petty and jealous? Darn right it was, and he was — jealous as could be. But he wasn't going to let her see that. No way. He'd stick to his original plan of being cool and friendly.

She'd struck hard and painfully when she accused him of not caring for Steffie. Of putting his daughter second to his work. It made him think. Wonder. Did he? In his mind he didn't. But he wasn't a six-year-old from a split family. He'd never been from a split family, had always known he was loved and wanted despite his father's harshness. Took it for granted. Could Steffie possibly doubt that her parents loved her? No! Chloe was wrong.

Hadn't she planned on going to a movie? She could've called to let him know if they'd gone on somewhere else. What if he hadn't made it at the last minute, and Simone had been here by herself? A late night didn't worry him, but it'd be different for Simone. She was yawning by eleven. Very inconsiderate of Chloe. Atypically so.

The credits were rolling when he heard the car roar into the garage. Half past two. Alex woke the cat, who jumped off his lap, and they both stretched. Where had she been? If she hadn't gone out with a policeman — and he'd met the man — he'd have been worried for her safety.

The roller door rumbled. The door from the garage to the house opened. The cat wandered away in the direction of the kitchen. Alex sat staring at the TV screen, glanced casually toward the door where she'd appear, returned to the TV, and glanced again. Back again to an advertisement for a car dealership. Chloe finally entered on a wave of cool night air, excited, sparkling eyes, golden hair tumbling loose about her face. Gorgeous. He pressed the mute button on the remote.

"Hello," she said. "Still awake?"

"Yes." He flicked the TV off and stood up.

"Simone's gone?" She tossed her little embroidered Chinese bag onto the nearest chair. It slid off and landed on the floor. She watched it fall but didn't appear to care. Alex stepped across and retrieved it, placing it carefully on the coffee table before replying.

"I sent her home."

His deliberately even tone must have cut through, because she glanced at him with a slightly raised eyebrow.

"She sleeps over if I'm late. You didn't have to stay." In other words, *Don't complain to me — you chose to sit up.* Off came her sandals. She threw herself onto the couch where he'd been stretched out. "Gosh, my feet are tired. Too much dancing." Toes wriggled, ankles flexed.

"If you're out late? I didn't think you went out much."

"Sometimes I have a late gig. A wedding or something. Thanks for staying."

His hands wandered to his hips. "I didn't have much choice."

She cast an appraising eye at his stance. Her tone altered. She planted her feet flat on the floor. "I told you, Simone would have stayed."

"I didn't know how late you'd be."

"We went on to a club. I haven't been dancing in years. It was great. Loud, though. My ears are ringing." She smiled.

It sounded horrible. Deafening music, flashing lights, semidarkness. He must be getting old.

"You have to be careful of drink-spiking

in those places." He sounded like her father. Except she didn't have one. He relaxed his hands from his hips and fished in his pocket for car keys instead.

"I didn't drink, Alex. I was driving, remember? Plus I was with a policeman."

The smile turned into a wide grin. Yes, the policeman. She sounded like a teenager. An errant daughter. Was she teasing him? Taunting? *Don't get into any of that. Be cool. Friendly.* "Well, I'm off. Glad you had a good time."

"Thanks."

"My pleasure. I enjoyed it. I'm happy to come again if Simone can't make it."

She actually smirked. "If you enjoyed it so much, you could come next Friday. I have a gig. Six till nine. I was going to risk leaving them on their own."

"I'll have Steffie next weekend. I guess I could bring her. If you won't be too late." He tried not to put undue emphasis on the last part but must have failed.

Chloe stood up. "I'll be home by nine-thirty," she stated. "Can she last that long?"

"Or they can come to my place. You could collect them on your way home." Cool as an ice cube.

"Fine. They'd like that. Thanks." Very polite. So brittle, she almost crackled.

269

She stared at him. Not moving. Was she expecting him to kiss her? A good-night kiss? He wasn't going to, because if he came closer than the two-meter gap they had between them, he couldn't answer for the consequences. He'd never seen her dressed to go out, in a satiny black sleeveless top and red shiny pants clinging to the gentle curve of her hips, with those sexy, strappy sandals she'd kicked off. He wanted to slide his fingers over her waist, slip those thin straps off her shoulders.

Leave. Right now.

"Bye." He smiled, turned.

"Alex." She was suddenly right behind him. No brittleness now. All yielding and pliable, tactile and desirable. Her perfume, the heat of her body, her breathing. He didn't dare face her, this close. The fabric of her top was too soft, low cut, revealing. He clutched his keys so hard, the metal cut into his fingers. He waited. She spoke so softly, he barely heard. "Brent doesn't mean anything to me — you know that. Not the way you do."

His breath caught, then jerked out in a gasp. "I know," he muttered. And he strode from the house.

Chloe closed the door slowly. Should she have apologized for her harsh words the last

270

time they'd spoken? Accusing him of not wanting Stephanie, of being selfish. Had she been too cruel? But she wasn't sorry she'd spoken. That was how she felt, and he needed to know. What sort of relationship could they have if she didn't speak her mind right from the start?

Here she was, thinking *relationship!* She'd also told him in that tirade that there was no way a relationship could work. He appeared to have accepted it, going by his behavior just now. Very distant. Polite and friendly. But distant. No kiss, not even a chaste good-night peck on the cheek.

Gave her an unsettled feeling in the stomach. A nervous churning. Unless that was the Thai food. No, it wasn't the dinner. It was Alex. After his confession and very potent demonstration of love, he didn't seem to care in the slightest that she'd gone out with someone else. Shouldn't he have been the teensiest bit jealous?

Swept off his feet? No. Instead, he comes over to babysit. And treats her to a diatribe on the dangers of nightclubs — just like a father. *Too confusing. Too tired, too late.*

Bed.

But sleep wouldn't come. The ringing in her ears was louder in the quiet of the night. They say if your ears ring, the hearing is

271

being damaged. Great outcome for a musician. Like Beethoven.

She wasn't Beethoven.

Chloe rolled over to stare at the luminous numbers on the clock: 3:41. She closed her eyes. She'd be a wreck at tomorrow's rehearsal with Amanda, for next Friday. A mini classical concert at the Mexican embassy. Jazzy background music during drinks, then two short performances between courses at the dinner. Flute and guitar. Fun.

Friday would be tough. She finished teaching at five. Barely enough time to change, drop the kids, and get to the embassy. Eat an apple in the car. Couldn't play hungry. If it went well, they might land more of the same. She'd played with Amanda once or twice and liked the rapport they had. Amanda was keen to make the duo a permanent entity, expand their repertoire, and advertise more widely. Try for music festivals. Record a CD.

Concerts. Recordings. Dreams. Like finishing her degree. Chloe lay on her back with her knees bent.

And where did Alex fit into her dreams? He didn't. Not into the music ones. He was in a whole other realm. He was the impossible dream, so far from attainable it wasn't worth hankering after. She loved him — she was fairly sure of that — but the strands of her life just didn't mesh. She had one focus for the moment, and that was rearing those children to the very best of her ability, and after Seb's little aberration she'd have to be extra vigilant. There wasn't room for complication and distraction in the form of a boyfriend. Alex was welcome to help out occasionally if he was so keen, but his enthusiasm wouldn't last long. Look how he'd failed when the first conflict of interest arose. The way Lachlan had failed. Bailed out when things got tough, when she really needed him.

She didn't need Alex. She had been coping without him and would continue to do so. While this first mad flush of attraction was upon her, she couldn't allow herself to weaken again. She mustn't let him touch her or kiss her. He'd lose interest fast enough. She had to be firm. He was the first man she'd been attracted to since Lachlan — that's all it was.

How very sensible she sounded. In theory. Lying in bed in the darkness. Apart from him. Safe from the smell and sight of him. The touch of his fingers, the feel of his skin, his hair, his breath, that certain way he looked at her. His voice. His kiss.

■ ■ ■ ■

On Friday afternoon Alex was at the Gungahlin building site wrangling with the
plumber over the misplacement of laundry
pipes. His cell phone jangled in the middle
of a heated explanation by the man, who
stomped away in disgust.

"Sorry," he muttered to the retreating
back.

"Knock-off time anyway," came the retort.
The plumber kept walking to his van.

"No," called Alex. "It has to be sorted out
today. The whole thing's behind schedule as
it is."

"Not my problem, mate."

The phone continued to ring. UNKNOWN
CALLER.

"Bergman," he snapped.

"Alex? It's Julian." A very frightened
voice, none of the usual confident, dry
humor. His stomach tightened.

"Julian? What's wrong?"

"Seb's hurt. I don't know what to do. Can
you come?"

Seb? Hurt? "Has he had an accident?
Where's Chloe?"

"Chloe's teaching, and she's got her gig
tonight. We didn't — Seb didn't want to

upset her. She can't stand blood." He was nearly in tears. The plumber stood watching, scowling, hands on hips. "He got beaten up."

"Where are you? I'll be right there. Does he need an ambulance?"

"No, I don't think so. I think his arm's broken and maybe his nose. It's all mashed. There's blood everywhere. We're at the ovals where he plays cricket. Near the school. They beat him up," he said again, his voice trembling after the gush of information. He drew in a noisy gasp of breath, struggling for control. "I had to leave him. I'm at the shops." Another gasp. "Gotta go in case they come back."

"Fifteen minutes," Alex said into the buzz of the disconnected line. He yelled to the plumber, "Sorry. Emergency. I have to go. Tomorrow morning, seven-thirty. Right?"

The man grunted, but Alex was already running to his car, heart pounding high in his chest. Beaten up? Who would do that? The rest of those thugs Seb hung out with? Someone taking revenge? Crikey! Seb was fourteen years old. A child.

The BMW leaped forward as he jammed his foot down, his mind already calculating the best route. Too early for the rush-hour buildup, but there were plenty of dawdlers in the way. Tempting to accelerate past the lot of them — the Beemer had the power — but no point crashing or having the police on his tail. He hovered just over the speed limit, ducking and weaving, charging through amber lights he'd normally slow for. Adrenaline pumped through his body, focusing his awareness, coordinating his limbs into smooth, effortless efficiency.

If Seb were badly hurt, it would almost kill Chloe. She'd blame herself. They'd suffered enough, that little family. A protective surge of anger almost choked him, and he had to force himself to wait at a red light at Belconnen Way instead of blasting his horn and ramming through the intersection like a fire truck. When the light turned green, he planted his foot. Someone changed lanes in front of him, then slowed to turn off. He swerved and accelerated again. So close, and now he was in a queue of cars behind a lumbering bus. Red light at Bindubi Street. Clear for the last stretch.

The boys were huddled under the trees near where they'd run laughing in the storm to Chloe's car. Julian leaped up, waving, then turned to help Seb to his feet.

Alex sprinted across the dusty dry grass toward them. What he'd thought was a design on Seb's T-shirt emerged as a bloody spatter pattern emanating from a large central splodge. Dirt caked the knees of his pants. Grit and dust streaked the blond hair like the work of an inept makeup artist. His lips and cheeks were already swollen and discolored, the nose twice its normal size. The left arm hung awkwardly, supported by the other. He winced as Julian's arm went around his waist.

"Ooh, mate," Alex murmured, his heart sinking with dismay he tried to hide. It'd be a miracle if nothing was broken, and that was just bones. He was no doctor, but he knew other organs could be damaged in a severe beating — kidneys, spleen, eyes, brain. Horrible to contemplate, but maybe this was panic, his brain in lurid overdrive. Too many TV shows, not enough info. He had no idea how bad Seb really was. *Stay cool for the boys' sake.* "We'd better get you to the emergency room."

"I'll call Katy and get her to tell Chloe we're at your place, okay?" asked Julian anxiously. "So she won't worry."

"Sure."

"Can I use your phone, please?"

"Here." He passed the cell to Julian and returned his attention to Seb. The boy's right eye was almost closed. Ugly, dark bruising contaminated his child's face.

Tears, sweat, dirt, and blood mixed in a frightening mess. His breathing was shallow — cracked rib? How did you tell? He'd need X-rays.

"Lean on me, Seb. Try to walk to the car, okay?"

They shuffled slowly to the BMW. Julian opened the rear door, watching anxiously as Seb sank gingerly onto the seat with a groan.

"Lie down," said Alex. "Hop in and support that arm for him, Julian."

"What about our bikes?" he asked.

"Chain them to a tree. We'll get them later. Toss your bags into the boot."

The hospital was only minutes away. Alex drove in tight-lipped silence. Seb lay breathing raggedly. Julian's white face stared at him in the rearview mirror.

"Will he be all right?" he asked. "There's so much blood."

"Noses bleed like crazy. Hurt like hell too. I got a basketball full in the face once." He forced a grin at Julian in the mirror. "Don't worry. We'll be stuck with him a bit longer. He'll live."

He was answered by a shaky smile from the backseat.

"You all right?" Alex asked, catching his eye again.

Julian nodded. "They didn't want me.

278

There were four of them. Two of them held me so I couldn't help Seb."

Gentle, creative, artistic Julian. A lover not a fighter. Alex's heart swelled at his unthinking bravery. If those thugs hadn't held him, he'd have been beaten to a pulp as well for trying to defend his brother. "Cowards always hang out in packs. Who were they?"

"Alan Simic," grunted Seb from the backseat. "And his mates."

"That's Zak's brother," said Julian. "Zak's the one Seb got caught with. He got six months in juvie. They said it was Seb's fault for ratting on him."

Alex nodded. "The police will be interested in this."

"No," Seb gasped.

"The hospital may have to notify them of an assault." He had no idea if that was true, but those thugs should be stopped, and he'd do it himself if he had to. That policeman friend of Chloe's should be told.

He pulled up as close as possible to the emergency entrance. "Take him in," he said, twisting in his seat to face Julian. "I'll park the car."

By the time he returned, Julian was reading a form with studied concentration, twiddling a pen in one hand. Seb slumped beside him. The waiting room, surprisingly, thankfully, wasn't very full. A tired-faced nurse appeared. She nodded briefly to Alex, then turned to Seb. "Let's have a look at you while your dad and your brother do the forms." She glanced at Alex. "I'll come and get you in a few minutes."

Seb stood up shakily.

"Twins?" she queried as they moved slowly away together, her arm around his middle.

"Did you say I was your dad?" Alex asked Julian when she'd moved out of earshot.

"Seemed easiest," he replied casually, frowning at the form. He wrote something carefully. "I didn't want them to call Chloe."

"She'll have to be told."

"Later. It won't make any difference to Seb, but it will to her. She'll have a fit."

"What about Simone?"

"What about her?"

"Perhaps we should call her."

"Why?"

"She's a relative."

Julian shrugged. "Okay, but she can't come. She's away — down at the coast with friends. I can fill this out, and you can sign it. They have to treat him. We can give them the insurance number later. I bet no one knows that by memory."

Alex sighed, shook his head. Chloe *would* have a fit. But Julian had a point. Her concert. She'd never play if she knew Seb was in the state he was in. He looked at his watch. 4:20. They'd probably be here for hours. He'd call Simone.

"I have to pick up Steffie soon," he said.

"I'll stay here."

"They'll want to X-ray him. Could take ages."

"I'll wait. You get Steffie. Pick up Katy too, so Chloe won't even know. She'll think we're at your place. It'll be easier for her anyway if we're not there. She's teaching until five-thirty."

Alex grinned despite his reluctance to join in with this mammoth conspiracy. "You're a real tactical mastermind, aren't you?"

"Yes, Mr. Bond," Julian replied in a guttural Goldfinger voice.

Alex chuckled, pleased to see he'd regained his usual confidence. "I'd better wait for that nurse first. I'll bring the girls back here to see how you're getting on, but then we might have to rethink. I don't want them sitting in the waiting room for hours."

Julian nodded. "Thanks, Alex. We knew we could count on you."

"Of course you can." Alex grimaced. "I hope Chloe sees it that way." Especially

281

when she discovered they'd all kept her in the dark. Somehow he doubted she would.

"Promise you won't tell her?" demanded Julian.

Chapter Twelve

After the performance the Mexican ambassador's wife insisted Chloe and Amanda stay and have dinner in a room off the main dining room where the guests were now enjoying dessert and coffee.

Amanda faced Chloe across the white-clothed table, grinning with delight. She raised her glass. Chloe clinked hers and drank. Nothing like the high after a good performance with an appreciative audience.

Amanda said, "Someone phoned today about doing a concert at a winery in Rutherglen. June, long weekend. We'd be away overnight. Can you manage that?"

A whole concert. A whole weekend away. Fabulous. Except . . . "Depends who else has what on," she said.

Amanda nodded and smiled. She ate a forkful of spicy chicken and rice. "I can find someone else if you can't, but I'd rather not."

Amanda was single, had finished her degree the previous year, and possessed energy, drive, plans, talent, and commitment. She freelanced — did orchestral work, played jazz, and wrote her own tunes. Very versatile. Unlike Chloe, she didn't teach and had none of the restrictions Chloe came burdened with: limited rehearsal availability, limited travel availability, the necessity of generous notice before gigs. No spontaneous anything.

How long before Amanda found someone else for her duo, permanently?

Half an hour later Chloe drove to Alex's house, humming snatches of melody from the program, smiling to herself. A whole concert in Rutherglen. She *had* to do it. This was what she wanted to do with her life. Play the guitar, perform. Perfect her art. Live, breathe, eat, and sleep music. If only she could take off whenever she liked, do what she wanted. Surely Simone could cover for her that weekend.

She was late again. Good thing the kids were at Alex's house, so Stephanie could go to bed. Not that she would, probably. Be far too exciting having Katy over to play. She wondered how Alex was coping with the whole tribe. Alone. Chloe snickered. Served him right for offering. Maybe she could ask

284

him to have them the Rutherglen weekend. If he was still interested in the Gardiners by June. The novelty might have worn off by then.

A police patrol car was parked in the street opposite the house. Neighbors having trouble? Didn't happen much in Aranda. The residents were predominantly law-abiding, well-educated, middle-class people. It was their kids who were the problem. Like Seb.

Chloe parked in Alex's drive. She skipped up the steps and tapped lightly on the door. A tingle of excitement shivered down her spine. She hadn't seen Alex since that tense little meeting on Saturday. Would he be more demonstrative tonight? A private glance, a smile? Steal a kiss? No! She'd made up her mind! But would he try?

Bundle the kids up, and get in and out quickly — that's what she'd have to do. Not allow herself to linger. Whatever had happened was over.

Chloe waited. Had she knocked hard enough? Were they all in bed? Engrossed in a movie, playing a game? She knocked again. Louder.

Alex, stern-faced, opened the door.

"I'm . . ." she started. If he wasn't so darn good-looking, she'd be able to stick to her

285

resolve much more easily. Her knees went weak just at the sight of him. *Stop it.*

"Come in," he said tersely, forestalling her apology. Chloe stepped inside, instantly alert. Something was wrong. Was he angry because she was late? "I'm sorry," she began again.

Then she saw the policewoman. And Seb. Sitting on the couch beside Julian, face half covered by a white bandage across his nose, the surrounding skin palely emphasizing the angry red right eye swollen shut. Sticking plaster across his temple. His arm in a sling. Wearing a T-shirt she'd never seen before.

Her whole body clenched like a fist. An unnamed fear sent ice through her veins. Memories of visions, nightmares conjured by a shocked mind. An unimaginable scene of death and destruction made real by photographs and news reports.

"What happened?" Her gaze flew wildly from Seb to Alex to the policewoman who had risen to greet her, back to the bashed and bruised body. Two rapid paces toward him. "Seb?"

"I'm fine, Chloe," Seb said thickly. "Nothing's broken."

"He was assaulted, Miss Gardiner," the policewoman said calmly. "It's not as bad as it looks. I'm Constable Diana Black. I'm just taking statements from him and Julian."

Assaulted? Battered, more like it. The quiet matter-of-factness steadied her. Reason asserted itself once more. Panic receded.

"But when?"

"On the way home from school," Julian said.

"But —" Chloe stared, uncomprehending. Hours ago. Before she left home.

"We didn't want to worry you before your concert," Seb explained, as if that were a perfectly legitimate reason to keep such a horrifying occurrence from her.

Silence, while they all waited for her reaction. Her mouth opened, closed. She shook her head.

"It looks worse than it is," said Alex from behind her. "Bad bruising, fair bit of blood from a minor cut on his head and his nose. We took him to the ER, and they X-rayed him." They were all speaking and acting as though it were nothing. As if Seb's being bashed was a minor event, of no concern to anyone. Not even worth telling her about.

"You knew!?" Chloe spun to face him.

"We called him," said Julian quickly.

"And not me?" Her voice rose in disbelief.

"You were teaching, and you had your concert," said Seb. "Alex came."

"You didn't *tell* me?" She glared ferociously at Alex.

"Miss Gardiner," interrupted Constable Black. "I need to finish taking the statements if you don't mind." She fixed Chloe with a stern eye.

Alex grasped her by the arm, his fingers cool on the bare skin. "Come into the kitchen." He dragged her through an archway, through the dining room, and into the kitchen, pulling a bifold door closed behind them. She went unprotesting, still floundering in the mess of deception and shock and this further, most damning proof of just how irresponsible and untrustworthy Alex was.

"How could you not tell me?" Tears of rage misted her eyes. His hand still held her forearm but lightly now, as though he'd forgotten the contact or didn't want to lose it. She snatched her arm away. "How dare you? Seb's my responsibility. Not yours. Mine! I take care of him and Julian. Where's Katy?"

He stepped back a pace, his expression stiffening to the remote, arrogant one she knew of old. "The girls are in bed. I thought it'd be best if Katy slept over."

"*Did* you!" Without asking. Assuming. Taking charge. Ignoring her authority.

His eyes narrowed. "Yes, I did. Keep your voice down. I don't want them witnessing this." His own voice dropped to a whisper redolent with suppressed anger. "What would you have done, Chloe? We were at the hospital for hours. You had your gig at six."

His blue eyes impaled her, demanding an answer.

"I would have stayed with Seb, of course." The answer flew straight back without a second thought.

A corner of his mouth rose in disbelief. "Would you?"

The second thought arrived. Would she have called Amanda and pulled out of the gig? Could she have done that to her? What would Amanda have done, stranded at the last minute? Impossible to let her down so badly. "I would have called Simone if I needed to."

"But she's away. Why not call me?" He folded his arms and glared at her, demanding an answer.

"I — you're not family."

"The boys didn't worry about that."

"No. I'm sorry they bothered you. They shouldn't have." Why hadn't they called home? Why call Alex of all people? Especially after he'd failed Seb.

" 'Bothered' me? It was no bother."

"They should have called me," she said,

but it was a feeble defense against his overwhelming aura of righteousness. The words wouldn't come to explain something so instinctive, something deep down she *knew* was right.

"Seb explained why. And we did call Simone. She couldn't help from Bateman's Bay, but she agreed with the boys." He was patronizing in his patience now. "You were teaching, and they didn't want to upset you before your concert. How did it go, by the way?"

"Well," she said dismissively. "And you thought that was enough of a reason not to tell me? What if Seb had been really badly hurt?"

"I'm sorry." He relaxed his stance. The arms dropped to his sides, rose, spread, lowered, matching his confusion and guilt. "I wanted to call you, but they were insistent. Both of them. The priority seemed to me to get him to a doctor. Of course I would have called you if there was anything serious. They wouldn't have treated him for a major problem without your permission. As it was, they X-rayed him and bandaged him up, and he'll be fine."

"I should have been there."

Alex ran one hand through his hair, released a sigh of exasperation, then let his hand fall to his side. "Chloe, you can't always be there. You have a life too. Seb and Julian understand that — that's why they called me. You're the one who can't see it. You're the one who can't let go. You can't have it both ways. You either let someone else help share the responsibility, or you don't have a life at all."

He had no idea! Absolutely no idea, and he was treating her like some clinging, overprotective imbecile! White-hot rage roared up through her body to erupt in a searing tirade. "What do you mean 'let go'? They're children. They don't know anything! They can't look after themselves. You don't know anything about bringing up children. You don't know how to deal with your own daughter. You've made quite an art of avoiding that responsibility."

"That's completely unfair," he hissed through tight lips. "I'll admit I'm not the best at understanding little girls, but I know what boys need. I was one." He leaned in closer, looming over her in his anger. His voice rose. "And what they don't need is to be smothered."

"Caring for them isn't 'smothering' them!" Chloe stood her ground, matching his volume. She was in the right, and he knew it; that's why he was attempting to use his height and physical bulk to intimidate her.

"I agree, but there comes a time when they need some slack."

" 'Slack'? Look what happened to Seb! You of all people can see the results of his being given some slack — us being at the police station in the middle of the night!"

"Daddy? Why are you and Chloe shouting?"

Two pajama-clad girls appeared in the kitchen doorway, clutching hands. Katy's face looked shocked, close to tears, Stephanie's frightened with a trembling lower lip.

Chloe gritted her teeth, her lips clamped tight and hard. Her lungs dragged in ragged gulps of air. Alex would never, ever understand. "I need to be in there with Seb. I'm his guardian," she said eventually, her voice tight and low. "Katy, we're going home."

"Let her stay, Chloe." Alex had moderated his voice now, making her seem the unreasonable, screaming one.

She shook her head. "No. It's not late. She can come home."

"I'll get my clothes," whispered Katy, and fled. Stephanie scampered to Alex's side. He bent to embrace her, and she buried her face in his neck as he straightened, holding her close.

292

Chloe shut her eyes briefly, then sucked in a deep breath. *Please don't let them have heard too much.* Katy wasn't used to adults arguing. Violence of any sort frightened her. She'd be upset as it was with Seb sitting there looking as though he'd insulted Mike Tyson.

"I'm sorry, Stephanie," she said. "It's nothing to do with you. I'd just like Katy to come home."

Alex carried his daughter from the room without a word.

Chloe stood immobile. For a moment her brain ceased to function. Too much information all at once. Shell-shocked. How had this unholy situation developed? Ten minutes earlier she'd been so happy.

Seb. She still didn't know what had happened beyond the fact that he'd been beaten to a pulp on the way home from school. Chloe slid the bifold door open.

Seb and Julian looked up with identical expressions when she reappeared — a mixture of apprehension and defiance. Had they heard the fight too? Must have. Two rooms away, but that door was only plywood. The policewoman smiled. Far too calmly, given the situation.

"We're finished," she said.

Finished? Surely that wasn't appropriate

293

without Chloe in attendance. "I don't even know who did this or what happened!" cried Chloe. "None of you seem to be taking this seriously."

"Believe me, the police will be taking this very seriously." Constable Black closed her folder and stood up.

"It was Alan Simic and his mates," said Julian. "Zak Simic's brother."

Understanding dawned. Finally some sense to be found in the mess. "Revenge for Zak."

And she'd chuckled privately to herself about Seb's request for police protection. Melodramatic, she'd thought, stupidly.

"Yeah. I told you I didn't want to tell who did the vandalism. I knew this would happen."

So now it was her fault again. Maybe in some way it was. But how could she protect him from thugs like those boys, short of driving him to and from school and never allowing him out without adult supervision? Ridiculous. What would Mr. Know-It-All Alex's solution to that little dilemma be? He'd say she was being overprotective and smothering, but when Seb went out alone, or even with Julian, he got beaten up.

"I'm sorry, Seb."

"The boys said there were independent

witnesses. Other students from the school."

"They saw but didn't help you?"

The eloquent moment of silence during which the twins glanced at each other told her what a stupid question that was. Julian said, "They were year seven girls."

Constable Black said, "Thank you both. I'm sorry it came to this, but I'll do my very best to see that those thugs get what they deserve."

"Thank you," the boys chorused.

"I'll see myself out. Good night." She strode to the door.

"Thank you. Good night," said Chloe. She turned to the twins. "Come on, we're going home. Julian, see if Katy's ready."

"She's in bed."

"No, she's not. She's getting her things."

"Why can't she stay?" asked Seb. Julian pulled a face but didn't argue. He helped Seb to his feet and left the room.

"No need," replied Chloe curtly.

"What's up with you?" So the bashing hadn't harmed Seb's tongue at all. He winced suddenly, filling her with remorse. It wasn't his fault. This time he was the victim, punished for bravely doing the right thing. What would he make of that lesson?

"Nothing. I got a shock seeing you, that's all." Tears unexpectedly filled her eyes. She hadn't been there. Again. That other time she hadn't been there. But if she had been with Mum and Terry and Bevan, she'd have been a victim too. She blinked rapidly. Sniffed.

"Chloe?" Uncertainty in his voice. The little boy looking to her for help. She *had* to look after them better. She had to be *much* better at it. "Seb." She touched his cheek gently. "Your poor nose. Are you sure nothing's broken? It looks terrible."

"It hurts, and I can't breathe properly."

"You need to go to bed."

"I won't be able to sleep."

"I bet you will. You look exhausted. Your body needs rest."

She held out her hand, and he accepted her support as they moved to the front door.

"How was your concert?" he asked.

"Went well. Thanks, Seb." They paused in the foyer. Why was Julian taking so long? She wanted to go home fast before Alex reappeared, so she wouldn't have to face his disapproval and her own bitter, hurt disappointment. "I would've come to get you. My students didn't matter."

"I know. That's why we called Alex. We didn't want you to."

How could he say that? Couldn't he see how hurtful that was? Cutting her out.

Keeping her at a distance while including Alex, a comparative stranger? The boys idolized him. She thought she might have loved him. Yet none of them really knew him.

Katy appeared with Julian, carrying a plastic shopping bag and wearing a miserable expression. She looked at Chloe with alarmed eyes. Chloe smiled, and the apprehension left the girl's pale face. Chloe held out her hand, and Katy clung on. Julian moved beside Seb.

Alex and Stephanie stood silently, watching from the hallway.

"Thank you," Chloe said stiffly to Alex's closed, blank face. The pain she glimpsed in his eyes she preferred to ignore.

"Chloe," he murmured, but she cut him off. "Good night, Stephanie."

"Good night, Chloe." Never had she heard such a subdued response from the child.

"Thanks for helping, Alex," said Seb. He added, "Sorry."

"No worries. See you, mate. Bye, Julian, Katy."

No one spoke during the short ride home. Plenty was thought, though, especially in the backseat, where the twins sat in absorbed silence, emanating waves of disapproval. Katy was first into the house. She took herself straight to bed without a word. Julian helped Seb out of the car while Chloe collected her music stand and guitar from the boot.

The roller door rumbled shut. Chloe followed the boys into the house, but they headed directly for Seb's room. She dumped her gear in the music room. If that's how they wanted to be, let them. One day they might understand. When they grew up.

Alex called the house midafternoon the next day. Dialing the number was as nerve-racking as calling his first girl for a date at the age of thirteen. Ridiculous how this woman did that to him. A couple of months ago he would have laughed anyone into the ground who'd suggest he could be so totally in thrall to any female ever again.

But more was at stake here. He had to maintain contact somehow, couldn't let her cut herself off. Cut him off from the boys and Katy. They'd trusted him. If Chloe answered the phone, he was prepared either for a hang-up or a torrent of abuse. Luckily, he got sweet little Katy.

"Hello," she whispered in a secretive voice when he identified himself.

"How's Seb?"

"His eye is a funny color. Lots of colors

actually, and it's swollen shut."

"Why are you whispering?"

"Chloe might hear."

His heart plummeted. Some small, forlorn shred of hope had lingered that she might have had a total rethink. "Is she still angry with me?"

"Yes."

"Oh, dear."

Chloe's voice in the background said, "Who's on the phone?"

The receiver scraped and went muffled as if Katy put her hand over it. He could just hear her say, "It's for me." A moment later she was with him again.

"She's angry with all of us. She was crying last night. I heard her."

His heart ached for her all alone with her hurt and anger. Totally unnecessarily. If only he could make her see how loving each other could conquer all those problems she struggled with. That ultimately they all wanted the same thing. "What should I do, Katy?"

"You could try flowers," she suggested.

"Think they'd work?"

"They might." Now she sounded doubtful. "Do you want to talk to Seb?"

"Yes, please, but I don't want to upset Chloe."

Her voice returned to normal. "It's all right, she's swimming now. Here's Seb."

"Hi, Alex."

"G'day mate. How are the battle scars?"

"I'm pretty stiff today, and my eye's really sore. Plus I can't breathe very well."

"Did you get any sleep?"

"Yeah. Kept waking up, though."

"Take it easy, then."

"Yeah. Chloe's really mad at us. I've never seen her like this."

"I should have told her straightaway."

"It's my fault. I wouldn't let you. We keep telling her that, but she won't believe us."

"She's right. I should have told her. I'm the adult. I'm the one who's supposed to do the right thing."

"You shouldn't take all the blame, though."

"Is that what she's doing? Blaming me?"

"It's like she wants to have an excuse for not seeing you or something. Or letting us see you. It's weird."

"She's confused. And very upset. You've given her a rough time lately, mate." So had he.

"Can you do something?"

"Like what?"

"I dunno. Talk to her?"

"Katy thinks I should send her flowers."

"Can't hurt."

"I reckon it'll take a bit more than that. I'll give it some thought, but I think we should leave it for a few days. Let her calm down. Also, I don't want to go behind her back. If she doesn't want you coming over, you'd better not. All right?"

"S'pose so. Send her some flowers, though. No one ever sends her flowers. Women are supposed to like that sort of stuff."

"All right. Look, Seb. You can call me anytime, you know?"

"Yeah, thanks. See ya."

"Bye."

Steffie, sprawled on the floor with an array of pencils, looked up from her coloring book. "Is Seb better?"

"He's sore and stiff, but he'll be fine." Alex sat on the rug beside her. He leaned his back on the couch and draped his hands over his drawn up knees. What a mess. If only he'd followed his gut instinct and called Chloe straightaway. But he hadn't. He could see the twins' point. Sometimes Chloe had to be protected from herself. And why didn't she trust him to take good care of Seb? What more could she have done that he hadn't?

"Chloe frightened me. Katy was scared too."

He reached out a hand to touch her cheek gently. "She wasn't angry with either of you, hon. She was angry with me."

"But she made Katy go home, and I wanted her to stay."

"I know. But she can sleep over another time. Chloe won't be angry forever."

"She'll get over it." That had a very Derek-sounding ring to it. Steffie selected a different pencil and returned to her picture. "See my house, Daddy?"

"It's very good." He looked more carefully. It *was* very good, and she wasn't simply coloring in as he'd originally thought. "Did you draw that?"

"Yes. It's my house. I'm going to be like you, Daddy, and draw houses for people to live in."

"I like the way the balcony goes right around." A swell of pride rose in his heart. How could he have missed this latent talent for design? By not looking — that was the sad truth of it. Never looking beyond the superficial. He'd seen caring for his daughter as a duty and done the right things without seeing the truth of the child. He'd missed the essence of Steffie. Chloe had hit the mark there. Painfully so. Strange that he had seen and clicked with the essence of Seb within a couple of hours yet missed so much in the six years of Steffie's existence.

"Do you know how to deal with me, Daddy?" She sat back to study her handiwork.

This time his breath stalled. Was she a junior mind-reader as well? " 'Deal with you'?"

"Chloe said, 'You don't know how to deal with your own daughter.' "

How much else had the girls heard? "Of course I know how to deal with you." He forced a smile. "All I need to do with you is feed you macaroni and cheese."

Steffie giggled.

"Hon, you mustn't be upset or frightened by anything you heard Chloe say last night. She was very upset about Seb. She was angry with me because I didn't tell her he was hurt, and I should have."

"Why didn't you?" She looked up at him.

"She had her concert, and we thought she'd be too worried and not play properly. Anyway, I took care of Seb."

"Yes, we all did," she said. "And Seb's going to be just fine."

"Yes."

If a six-year-old could understand the logic, why not Chloe?

CHAPTER THIRTEEN

By the end of the week Seb was reasonably mobile, but Chloe wouldn't let him play cricket for at least another week, which annoyed him intensely.

"They need me!" he shouted after reluctantly relaying the news to his coach on Thursday evening. "I can't just not turn up. I'm part of a team, and I'm the best bowler."

"I don't care!" she yelled. "What if you get a cricket ball in the face?"

"Don't be stupid."

"You wouldn't be much use anyway. You're still too stiff."

Seb glared at her, his eyes glittering through the purple-red swollen flesh, and stomped down the hall to his bedroom, where he slammed the door. Hard.

Chloe heaved in furious gasps of air. Why couldn't they understand? Men! Dense as tree trunks. Bodies were fragile. They broke and bled and needed care and attention.

Sometimes they died, blasted to pieces. She clenched her fists until her nails dug into her palms. This wasn't Bali. There weren't suicide bombers here intent on destruction.

Get a grip.

He'd sent roses. Red roses. They stood in a tall glass vase on the kitchen counter. In full view. Katy insisted they go where everyone could see them, fussing about choosing the right vase. Katy didn't read the note, though. That was private.

Forgive me. Love, Alex.

Could she forgive him? Probably, in time. Did she want to rekindle what had flamed so briefly between them? Staring at the roses, breathing in their deep perfume, holding the card and gently running her finger over the words. *Love, Alex.* Drinking in the meaning, absorbing it through the skin on her fingertips. She did love Alex. As deeply as the roses were red. She'd go on loving him long after the flowers had shriveled and died.

But he didn't fit into her life. He couldn't fit. He didn't know how. Loving and wanting weren't enough. There had to be understanding and empathy, and most of all there had to trust. Bevan and Mum had had it. Trust, honesty, openness.

In some ways it was fitting they had died

together, because she couldn't imagine either of them surviving without the other. Mum said Bevan was her savior. He said she was his life and that he hadn't any idea of what living was all about until he met her. They met and knew, Mum and Bevan. Instantly.

Was her love for Alex like that? Was his for her like that? She had no way of telling. The trust wasn't there — she knew that.

She wrote a brief, polite, thank-you note and dropped it into his letter box the following day, scurrying back to her car in case he spotted her and came out. Impossible to face him yet.

Simone paused with her hand on the latch. "What are you doing for your birthday?"

Katy smiled and looked at Chloe quickly with sparkling eyes. Those two terrors had secrets. Chloe shrugged. "Nothing."

"You should throw a party. Cheer yourself up a bit."

"I'm cheerful."

"No, you're not."

"I am." No doubt that pair had been discussing things that were none of their business. Chloe put her guitar case down to take off her jacket, turning her back for a moment in order to hang it up and to forestall further unsolicited comment on her state of happiness. *Fragile* was the best description. Incapable of withstanding Simone-style scrutiny.

Alex hadn't called or visited for two weeks. Not since the roses. She'd had no idea not seeing him would be so torturous, hadn't thought he might take her anger at face value and completely withdraw from her life. All their lives. As far as she knew, he hadn't seen the boys either. No one had so much as mentioned his name. It was as if he'd ceased to exist except in her heart and her memories. Wasn't that what she'd wanted?

She faced Simone, expression and voice composed. "Thanks for coming over."

"How were the weddings?" asked Katy.

"Fine. The second bride had a lovely dress, very elegant."

Simone smiled. "You've had a busy weekend."

"It's been great." It *had* been wonderful, the musical part of her life. Around the gaping hole that had developed at the core. A wedding yesterday. Two weddings today, with an hour in between to relocate. Most of the weekend being a musician. "Thank you for being here for us."

"I loved every minute of it — you know

that." Simone offered her cheek for a kiss. "I have to run now. Dinner with the girls."

"Bye-bye, Gran." Katy zeroed in for a hug and kiss.

"Thanks again, Simone." Chloe shut the door.

"Gran brought Easter eggs," said Katy, skipping ahead of her down the hall. "Even though it's not Easter yet."

"It nearly is. Any left for me?"

"Heaps."

The boys were sprawled in front of the TV, watching *Ben Hur* and eating chocolate eggs. Charlton Heston was striding down into the leper colony to find his mother and sister.

"You won't eat dinner," said Chloe on her way past.

"Wanna bet?" asked Julian. He tossed a ball of colored foil at Katy, who squeaked and threw it back.

"What *is* for dinner?" asked Katy.

Chloe sighed. *Back to reality.* "Tuna casserole."

"Great," Seb groaned.

"You could have organized something else."

He grunted and returned his attention to the lepers and Charlton.

Chloe went to her bedroom to change

from her black pants and deep red blouse into jeans and a sweatshirt. They'd played well today. She'd sung a couple of Amanda's new songs. Another wedding a week from Saturday to look forward to, plus they'd devised a rehearsal schedule for the long weekend concerts. Plenty of practice, plenty of playing. Plenty of activity to take her mind off Alex.

During that first week the tidal wave of her anger had carried her across the gulf of their separation. She was glad he didn't call; she never wanted to see him again. He couldn't be trusted, he'd undermined her authority, he'd usurped her role as protector and carer.

Toward the end of the week it became clear he wasn't going to attempt a reconciliation beyond the roses. He hadn't responded to her card. He'd gone on with his life. The Gardiners had ceased to exist for him. Or was he waiting for her to make the first move?

During the second week more doubts began to creep in. As her anger dimmed, the memories glowed. Memories of intimate words spoken in love. Memories of kisses, scents, touch. Memories of a man she adored. A man she'd shunned and abused. And ultimately discouraged. A man who said he loved her, was willing to help and share. Gone. Here she was, stranded, high and dry on the shore after that wave of rage had receded. Alone.

Served her right.

In the kitchen she began preparing the casserole, opening the can of tuna, peeling veggies. Katy came in to help. One week of Easter school holidays down, one to go. No work in the shop this time, no students. Plenty of time to think. Or mope. *No!* This was what she'd wanted, this was what she'd gotten. No distraction in the form of Alex. Time to practice, which she needed. Time to focus on the kids and head off future disasters before they happened.

"What do you want for your birthday?"

Chloe smiled. "Nothing special. I'd like Seb to stay out of trouble."

Katy giggled. "Gran said he looked like Muhammad Ali. Who's he?"

"A world-champion boxer."

"Seb can't box."

"Apparently not."

Katy opened a tin of cream of celery soup and poured it carefully into the casserole dish. "Alex could help him."

"Alex?" Chloe's hand froze over the carrot she was peeling. "He can't box, can he?" Was Alex secretly contacting the kids behind

310

her back? He'd better not be!

"I don't know. But he's a man."

"What's that got to do with anything? I don't want Seb fighting anyone, anywhere."

"S'pose not. Are you still angry with him?"

"Who?"

"Alex."

Chloe chopped the knife into the carrot. *Hack, hack, hack.* "No," she said tersely. "I don't think about him." *Hack, hack* — with even more vigor. "Have you seen him lately?"

"No." Katy didn't say anything more, but the doubtful tone made Chloe glance suspiciously sideways at the intent face. The knife sliced into her finger. "Owww!"

"Eeek!" shrieked Katy. "There's blood everywhere!"

Chloe stared at the flood of bright red flowing from her index finger. Strangely, it didn't hurt. She put the knife down and turned on the cold tap. Bloody water swirled around the sink, mesmerizing, around and around.

"What happened?" Julian peered over her shoulder.

"I cut my finger." Now it was beginning to hurt. A sharp, clinical pain that made her gasp and brought tears to her eyes.

"Stick it under the tap," he said. "Chloe?"

She did as he said, dumbly, incapable of coherent thought. Blood still poured out, unstoppable. Her life's blood washing away down the drain. Like her life. Tears streamed down her cheeks. They wouldn't stop. The blood wouldn't stop. A chunk of flesh hung away from her finger, gaping crimson. Julian yelled something at Katy.

He turned off the tap and wrapped her hand clumsily in a tea towel. Blood seeped through as she watched. Her knees gave way, and she sank to the floor, clutching her wounded hand and sobbing. The pain clawed up her arm, biting and snapping like a vicious animal. She moaned in between heaving gasps of tears, bending forward to find relief but without success.

"Chloe, please." Julian's face swam before her, blurred through the tears — frown lines, wide, frightened blue eyes. "What should I do?"

She shook her head, but no words formed in her mind.

"You have to go to the doctor," he said.

When she didn't reply, he stood up and went away. Chloe rested her forehead on her bent knees. A drop of blood oozed through the makeshift bandage and fell to the floor. She clamped her hand over the tea towel, pulling another corner across to

312

stem the seepage.

Julian knelt before her again. "I rang the doctor, but I got an answering machine saying go to the on-call doctor in Weetangera."

"Can you drive?" Seb's voice now.

"She can't drive." Julian answered for her, his voice taut. "I think she's in shock."

As if in response, Chloe shivered. The tears had eased, but her body had no strength. She doubted she could stand without assistance. The shivering took hold. Her lungs dragged in air.

Julian and Seb grasped an arm each and pulled her upright. Katy fluttered in front of her, face pale and anxious.

"What will we do?" she cried.

"Sit her on the couch," said Seb. "I'm calling Alex."

"Chloe'll be angry," said Katy.

"Too bad. Alex will know what to do."

Chloe, slumped on the couch, was beyond caring. Her whole hand hurt in sympathy with the cut finger. Every now and again her body was wracked with convulsive shivers. Katy snuggled next to her and slid her arms around as much of Chloe's body as she could manage. Comforting, familiar. Loving. More tears slid down her cheeks.

"You'll be all right," Katy whispered. "We'll take care of you." Chloe rested her cheek on Katy's head. Furry, warm Simba rubbed against her ankles.

"He's coming," Seb announced. "He'll drive you to the doctor."

Alex, rushing for the second time to assist an injured Gardiner, wasn't prepared for the sight of the pale-faced, tear-sodden woman sitting on the couch with Katy cuddled beside her and the cat sitting at her feet. Julian and Seb hovered anxiously, both looking to him for guidance. Resilient though they all were, when Chloe collapsed, they floundered. She was their rock. He'd expected her to be injured and incapable of driving but not in this state of collapse. He'd readied himself for a chilled acceptance of his chauffeuring.

He swallowed his fear, steadied his voice, composed his expression, but she barely glanced at him as he knelt before her and carefully unwrapped the blood-soaked tea towel she clutched in her hand.

"Get ice and a clean towel," he said. "A packet of frozen peas will do." Julian darted away.

Her hand lay lifeless in his. He examined the wound as well as he could. The bleeding had slowed, but the unwrapping movement started the rush again. She'd chopped down half the length of her index finger, slicing deeply through the flesh to carve a strip away from the bone. Sickening. He winced. Looked as if it needed stitches. He took the clean tea towel from Julian, swiftly rewrapped the hand with the ice pack, and stood up.

"Come on. We're going to the doctor."

"All of us?" asked Katy.

"If you'd like. But we'd better go now."

"Lock the house," said Seb. Julian and Katy dashed away. Seb collected keys from a dish on the kitchen counter.

Alex helped Chloe to her feet. He supported her stiff body with an arm around her waist as they headed for the front door. She hadn't spoken a word. There was more going on here than a cut finger, shocking as that might be. Chloe was deeply upset. Shattered. He'd never seen her so distressed and compliant.

"Chloe, it's just a cut," he said. "The doctor will probably stitch it, and you'll be as good as new."

She turned her head then, but the eyes that gazed at him were dull. "You don't understand." The words emerged hoarse and uneven with an undercurrent of bitter resignation. "You never do. It's my finger — I can't play. If nerves are damaged, I may never play properly again."

That aspect had never entered his head. She sounded so melodramatic. In reality, she was terrified. Alex's fingers tightened around her waist. He brushed his lips across her cold cheek. "You'll be fine, sweetheart. Don't think that way."

She turned her head away without a word. Seb flung the front door open. "Ready?"

"Yep." *Would* she be all right? What if nerves *had* been severed? Or a tendon? Reduced finger flexibility would be disastrous for a musician wanting to make a career as a performer. He'd heard her play. She was very, very good.

Some of the chill from her fear seeped into his own belly.

Chloe sagged into the couch. The painkillers the doctor had given her made her sleepy, or maybe it was the aftermath of shock giving her this warm, indolent feeling. But her hand didn't hurt quite so much. She stared at the white bandage neatly covering the injury. No visible blood. So much had poured from the wound. . . .

"Hurting?" asked Alex softly from the armchair opposite.

She raised her eyes to discover those blue, blue eyes watching her closely. So reassuring and right to look up and see him there.

Much of the comfort and warmth radiated from him, from his presence in the house. From his soul to hers.

"A bit." Chloe picked up her cup of hot cocoa. The sweet liquid scalded its way down her throat. She hastily put it down. Hot chocolate wasn't a favorite, but Alex had suggested it as a soothing pre-bed drink. He'd been amazingly supportive. He'd taken control the instant he walked through the door. Fortunately. The kids didn't know what to do and she . . . Hopeless. What a sight they must have been. So much for her protestations about being in charge of things.

"I'm sorry I was in such a mess earlier."

"You were in mild shock, the doctor said."

Chloe grimaced. "I've never felt like that before — it was weird. My brain wouldn't work. And all that blood." She shuddered. "It reminds me of — you know. Bali."

He nodded. "You've had a lot to cope with lately."

"I suppose so. But I always managed before." She glanced up defiantly.

"But it wasn't you who was injured before," he said gently.

"No." She closed her eyes briefly. "Missed the tendon by millimeters, he said."

"I know. You were lucky." He smiled. "Well

— sort of."

She returned the smile, lingering, with her eyes exploring his face. Such a strong jaw-line, straight nose. So comfortable here together, just the two of them. The kids had absented themselves pretty smartly after they'd eaten. Curiously so, considering how much they liked Alex. "Thanks for cooking dinner."

"I only helped Katy finish what you'd started. She told me what to do. She's ter-rific."

"Yes, she is."

She gazed across at him, dreaming, imag-ining. Silly things, the product of a doped-up mind. What if he was always here like this? He lounged in the chair, quite at home with his tie loosened and top button undone. He'd thrown his jacket across the back of one of the dining room chairs. She frowned as small details registered for the first time. A tie? Alex never wore ties, not that she'd seen anyway. A quick glance at the jacket and back to his pants confirmed the fact that he was wearing a suit.

"You're all dressed up," she said, blinking to throw off the drowsiness and the love-induced stupor. "Were you going out?"

He nodded.

She sat up straight. "Where?"

"A dinner." He didn't move.

"Friends?"

"The Housing Industry Awards dinner."

"Why didn't you say so?" Chloe demanded, horrified. "You can still go. It's only nine-thirty."

He didn't move a muscle. "I'd rather stay here."

"But what if you've won?"

"They'll call me."

Chloe sat staring. Dumbfounded. "You came here instead?"

Alex drew in his feet and stood up.

He hadn't asked her to the dinner. She couldn't blame him. But her mouth drooped in dismay.

The daydream sweetness lingered in her mind. He fit here in the living room, in her house. He fit in that empty hole in the center of her heart. She wanted him to stay.

He stared down at her. She met his gaze briefly and looked away. Picked up her cocoa. Could he tell how much she wanted him to stay? Could he tell and was thinking of a polite way of saying he wanted to leave? If she'd killed his love for her with her harshness, she had to make it easy for him. *Don't cling.* Not now, when they'd reestablished a comfortable, friendly relationship.

She stretched her lips into a smile. "Go-

319

ing to collect your award?"

"Would you rather I did?"

"No." She stopped, unsure of herself, unsure of him. She replaced the cocoa mug on its coaster.

He stepped around the coffee table and sat on the couch beside her. Close. Could he hear the thumping of her heart? His thigh was warm against hers. His shoulder rubbed hers, but he lifted his arm and slid it around her, drawing her body against his. A sigh escaped. She fit perfectly there in his embrace. He smelled so good.

"Was that a happy sigh?" he murmured, turning his head to study her face.

"Yes." His lips were so close, he could bend his head a mere fraction and kiss her. He didn't.

"You gave me the fright of my life," he said.

"Did I?"

"When Seb called and said you were hurt, all I could think was that I had to be with you."

"I'm glad he called you," she whispered.

He shifted slightly to study her face intently. "Are you still angry with me?"

She smiled and snuggled closer. "Do I look angry?"

"No. But you were right. I should have

called you the day Seb was hurt and not listened to the boys. I could have persuaded you to go to your gig and looked after Seb as well."

"I overreacted. I'm so used to being the one in control, the one they turn to when they're in trouble."

"It's a big responsibility, caring for three children. You've done an amazing job."

"When our parents died, there wasn't anyone else. Simone couldn't cope. The alternative was foster care. We wanted to stay together. It was up to me to keep us together." She only realized she'd clenched her uninjured right hand into a fist when Alex placed his hand over hers and gently opened the tensed fingers.

"You don't have to do it on your own anymore, Chloe," he said.

Alex felt her give a little start of surprise. He squeezed her softly and interlaced his fingers through hers. He had to choose his words so carefully. Anything might set her off, any hint that he thought she wasn't coping and that he could do better. Any inference that he wanted to take over the family, her responsibilities. He stared into her eyes. His mind went blank. There was really only one thing to say when she gazed at him with such an expression, when her lovely face

was so close, the merest fraction of movement would close the gap between their
mouths. "I love you."

She moved that mere fraction and met his
lips, soft and sweet. Too long between kisses.
Her kiss didn't lie — she didn't need to say
it. He could tell. She loved him right back.
The disappointment of her anger, the hurt
of her words, his own anger at her distrust,
the misery of her dismissal of him from her
life, the pain of not knowing — all melted
in the heat of the passion in her lips.

An age later she pulled away. He pulled
her back for more, and she came willingly.
Much later she said, "What were you going
to say? Do what on my own?"

"Raise the children." He nibbled at her
throat, reveling in the softness of her skin,
feeling the pulse of her blood, her heart,
under his lips.

"I can do it on my own."

"I know, but you don't have to — I want
to help." He raised his head to look into her
eyes and better emphasize his words.

"You already do," she said.

He shook his head in frustration. She
wasn't listening properly, wasn't understanding, wasn't reading between the lines.
His love for her was boundless and overflowing, and she had no idea of its depth. "No,

that's not what I mean. I want to be part of the family. Properly. I want to marry you," he blurted. "Will you? Marry me?"

Chloe's eyes opened wide in astonishment. Not the reaction he'd desired but probably what he should have expected. He hadn't intended to propose. Not yet. He'd surprised himself as much as her. His heart sank as he saw the doubt cloud her expression. She didn't think he meant it. He had no doubt he meant it, but the timing was off. Too late now — he'd played his hand. She had to understand how sincere he was.

"I love you," he repeated. "And I would like nothing more than to spend the rest of my life with you and have our own babies. Our very own family."

"You've already been married," she said. "You already have a daughter."

"Yes. But that's got nothing to do with how I feel about you. I know what love is now, since I met you. What Lucy and I had was a pale imitation. I love you, and I will always love you." He gripped her hand tightly.

"But I don't want babies," she cried. "I've never thought about getting married. I want my life back."

"Can't I be in it?" She was slipping away, and he had to hold on like a desperate drowning man to a life raft.

"You already are."

"Not as much as I'd like. I want to be your husband. I want to be with you for the rest of our lives."

The expression on her face was near to panic. "I'm sorry." She leaped off the couch, tearing her hand from his grasp. The cat scooted across the floor. "I can't think. My head's muzzy. I'm too tired, and my hand is hurting again."

Alex sprang to his feet. He seized her face between both his hands and pressed his lips onto hers. She resisted very briefly, and then her body sagged against his, and he had to release her face and hold her up instead, never losing contact with her mouth. She sighed when he eventually drew away, and he smiled. "Remember that," he murmured. "Take it to bed with you, and think of me."

She stretched up for another kiss, which he willingly granted.

"I know you love me," he said into her mouth.

"I can't commit myself, Alex. I can't go from raising the kids straight into a relationship with all its expectations. I can't load on more. I want to be by myself after Katy grows up. I want to be a musician. I don't want to answer to anyone."

"Even someone you love?"

"I think so," she said slowly. "Yes."

"But you'll let me hang around, won't you?" He gripped her by the shoulders to peer down into her upturned face. The green eyes, which moments before had swum with love, turned glassy and hard. Chloe firmed her mouth, and a chill shivered its way down his spine.

"I'd feel trapped, knowing you were expecting me to marry you one day." The words hit like rocks, painful, sharp. Wounding.

Despite his attempt to maintain control and a semblance of dignity after such a baring of his soul to her scorn — wanting to howl in despair at the insanity of her statement — his voice rose on a surge of anger. "We love each other, and you deliberately want to stay apart because in seven years' time you want to do your own thing?"

"I don't want to be responsible for another child."

"You won't be. Steffie's mine."

"If we're together, of course I'll be responsible. That's what you just don't get, do you?"

"No, I don't!"

"I can't not be responsible for your daughter if we're in a relationship. I can't ignore her the way you do and say she's her mother's problem. I'm not like that."

"I don't ignore her."

"Don't you? You fobbed her off onto me quickly enough."

He flung his hands into the air, shaking his head. "I admit, I did do that — or at least you could see it that way — but I've learned how to be a better father from your boys. I want to be a better father, much better than mine was. You love me, I love you. It's simple. Unless . . ." That icy chill rushed through his veins, freezing his blood, stifling the red rush of anger. "Unless you don't really love me, and this is just an excuse. I know I love you, and I won't love anyone else. Don't you believe me?"

Chloe regarded him from behind those cool green eyes. She looked away. "I don't know."

Alex froze in place for a moment; then his limbs jerked into action. He snatched his jacket from the chair and headed for the front door, thrusting his arms into the sleeves as he went. Chloe didn't move to stop him. She wanted to say more, but the words wouldn't come. She wanted to tell him she was honored and flattered and excited by his proposal, but it had truly astounded her, struck her dumb. He was asking questions of her she hadn't considered. They deserved well thought out answers. These were questions that dealt with the rest of her life. Her whole life. If and when she married, it would be forever — with the kind of love Mum had had with Bevan. How did anyone know?

She'd loved Lachlan and believed he loved her. Wrong. Granted, they were young, neither ready for a lifelong commitment. But was she ready now? Alex asked if she knew she would never love anyone else — how could she possibly answer that? It felt that way at the moment, but anything could happen at any time.

"Has Alex gone?" Seb's voice cut into the seething morass of her thoughts.

"Did you know he was supposed to go to that awards dinner tonight?" Chloe turned, ready for an attack. She'd come to expect that from Seb. Ever since his beating. He hadn't forgiven her for her actions that night. Julian and Katy were less forthright in their disapproval, but they were wary of upsetting her. Until now, until her accident and Alex's appearance as savior.

"He said it didn't matter." His voice was surprisingly gentle. A tear popped into Chloe's eye and ran down her cheek. *Didn't matter?* An accolade like that to a man who put his work before everything? Didn't he?

Seb smiled uncertainly and shoved his hands into his pockets. "You should go to bed."

"Yes." Chloe sniffed. She walked across to switch off the lamp on the bookshelf in the corner.

"Are you still mad at him?"

In the semidarkness she could see the anxious expression. "No." Her voice shook, and she couldn't stop her lips from quivering. Several more tears followed the first. She gulped and swallowed, then rubbed the heel of her undamaged hand across her cheeks. "He's mad at me now."

"Why?"

Chloe hesitated, but whom could she confide in? Who else, of all of them, had a special relationship with Alex? It was through Seb that they'd met. Seb with his instinctive assessment of Alex as a good bloke and his dogged defense of their friendship. "He proposed, and I said no."

With streams of tears washing her face, Chloe fled to her bedroom. But she should have known a closed door would provide no sanctuary from her siblings. Within minutes the door cracked open and two identical, concerned faces peered carefully around the door frame.

"Go in." Julian pushed the door wider, letting in a stream of light from the hallway.

Chloe, collapsed on her bed in the dark, barely managed to lift her head when they sat one on either side of her. Two hands patted her clumsily. Julian shoved a tissue into her lifeless fingers, and when she didn't move, he took it and mopped her face as best he could. Seb closed the door and switched on the reading lamp, turning the shade so the light was muted and the room in soft shadows.

Gradually the sobs slowed. The boys sat silently, waiting. Unusually for them they said nothing, but their presence was comforting. Chloe stirred and rolled onto her back. Julian handed her another tissue. She blew her nose, awkwardly with her bandaged finger.

"Why did you turn him down?"

Chloe bit her lip and drew in a shuddery breath. "I don't want to get married."

"To Alex?" asked Julian.

"To anyone."

Silence for a few moments while they digested that information with furrowed brows. Seb ventured, "He loves you."

"I know, and I love him." A couple of late tears escaped.

"We thought . . ." Julian glanced at Seb

for assistance.

"We reckon you'd be perfect together."

Chloe sighed. She picked at the edge of the bandage with her free hand. The cut was throbbing gently, but that pain was nothing to the slashing wound she'd made in her heart. "I don't know him very well."

Julian shrugged. "You know enough."

"I want to do other things. I want to finish my degree."

Seb cried eagerly, "Alex won't stop you from doing that."

"You don't understand." She didn't properly understand herself anymore. He'd rushed away from that building site to help Seb. Twice he'd put the Gardiners first. Without complaint. Like a father. He'd changed.

"Tell us."

"I can't. I just don't think it's the right thing to do."

"I reckon you're just scared," said Seb. "Mum said she was scared before she married Dad, but it turned out to be the best thing she ever did."

"Mum never said that!" cried Chloe.

"Yes, she did," Julian confirmed. "When we were in primary school, and we had to sing at assembly. She said things you're scared of rarely turn out to be as bad as you thought, and sometimes they're way better. Like marrying Dad."

"I always thought they fell in love at first sight, and that was that. She told me she knew straightaway."

"They did, but it didn't stop her being scared of getting married," said Seb. "Maybe because of how your dad had treated her."

"You don't have to marry him," Julian said. "Can't you just be engaged or something?"

She would have laughed at their serious, knowing expressions if she hadn't been so close to tears again.

"Go to bed," she said. "And thanks for looking after me."

"We love you too, Chloe," said Julian. They both stood up, and the mattress bounced back into place.

"I know, and I love you."

Two faces smiled down at her with relief. Chloe's smile faded. "Do you think . . ." They waited. She ran her tongue over her lower lip, swallowed, gazed up at them. "Do you think it's too late to change my mind?"

CHAPTER FOURTEEN

Countless times Alex had his hand on the phone, even dialed several digits before he lost his nerve. She couldn't possibly be serious about not seeing him. There was no earthly reason for such a drastic decision. It must have been shock and the drugs the doctor had given her messing with her mind.

He paced about the house, thumping his clenched fist into his palm, and then, when the house became claustrophobic, he flung the sliding door open and paced about the garden in the crisp autumn air. He was mad, temporarily deranged, to have blurted out that marriage proposal.

But he'd been permanently deranged since he fell in love with her. He knew the instant she smiled at him that day in the car. When did she know? He hadn't even had time to ask all those senseless questions new couples ask each other, all those trivial little things. When did you first notice me?

When did you first fall in love with me? Did you know I loved you?

There'd been no time — she'd broken up before they'd gotten properly started. It was his fault. He'd frightened her; he'd seen it instantly in her face. Again. He'd terrified her the first time they met and later the same day in the shop. Her expression was identical — bewildered, confused, trapped. He did nothing but scare her. He was a crass, blundering fool in love. Too impetuous, too eager where she was cautious. She was right to turn him down. He'd given her no chance to think or absorb the fact that he loved her before he was asking her to commit herself to a lifetime with him. Crushing her under the weight of his passion without giving a thought to how she felt. Assuming everything. Arrogantly blind in his own desire.

He had to tell her. Apologize. Retract his rash statement, his proposal. Make her understand it was his fault and his excessive passion. His problem, not hers. Leave her be. In peace. To heal.

Alex ran inside, grabbed his car keys, locked the house, and ran to the BMW.

But Chloe's house was empty. No one answered his knock. Alex stood undecided on the front steps. He could leave a note to say he'd stopped by. He had a notepad in the car, maybe even a business envelope.

Darling Chloe,
   Please forgive me for my rash statements yesterday. I know I took you by surprise and perhaps even frightened you, and you were right to turn me down. You're not ready for marriage or a lifelong commitment, and on reflection I realize I'm probably not either. I'm sorry. Believe me, I'll do as you request and not bother you again.
   Be happy.

All my love,
Alex

Some of it was true; some of it wasn't. He wouldn't bother her again, and he did want her forgiveness, but he *was* ready for commitment and marriage, and he loved her, adored her. Loved her so much that what she wanted she would have, and if that was to pursue her dreams without him, so be it.
He stuck the envelope with her name printed on it into the screen door. Suddenly Aranda seemed claustrophobic. The houses crowded in on him; the suburb lay drab and uninteresting. The remainder of the Easter break stretched before him. He needed to

get away. He could stay away until Wednesday at the latest; after that, work commitments would be unavoidable.

Alex went home and threw clothes and essentials into an overnight bag, tossed it into the car, and left town with nary a backward glance, a heavy rock track pounding out his sorrow on the sound system.

Julian lifted the two bags of fresh apples from the backseat and headed for the front door. Seb waited for Chloe to get out of the car, then walked with her to the house, carrying the bags of vegetables. The boys hated going to the markets as a rule, but today both had offered, even insisted when she said she was capable on her own. They were worried about her, she knew. Her collapse must have frightened them all, although Katy was happy enough to visit her friend Annabel as planned. But she hadn't witnessed Chloe's teary confession. The boys had.

Was it too late to change her mind? Would Alex's be a once-only offer? Take it or leave it? Was his pride stronger than his love for her? The questions burned into her brain as she randomly chose apples and potatoes at the markets, finally arriving at the answer. There was only way to find out. Ask him.

Now, as soon as they got inside and stowed away the food.

Seb began unpacking the vegetables. He wouldn't allow her to help.

"You'll hurt your finger," he said.

"That letter was stuck in the door for you." Julian continued stacking apples in the fridge. The envelope lay on the counter.

Chloe glanced at it on her way to pick up the phone and take it to her room. "Probably from a student."

"It's from Alex."

"How do you know?" She snatched up the letter. BERGMAN DESIGN was printed on the top left corner. She ripped it open with a chill of foreboding. A letter was very formal. What was he writing that he couldn't say to her face? Or on the phone?

Her eyes flew over the words, scanning the phrases, absorbing the meaning in snippets of understanding: *rash statements . . . not ready for marriage or lifelong commitment . . . not bother you again.*

She sagged against the counter, the paper clutched in her fingers.

Good-bye. That's what he couldn't say to her face.

Chloe didn't celebrate her birthday on Tuesday. The family did. Simone took them

336

out to dinner, and they all gave Chloe gifts, which she admired through her haze of misery, and they sang "Happy Birthday to You" in the restaurant, which embarrassed her. Nobody mentioned Alex, but it was as if his specter sat with them at the table. He'd become so much a part of their existence, they must miss him as much as she did. Or was she the only one thinking that?

The boys hadn't said anything more about her teary confession or his letter, but they'd treated her with extra care and consideration. Like an invalid. Which outwardly she was, given her finger. Seb was especially solicitous. Alex had forged a bond between them not only with his presence but with his absence.

The following weekend, on the Sunday before school resumed, Seb interrupted her practice. Her finger had healed enough to accommodate a short workout. Chloe looked up in annoyance when he pushed open the door. He knew she hated being disturbed in the middle of a session, and this was the first time she'd been able to take her guitar out of its case in a week.

She missed playing. The guitar vibrated with passion in her hands, sang to her, interpreted her feelings the way nothing else could, expressed her emotions better than words. It was also her refuge. She hugged the instrument to her, waiting for Seb to state his business.

"Have you spoken to Alex since . . . you know?" he asked, keeping his voice low. He stepped into the room and closed the door.

"No." Chloe ran her hand up and down the fingerboard, silently practicing the pattern she'd been working on when he came in. Her index finger was stiff and unwieldy, still painful, and some positions were impossible.

"Are you going to call him?"

"I don't know. No, I don't think so." She stared at the piece on the music stand, then turned the page, even though she hadn't finished that section.

"Can I?"

"Don't interfere in this, Seb!" She glared at him so fiercely, he held his palms up to ward off her anger.

"I'm not. I won't say anything about you. But I don't see why I shouldn't see him. He was my friend first."

Chloe strummed a chord. She adjusted the tuning, strummed again. "Fine."

"Good." He hesitated with his hand on the doorknob. "What will I say if he asks about you?"

Chloe shrugged. "Whatever you like."

Seb heaved a sigh of total exasperation and opened the door. She resumed her practice.

The phone was ringing when Alex came home after dropping Steffie at Lucy's. He didn't rush to answer it, allowing the machine to do its job while he removed his jacket and went to the kitchen to make coffee. He couldn't be bothered talking to anyone, didn't feel like going out, didn't want to stay home, didn't want to work. Steffie had roused him from his torpor briefly, but with school resuming tomorrow, she'd gone home earlier than usual.

"Hi, Alex." Seb's voice floated into the room, and Alex raced to snatch up the receiver. A lifeline. A link to his love, albeit secondhand. He'd thought, in his deepest depression, she might forbid the boys any contact, and that pained him on a whole other level.

"G'day mate. How are you?"

"Fine. School starts tomorrow." Glum.

"I know. Steffie wasn't happy about it either. What have you been up to?"

"Not much. I wanted to call you before, but I wasn't sure if I should."

"You can call me anytime, Seb. I told you that."

"I know, but . . ."

"Did Chloe tell you not to call me?"

"No! Why would she do that?" Too fast, that reply. Too anxious to reassure. Did Seb know about the proposal and its aftermath? How much did the Gardiners confide in each other?

"What, then?"

"I didn't know if you'd want me to. You didn't say good-bye."

Alex smacked himself on the forehead. So that was it! *Dope!* That last night he'd charged off without so much as a yelled good night to the boys. "Sorry, Seb. I left in a bit of a rush. I've been away for a few days, and I turned the cell off — didn't want to be bugged by work stuff. Nothing to do with you." He gave an unconvincing-sounding laugh. "How's Chloe's finger?"

"Getting better. She played today for the first time." To his relief Seb's voice lightened, the excuse for his rudeness accepted.

"Good."

"She's not very happy, though." It was said in a stiff, awkward way, as though he'd prepared the words carefully before delivery. Why did he feel there was a subtext here? That Seb was working toward something? Warily, like a stalking cat.

"Why do you say that?" Equally awkward,

equally stiff.

"She hardly says anything. And she hasn't smiled for ages. She's like a zombie," he added.

That made two of them. Two miserable people in love with each other. Apart, when they should be together. He'd never considered that she might be feeling the same way. She'd seemed completely in control, her green eyes flinty. She'd seemed to know exactly what she wanted, and it wasn't him.

Was she having second thoughts? He certainly was. The grand gesture of denial, of martyring himself and his love to her wishes, was far more difficult than he'd imagined when he dashed off that spontaneous note and stuck it into her screen door. It was downright impossible. By the second day he'd begun to suffer withdrawal symptoms.

"What can I do?"

"I dunno. Come and see her. Talk to her or something. Bring her flowers again. She liked the flowers."

Red roses to symbolize true and lasting love. A simplistic solution to a complex problem. To a fourteen-year-old it would all appear quite straightforward.

"I don't think I can help you this time, Seb. I don't think she wants to see me."

"Don't take any notice of *her*." It was said with such disdain, Alex smiled despite the ache in his chest. "We reckon you and Chloe should get together."

A huge weight was lifted from his chest. He had reinforcements, spies on the inside. He could mount a campaign, a siege. Think it through this time. Plan. "Would you like that?"

"Yeah, it's obvious."

"I think so too. Chloe doesn't."

"She's just scared."

That jolted through him like a shock from a cattle prod. "What of? Me?"

"No. Not you. Maybe because her dad left our mother, and that dropkick Lachlan dumped her too."

"I think it's more complicated than that, Seb." If only it were simply a case of untrustworthy men in her life. He'd proven his worth; he was sure of it. She'd accepted and forgiven the misjudgments over Seb. She'd been amazed that he'd ditch the HIA awards to take her to the doctor, when in truth he hadn't hesitated. She knew he was willing to take on the children. It wasn't lack of trust in him that scared her now. It was commitment. The sacrifice of her potential freedom, as she saw it. Ironic, really. That had been his stance, initially.

"I just think you should come over."

"I'll see." Into the disappointed silence from the other end of the line he said, "What about you? We could get in an hour or so at the basketball courts before dark."

"Sure." The change of mood was astounding. Seb positively bubbled with enthusiasm.

"Meet you at the school in ten minutes."

"Great!"

Chloe could only nod her approval when Seb and Julian told her they were meeting Alex. It was easy for them. They could call him anytime they liked, whereas she, who adored him, couldn't. He wouldn't welcome contact from her. She'd thrown his proposal into his face and, together with that, his passion, told him — ridiculously and stupidly beyond imagining — that she didn't want to see him again.

What had she been thinking?

He was a proud man, an attractive, popular, successful, busy man. He wouldn't be wasting any more of his time on such an idiot; he'd made that clear in his note. If she went to him and begged forgiveness, what else would he say other than, "Sorry. I've had enough."

Simone had told her in no uncertain terms not to fool around and play games with a man's heart. She'd meant in relation to using Brent Burrows to make Alex jealous. Chloe hadn't meant to play games, but she had. And she'd lost.

She'd had a week to regret her foolishness, and she had, during every tortured, sleepless moment. Experience had taught her that the sharp edge of pain dulls in time. The sense of loss doesn't go away, but it can be lived with, covered and obscured by other things, mundane things that take up the days and prevent one from sinking into a morass of destructive self-pity.

Five years ago the children had been her savior; they would be again. She had no time to wallow in her misery. Her guilty conscience would have to fend for itself.

The boys returned an hour later, bursting with surplus energy and starving. Chloe, peeling potatoes in the kitchen with Katy, strained her ears as they crashed in through the front door. Three voices? No, only two. Alex wouldn't come home with them. Not anymore.

"What's for dinner?" called Julian as he passed on his way to his room.

"Bangers and mash," yelled Katy.

"Good."

Seb appeared and headed for the fridge. "Have fun?" Chloe asked.

"Yeah." He held the door open while considering his options.

"Get the carrots while you're there. Don't eat anything."

He dumped carrots onto the counter. "Alex asked how your finger was."

"It's better."

"That's what I told him."

Chloe picked up the knife. Seb moved across and took it from her.

"Don't want you to amputate any more fingers," he said. He began cutting the potatoes into cubes. "Alex went to Sydney for a few days." Chloe busied herself with a carrot and the peeler. "He doesn't think you want to see him again."

"Why not?" asked Katy. "I like him."

"Don't interfere, Seb."

"I'm not. I didn't say a word."

"What are you talking about?" demanded Katy.

"Nothing." Chloe threw down the peeler. "You can finish doing this, Seb."

"You should talk to him," he yelled as she strode from the room. "You're both being stupid."

Talk to him? When she talked to Alex, she said the wrong things. Things that weren't in her heart but in the dark recesses of her mind. They got mixed up with the purity of her love for him. Confused and fouled by doubts and hidden fears she wasn't even sure of and didn't know she had until they emerged as hurtful arrows, aimed at the one person she wanted above all to love her.

If only she could speak to him without words. He knew how she felt when she kissed him, but she couldn't knock on his door and throw herself on him without warning. She had to let him know she was sorry for trampling on his proposal and let him see she'd changed her mind. Beyond that it was up to him. Her conscience, at least, would be clear. In time she might even sleep peacefully again.

That night when the children were in bed, Chloe tapped on Seb's door. He shifted so she could sit on the edge of his bed.

"Do you think I should go to see him?"

"Yes."

"What would I say?"

"Tell him you've changed your mind."

"He might have changed his."

"He hasn't."

"How do you know?"

"I can tell." He stared at her with a confident smirk.

Chloe held her hands to her head and screwed up her face. "Aaaargh. I don't know what I'm doing anymore," she wailed softly.

"Taking romantic advice from a fourteen-year-old." But she tempered the groan with an anguished smile. "Thanks, Seb."

He picked up his book. "No problem. Just get it sorted out, will you? The sooner the better for all of us."

Too early for bed. Not that sleep would come any more easily this night. Chloe went to her music room and opened the guitar case. She couldn't express in words what was in her heart, but she could play it and sing it. She sat down and began softly strumming chords and humming. Amanda had done clever arrangements for the duo, making the most of the lush chords and beautiful melodies of jazz standards. The lyrics of those old tunes were fantastic, so poetic and emotional. Fitting perfectly with the melodic line. So expressive.

"I've Got You Under My Skin" said it all. This version was slow. The drawn-out phrasing emphasized the pathos of the words, the hopeless, captured, lovelorn state of the singer. Exactly how she was at the moment.

Chloe stopped mid-bar. Maybe she should play to Alex. Sing. Not "I've Got You Under my Skin" but a different song. She frowned. Something that said *I love you* very clearly. She flipped through the folder of tunes.

Stopped. A favorite. Van Morrison. "Have I Told You Lately That I Love You?" Perfect! It said everything she wanted to say in a far better way than she could. She glanced at her watch. Now? Ten past eleven. Not too late. She stood up.

Sat down.

Stood up. If she didn't act immediately, she wouldn't be brave enough.

Go.

She packed her guitar into its case and snapped the catches. Seb was still reading when she peeked into his room.

"Turn out that light," she said. "I'm popping out for a few minutes."

"Alex?"

She nodded. "Wish me luck."

"You won't need it," he said, and he switched off the light.

At first she thought Alex must be in bed, because all the windows were dark, but as she approached the house, walking carefully up the driveway, a dull glow showed through the living-room curtain. The sensor lights came on, illuminating the path to the door. The path to her future? Happiness?

Her gloved fingers clutched the handle of the guitar case. Her insides writhed. This was worse than any recital she'd done, worse than performance exams. Worse than

Seb in court. What if he laughed at her choice of song? Or at her voice? Maybe she should just play instead. But if he didn't know the words, the whole thing would be meaningless. What would he think of her coming around in the middle of the night to play some tune he'd never heard? Another ridiculous act on the part of Chloe Gardiner.

She extended a finger to the doorbell. Withdrew it.

No.

Go home. This is insane. She backed away slowly. Turned and took a shaky step down. Her stomach churned. She might be sick.

The front door opened.

"Chloe?"

She froze.

Alex's heart thudded like a pile driver as he stepped outside. Was it really her, here on his porch in the middle of the night? She half turned.

"Sorry, I didn't mean to wake you." Her expression was blank, her mouth tight.

"You didn't. Come inside. It's cold."

He extended his arm, and she hesitated, then stepped up and into the house. What was she doing here? His amazed gaze dropped to her guitar. On the way home from a gig? Come to ask him not to encourage the boys, perhaps? His jaw tightened. Not fair if that were the case. He closed the door and followed her into the living room.

Chloe held up a gloved hand. "Please. Don't say anything." She glanced around helplessly. "Sit down."

Too astounded to do anything else, he did. Chloe removed her gloves, revealing a slim white bandage over her injury, took her guitar from its case, and perched herself on the edge of the couch. She played a series of beautiful chords, a rising progression of notes, set up a slow, rhythmic pulse. It sounded familiar, but he couldn't tell what it was until she began to sing. His breath caught as her soft, clear voice delivered the opening line.

For him. She was singing for him. Tender, loving, special. Wonderful. He couldn't move, riveted to his seat by the depth of the love pouring from her fingers and voice. This message was as clear as if she'd shouted it at him. It stunned him with its weight and its total, wondrous unexpectedness. If he shifted even the smallest muscle, he knew he'd collapse in a blubbering heap.

Chloe plucked the last chord, allowing the notes to fade into the silence of the room. Her voice had been shaky from nerves, and she'd missed a couple of notes. Alex sat like a statue. The swift, covert glances she'd managed while she played had revealed his stern expression and stiff posture. She remained with head bent. He was waiting for her to leave. She'd failed. He didn't know what to say to her, how to let her down gently. Too embarrassed by this display. A tear dropped from her cheek and plopped onto the shiny wood of the instrument cuddled in her arms.

Then the guitar was lifted from her embrace and laid aside carefully. She raised her head to discover Alex kneeling before her with tears in those beautiful blue eyes. He cupped her face in his palms and ever so gently pressed his lips to hers. Chloe slipped from the couch into his arms and into his kiss, into his life. Into her future.

"I didn't sing very well," she murmured when she was able.

"Yes, you did." He rose to sit on the couch, pulling her into his lap, where she snuggled into his arms. "Old Van and Rod have got nothing on you."

"I'm sorry I turned you down."

"It doesn't matter now," he whispered against her cheek.

"It does. I couldn't bear it. I didn't know how to make it right. I thought . . . after that note . . ."

He grimaced. "That stupid note!"

"Will you ask me again?"

"Yes. One day. When you're ready." He grinned and kissed her again.

After a time Chloe said, "I will marry you, Alex, but I want to finish my degree first. I only completed half of it."

"You can do whatever you want, my darling, as long as I'm involved. I couldn't bear it when you said you didn't want me in your life."

"I'm sorry. I was stupid. Actually . . ." She giggled. "Seb said we were both stupid."

"Smart boy."

Chloe nuzzled her face into his neck. "I should go home. They're on their own."

"I'll come with you."

EPILOGUE

Alex sat next to Simone on an uncomfortable plastic chair in a school hall packed with parents and relatives. Katy sat beside Simone, and on Alex's other side Seb and Julian joked together in their usual fashion. He was surprised when they said they'd come tonight. At seventeen, a primary school music concert wasn't their usual choice of entertainment on a Friday night.

"I think I'm more nervous than they are," he said to Simone.

"They'll be wonderful."

"They should be. It sounded great at home. But, well . . ."

"Don't worry. Chloe's a full-fledged professional now."

It wasn't Chloe he was concerned for. They'd all been to her recent graduation recital. He knew she was brilliant. No, these nerves were for the just turned ten-year-old making her debut as a performer.

Mrs. Purcell, the principal, took the microphone and began talking about the benefits of music in a child's development and how proud she was of all the students taking the stage tonight and how difficult it was to stand up and perform in front of a crowd.

"Most people would prefer to jump out of an airplane," she said.

"I wouldn't," Simone muttered.

"Neither would I." He looked at the program again. First up was a little girl playing the piano, then two flutes, a clarinet, another piano, and then they were on.

The Owl and the Pussycat, Stephanie Bergman, voice, accompanied by Chloe Gardiner, guitar.

The first performer was so nervous, she had three false starts before charging through her piece so fast that half the notes were missing. The flute duet was very good; the clarinet squeaked and sounded like a duck. Alex had to dig his elbow into Seb to stop him from laughing.

"Shh. What if people react that way when Steffie and Chloe play?" he whispered during the relieved applause.

"Don't be ridiculous. They won't sound like that."

"That's not the point. It's rude."

"Sorry, but I didn't know you could get noises like that out of a clarinet. That kid's got a rare talent."

Julian snickered. Alex shook his head, grinning. Those boys were incorrigible, way too smart for their own good.

Only one more piece, and they were on. His mouth had gone dry. He needed a drink of water. Would Steffie need a drink? He hadn't given her a water bottle. The next boy played the piano like a virtuoso, earning a thunder of well-deserved applause. Hard act to follow. But Chloe was a professional; she'd support Steffie and cover up any mistakes. What was he thinking? They wouldn't make mistakes. They'd be brilliant.

His two beautiful girls walked onstage and bowed. Seb gave an ear-piercing whistle, while the rest of the family clapped like lunatics. Steffie giggled and glanced at Chloe, who was smiling calmly and setting her fingers on the guitar strings.

Great deliberation, overseen by Katy, had gone into their dress tonight, resulting in tones of blue. Steffie in sky blue, long silky hair pinned back with a sparkly clasp courtesy of Katy, Chloe in dark blue. Both lovely, one dark-haired, the other golden.

Chloe strummed a chord. Steffie drew a breath and began to sing.

Her voice was pure and clear and perfectly in tune. Who knew she could sing like an angel? He hadn't, and neither had Lucy, sitting two rows back, as proud as he was. Chloe was the one who had discovered this talent. Chloe, who coaxed the love of music from his confused, difficult little girl and produced the confident, happy child onstage.

In the chorus Chloe sang harmony, her smooth, mellow voice supporting Steffie's. Alex closed his eyes briefly as the memory of that special, wonderful night, the night she sang her love for him, flooded back. The first time he'd heard her sing. Three and a half years ago now, and it still choked his throat. Thank goodness she'd decided after a few months that she couldn't wait years to marry him, and they'd tied the knot before Christmas.

The song ended. His beloved adopted children jumped to their feet, cheering and applauding their sisters. Simone dabbed at her eyes with a tissue in between bursts of clapping.

Alex pounded his palms together, gazing at two of the people he loved most in the world, holding hands and bowing now as they acknowledged their applause.

He would've waited for Chloe forever.

MR. S